Two Sides of the Same Coin

Ashlynn Carter

Copyright © 2024 by Ashlynn Carter

All rights reserved.

No part of this publication may be reproduced, distributed, or transmitted in any form or by any means, including photocopying, recording, or other electronic or mechanical methods, without the prior written permission of the publisher, except as permitted by U.S. copyright law. For permission requests, contact Ashlynn Carter at ashlynn.carter@proton.me.

The story, all names, characters, and incidents portrayed in this production are fictitious. No identification with actual persons (living or deceased), places, buildings, and products is intended or should be inferred.

Book Cover by Ashlynn Carter

First edition 2025

Chapter One

Cruz

The sky was dark and starless. Storm clouds had rolled in, making the already moonless night even darker. That suited me just fine. I wore my specially made night vision goggles that wrapped around the sides of my face, giving me more visibility without having to turn my head. Without moving a muscle, I let my gaze slowly sweep across the landscape again. Nothing seemed to be out of the ordinary. The two sentry towers showed no sign of anyone inside, even though I had watched the shift change.

I pressed a button on the side of the goggles so that I could check for heat signatures. I counted four people in each tower, just like an hour ago. I waited another few minutes before silently making my way to the top of the hill five hundred yards from my current location. I blended with my surroundings, becoming one with the environment. There were four sentries stationed in each of the two towers on top of the hill. I marveled as I crouched at the base of the first tower. None of them had spotted me approaching.

Then again, I have been at this for six years, sharpening my skills. I wasn't the typical soldier. I was the one they called in when they couldn't get the green light from the higher ups to send in normal soldiers. I was a weapon used when there was no hope left. I was a ghost. No one knew my real identity.

My family all believed that I worked with my uncle at the Federal Bureau of Werewolf and Human Affairs. I guess in a way, I still did. However, most of the time I was sent on off-the-book missions. The kind the government would deny being a part of if I got into trouble. Uncle Miles and Garret Martinez were two of the three people who knew what I really did. They were the go-betweens for the ones assigning missions, and me.

Tonight's mission was simple. There was a hostage that had valuable information on a pending terrorist attack on the royal family of the Northern Kingdom. Both the Northern Kingdom and my government had tried to extract the contact twice and failed both times. Seven men were killed in the attempts. My job was to get the target out and back to Miles and Martinez unharmed enough to share the information he had.

"Are we going to take them out before or after we collect the target?" Caspian asked.

Caspian was my wolf. I have been able to communicate with him since I was eighteen, but we haven't been able to shift. My mother is a hybrid, part werewolf, part human. She is the first of her kind. She had not even known her father had been a werewolf until she met my dad, her mate.

Werewolves have a destined mate that is essentially their second half. She shifted for the first time after her bond with my dad was fully formed by them biting into each other's necks, creating the mate's mark. When both mates mark each other, it seals their bond. The two are connected on a deeper level, allowing them to even feel some of the other's emotions.

Then me and my sister came along. No one knew how being a hybrid would affect us kids. My sister Molly shifted at sixteen like a normal werewolf. I was human, except for the fact that I could talk to my wolf. He was in there, just locked away. I was twenty-four years old and didn't see shifting ever happening for me. Sometimes I was envious of my sister's werewolf abilities. It would be nice to be stronger and faster than humans or to have accelerated healing. I never hated her though. She is my best friend, the only person I have confided in about work.

"We will take out the towers first." I started climbing one of the legs of the tower. "I do not want any alarms raised or reinforcements called. This is a stealth mission."

Caspian's grumbling caused me to smile. He was a very aggressive wolf. Probably made worse by not being able to shift. He enjoyed our line of work. It allowed us to freely release our pent-up anger on people who deserved it. I knew that under all of Caspian's gruff, was a caring and protective creature. The two of us were not much different. However, these days, we haven't shown much of our softer side. That side of me only came out with my family.

I only made it home every few months, and by then, I was usually a ball of aggression. I had accidentally put three of our pack's guards in the hospital after a sparring match a few years ago. Molly was my saving grace. She was the only one that was able to quiet the beast inside. After the incident with the guards, I would spend several hours with Molly after getting home, before letting anyone else know I was back.

I reached the top of the tower and carefully peeked over the edge. All of the guards were inside. What kind of guard tower didn't have someone patrolling the outside of it? A lazy one, that's what. I slipped onto the walkway and made my way to the door. I mentally shook my head. Three of the four guards were at a small table, gambling. The fourth man was sleeping.

"Pathetic." Caspian snickered. *"This is going to be easy."*

"Let's go to work."

I quietly pushed open the door. I was embarrassed for these guys. No one turned in my direction. I sprang forward, throwing a fist into the nearest man's jaw before spinning and throwing my knife into the next man. The third man came at me with fists flying frantically. I inwardly rolled my eyes as the man tripped over his fallen comrade. Caspian snickered as I snapped the man's neck. The fourth man let out a loud snore. There was an empty whiskey bottle next to the bed.

"Wow." I shook my head. This just got more and more humiliating. I pulled a syringe out of my belt and injected him with a sedative. It didn't seem fair to kill the man in his sleep. Let his superiors take care of him for sleeping on the job. *"On to the second tower."* I told Caspian with a sigh. I had a feeling those in the other tower were going to be just as untrained as those in the first.

With both towers no longer a problem, I moved to the shed-like structure at the base of the hill. The intelligence I had received said that the shed sat on top of a bunker, and inside was my target. I approached cautiously, keeping behind cover. I paused when I saw a camera on the exterior of the shed. I checked my firearms before tucking them back into their holsters. I didn't like using them if I could help it, but if it came down to it, I needed them to be ready.

The FBWHA didn't hold back any resources or money on my equipment. Everything I had was top of the line and usually, no one else had them. My bow was compact and clicked into my belt. With a single flick of my wrist, it snapped out to a full-sized bow. The arrows were no bigger than a bullet, but when I squeezed the right spot, they extended. I had used one on a guard in the second tower as a knife. I pressed it to the man's chest and squeezed. Quick and relatively painless. Well, the man hadn't screamed, so I was assuming it wasn't too painful.

Drawing back on my bow, I took aim and shot out the camera. I waited for several minutes, but no one came out. I had assumed someone would have been watching the cameras, apparently not.

I moved to the door quickly and slipped inside. The door hadn't even been locked. *"Do you think this is a set up?"* I asked.

"I'm not sure." Caspian said thoughtfully as I jumped down into the opening in the floor. *"This has to be the sloppiest hostage operation I have ever seen. How had these people managed to kill seven men, prompting our involvement?"*

Voices up ahead had me slowing my steps. A door was cracked open at the end of the narrow hallway. I moved down the hall while checking each room I passed as quickly as I could. I finally got to the cracked door, and I peeked through the opening. What I saw had both Caspian and me seeing red.

A young boy, no older than six or seven, was being held down on a table. A girl about the boy's age was being held nearby. The man holding her had a fistful of her hair, forcing her to watch. Another man slowly ran his hand over several surgical-type instruments as he observed the boy. I counted eight men in the room, including the one chained to the wall.

"Which one is the target?" Caspian asked.

"We can sort that out after we get the kids out of harm's way." I said, and Caspian perked up.

I was planning which of the men to take out first when the man near the instruments spoke. "Now, I will only ask you this one more time, where is it?" The boy spit at the man. I smiled at the kid's spirit. In a flash, the man grabbed the boy's arm. A sickening crack broke the silence left behind by the boy's show of defiance. The boy's scream of pain echoed through the room.

I pushed the door open as I threw my knife at the man holding the little girl. For the length of a breath, no one moved, and then it was chaos. Caspian thoroughly enjoyed ending each and every man's life in the room. We hated it when innocent people were injured, but kids? People who could injure a child were not worthy of life.

I was breathing hard by the time the seventh man fell. I took a deep breath and looked around the room, searching for the kids. The bodies of the men were everywhere. The girl had her arms around the boy as they huddled in the corner. Both were watching me with wide eyes.

Moving slowly, I walked toward them. They pressed themselves more into the wall as I approached. Standing six foot three and two hundred and fifty pounds of solid muscle, I was an intimidating sight on my own. But on missions, I wore a black face mask that covered everything from my eyes down to protect my identity. It also masked my voice by dropping it a little.

Once I was within five feet of them, I crouched down. I was tempted to remove my mask, but we were still in hostile territory, and there was the man chained to the wall. I studied each child in turn. The boy had tears running down his pale cheeks. He cradled his broken arm close to his chest and he was shaking. The girl held the boy tightly as silent tears coursed down her cheeks. Both had black hair and dark brown eyes. My guess was that they were siblings.

"Are either of you hurt? Besides the broken arm?" I asked softly. Neither child spoke. "Why are you two here?" Again, my question was met with silence.

"Leave the kids alone." The man chained to the wall snapped.

I turned my head to the side to look at him. "And why would I do that?"

"They are only kids." The man said.

"Kids who happen to be in a bunker being tortured. Which begs the question, why?" I turned my gaze back to the kids who looked even more scared. "Let's start with something simple then…what are your names?"

"Anabelle Williams." The girl whispered.

I smiled, even though she couldn't see it. "How long have you been here, Belle?" My intelligence said that my target had been at this location for at least three weeks.

"Everyone calls me Ana." The girl corrected with a scowl.

"Ah, but Belle means beauty, and you are as pretty as a princess. I would love to help get you and this young man back to your parents. So, how long have you been here, Belle?"

"I don't know." Hope flashed in her eyes before she glanced over my shoulder. Fear was etched in her every feature.

"She is scared of the man in chains." Caspian observed.

"I guess there really isn't a way to tell time down here, is there?" I said as I looked around. "Did you get here recently, or have you been here a while?"

"A while." She squeaked. Her anxiety seemed to be climbing.

"And the man in chains, was he here before or after you?" I asked. "I am looking for someone specific and I can't leave without this person."

"I am the one you are looking for. I am the one with the information about the royals." The man claimed. His voice was firm and there was an angry tone to it.

I didn't look at the man. I pretended the man hadn't even spoken. I never said I was looking for someone with information on the royal family. I could have been looking for anyone. My suspicions about the man rose.

"He came here with us." Belle said.

"Hmm." That didn't make this any easier. I needed to figure out who my target was, and I needed to get these kids to safety, but my exit plan had limited space. I wouldn't be able to take all three people with me. And the terror in Belle's eyes made me think the man was not actually a hostage. I lowered my voice so only the kids could hear me. "Has that man hurt you?"

Tears filled the girl's eyes again. "No, but he told the others to." The boy said, through his pain.

"Can you two do something for me?" When both hesitantly nodded, I continued. "I need you to close your eyes until I tell you that you can look."

They had both seen me kill seven men with my bare hands, but I didn't want them any more traumatized than they already were. The boy squeezed his eyes closed and the girl buried her face in the boy's shoulder. I quickly pulled my gun from its holster and fired a single shot into the man's head. The kids jumped, but didn't open their eyes.

"You are doing great. Keep them closed." I praised as I started dragging bodies into the room across the hall. I needed to move quickly. Travelling with two kids was going to be slow going, and chances were, the man had triggered some sort of distress signal.

I returned to the kids and knelt down by the boy. "You guys did amazing. You can open your eyes now." I pulled a syringe from my med kit. It was a strong pain killer, and the boy could use it. "Can I get your name, young man."

"Nash."

"Belle and Nash, I am here to take you home." I told them. "I am going to give you something for the pain, Nash. Then I can splint your arm so we can get out of here. How does that sound?"

* * *

Nash sat in front of me on my motorcycle while Belle clung to my back. We had been driving for hours. We were almost to the helicopter that would take us to an abandoned airstrip where I had a vehicle stashed.

"You are doing great, Nash. Just a little bit farther." I called above the roar of the machine. The boy gave a small nod but didn't say anything.

Ten minutes later I pulled off the road and cut the engine. Belle looked around and her grip tightened on my shirt. We were in the middle of a forested area. Not a soul in sight. Miles and Martinez were to meet me at the airstrip, but I wanted to approach them from a different angle. Nash had become talkative due to the pain meds.

I learned that both kids had been on a trip with their father, Alpha Max. Their dad had been in a meeting, and they were outside playing when they overheard a conversation about the royal family. They were seen and immediately kidnapped.

How had our intelligence not known that we were looking for two kids? That was something I planned on asking Miles before bringing the kids out in the open. I got off the bike and turned to face them.

"We are going for a little walk." I told them.

"But you said you were taking us to a helicopter." Belle looked near to panicking.

"We are, Belle. We are just going to do things a little different." I explained. "We are going to walk the rest of the way. I am going to have you and Nash wait in the trees while I make sure the helicopter is safe and my pilots are good to go."

The pain meds were beginning to leave Nash's system, and he winced when I picked him up. Belle clung to my side as we headed into the trees. We walked for twenty minutes before I saw the helicopter through the trees. I found a tree that had tipped over and hid the kids in the tangle of roots, dirt, and other foliage.

I took five steps into the clearing before stopping. I didn't want to get too far from the kids. "Hello?" I called in a loud voice. "Is anyone here? I got lost on a trail and cannot find a ranger station." It was our code to let each other know who we were.

Miles and Martinez materialized out of the early morning shadows near the helicopter. "Took you long enough. We expected you hours ago." Martinez smiled, and I glared at them.

"The contact I was supposed to find, who is it?" I asked.

Miles looked at Martinez with a furrowed brow. "All we know is the person had information about the royal family. We were not even aware if they were male or female."

"Try both." I growled. How had I not thought to get more details? The helicopter was a four-person machine. If I didn't trust Miles, I would kill one of them and get the kids out. As it was, I was going to have to trust the kids with these two and meet them when they landed.

"Both? What are you talking about, Shadow?" Martinez asked, using my Codename.

Before I could say anything, a scream shattered the quiet morning. My feet were moving before I fully registered that Belle had been the one to scream. When I got to where I left them, I saw a man standing over the kids.

"The famous Shadow has a weakness for children." The man drawled.

"You better pray that neither child is harmed." I growled. I heard Miles and Martinez coming up behind me. The man scowled as he took a step away from the fallen tree. "Belle, are you okay?" I asked as I slowly approached, and the man slowly backed away.

"Shadow." Belle's terrified voice cried from where I had hidden them.

Pressure built in my head while pain slashed through my body. I gritted my teeth against the familiar pain. When I got to the tree, I glanced down. Both kids were there with wide scared eyes. A stick broke and an image of the man aiming a gun at the kids filled my mind and I dove forward, shielding the children with my body. A gunshot rang through the air, just as pain ripped through my shoulder. More gunshots were followed by Miles and Martinez shouting.

Everything around me moved slowly as I looked at the kids. In my head, I could see Miles and Martinez running after the gunman as he fled the area. Suddenly the pressure in my head was gone and everything sped back up. Most of the pain disappeared, leaving only a burning in my shoulder. Being a hybrid, we had special abilities. Mom could control her pack rank and aura. Molly could see the many different outcomes of a single decision. I was able to see all around me in slow motion. It helped in a fight for sure, but Caspian had to really push for us to use it. Usually, it was when my life was threatened, or he was trying to shift. I am sure if we could shift, we would be able to use the ability at will.

"Come on, Shadow. Let's get the girl and get out of here." Miles said as he helped me up.

"What about my brother?" Belle asked, clinging to Nash.

"He is coming too, Belle. Miles just didn't know about him." I said softly as I lifted Nash out of the hole and passed him to Miles. "Come on, we need to hurry."

I carried Belle as I ran for the helicopter with Miles at my side and Martinez covering us. I put her inside and stepped back so that Miles could do the same with Nash. "Two kids? How did they not tell us?" Miles whispered.

"I asked myself the same question." I told him. "Nash has a broken arm and is in quite a bit of pain." I took a step back as Martinez started the engine.

"Aren't you coming with us?" Belle nearly jumped out of the helicopter as she reached for me. Her arms went around my neck, and I winced. "You're bleeding!"

"Miles will take good care of you, Belle. You and Nash are in good hands."

"But..."

"There aren't enough seats, and you and your brother are my priority." I gave her a hug. "I will see you again, Belle. I promise." I whispered in her ear before pushing her back into the helicopter and closing the door.

I stepped back as Miles strapped the kids in. I watched until the chopper rose into the sky and flew off. This was going to be painful, but necessary. Caspian was going to have to try to shift again in order to heal me, which meant feeling like every bone in my body was shattering all at once. I needed to find a safe place to be able to do it.

Chapter Two

Cruz

I stood in the gas station parking lot waiting for Miles to show up with the kids. It had been two weeks since I had rescued them. Nash's broken arm had needed surgery, and they didn't want him travelling so soon afterwards. I requested the task to take them back home and Miles had made it happen.

He had been livid when he called me to meet him here. Apparently, no one had allowed the kids to call home, and no one let their parents know they had been rescued. Miles was under the assumption that they were trying to convince the kids to tell them what they overheard, but neither one was talking. When he told The Board that Shadow had taken a special interest in the kids, and had promised to check in on them, The Board had started plans to get the kids home.

A black SUV pulled into the gas station. The windows were tinted, and I couldn't see anyone inside. I remained in the shadows of the building as I watched a man climb out of the driver's seat and start filling up with gas. He removed his baseball cap and wiped his brow. Miles. I smiled as I used the many vehicles to mask my approach. I was on the other side of the pump when I heard the click signaling the tank was full.

"Took you long enough, old man." I whispered, and Miles cursed in surprise.

"Do you always have to do that?" He stepped to the side of the machine as he tossed his receipt in the trash can.

"What kind of shadow would I be if I was visible all the time?" I grinned at him. "That's a nice hat."

Miles shook his head and tossed it to me. "How's the shoulder?"

"Healing. How are the kids?" I put the hat on and passed him mine. I hadn't been able to have Caspian heal me. There were too many hostiles in the area, and I had to make my way out with just a makeshift bandage to control the bleeding.

"Both are asleep in the back. They were up really early so they will probably sleep most of the way. I should let you know that your parents and Molly are visiting the Silver Moon Pack." Miles slipped the hat on. "They were invited by the niece of the Alpha King so they could learn more about hybrids."

"Thanks for the heads up." I said before climbing into the driver's seat and starting the SUV.

I had been driving for several hours before I heard a noise in the back seat. I glanced in the rearview mirror and saw that both kids were awake. They watched me with guarded eyes.

"I think they recognize us a little." Caspian chuckled.

"You are not Miles." Nash finally said.

"You are correct, Nash. I am not Miles." I smiled at him through the mirror.

"Who are you?" Belle asked slowly.

"Who do you think I am?" I asked instead.

"Miles said the Shadow always wears a mask, but you are as big as he is." Belle stated. "And your hair isn't black. Your voice is different, too."

"I have heard that about the Shadow." I chuckled. "My name is Cruz Storm. I work with Miles at the FBWHA. He needed to be home with his family, so I get to drive you the rest of the way to the Silver Moon Pack. Are you guys hungry?" I asked.

We were five hours south of the kids' home pack. I wanted the kids to be happy and fed before I took them home. Caspian and I also wanted to make sure that the kids had been treated well over the past two weeks.

We sat in the shade of a large tree as we ate the sack lunches Miles had prepared for us. "How did your surgery go, Nash?" I asked.

"It went well, I guess. It still hurts some." Nash shrugged. His arm was in a sling, and he was on prescription pain meds. Even though he was a werewolf, he was too young for his wolf to help heal him. It had been a really bad break, and his healing was more like a human than a werewolf at this point.

"Have you met Shadow?" Belle asked.

"I have. Why?"

"Does he keep his promises?" Belle glanced at me as she put her barely touched sandwich down.

"He always keeps his promises, Belle. Always." I said firmly. Nash and Belle looked at me with wide eyes and I winked at them. "Eat up, little princess, so we can get you home." Both kids gave me the biggest grins. "I need you two to do something for me."

"What?" Nash asked excitedly.

I lowered my voice. "No one can know that I am the Shadow. It would be very dangerous for my family if anyone knew."

"We understand." Belle nodded her head.

"Even if you think you can trust the person, no one can know. And you shouldn't talk about me to each other either. We wouldn't want someone overhearing you."

"Like how we had accidentally heard those guys?" Nash asked.

"Exactly." I said. "You told me a little of what you heard, but would you be willing to tell me more?" I asked.

Belle and Nash looked at each other before turning back to me. "The woman said that she couldn't wait to get revenge on her. The man kissed her as he told her to be patient. That they just needed to wait until the plane goes down." Belle whispered with wide eyes.

"The second man rubbed his hands together and said that the girl was pretty enough that he could enjoy a life with her warming his bed." Nash added. "The men said good-bye to the woman and started walking away. They found us on the path."

"They looked at each other before they grabbed us and jumped in a car by the stables." Belle shivered.

"Did you recognize any of them?" I asked.

Both shook their heads. I leaned back as I thought. A plane going down? My stomach knotted with dread. I hated planes. The kids had been kidnapped a month and a half ago, which meant the plane was going to be going down soon. I needed to get the kids home and call Miles. Hopefully, we can figure out what plane they were talking about before it crashed.

I pulled up in front of a large packhouse and put the vehicle in park. I took a deep breath before turning to look at the excited kids in the back. "Stay here until I know your parents are here." They looked disappointed but nodded.

"Do you think our family is here?" Caspian asked.

"Only one way to find out." I said as I stepped out of the vehicle and locked it.

I walked up the stairs and knocked on the door. I didn't have to wait long before the door opened. A beautiful woman stood there. She had startling green eyes and light brown hair flowing around her shoulders. The smell of a salty ocean breeze filled my lungs. I mentally shook my head. We were too far inland to smell the ocean.

"She is our mate!" Caspian yelled in my head.

I blinked in surprise. *"How do you know?"*

"Because I am a wolf you dimwit. She is our mate. I can smell her." Caspian said in irritation.

The woman took her time eyeing me up and down before her eyes settled back on my face. "Can I help you?"

"I...Uh..." I cleared my throat. "Is Alpha Max and Luna Jackie in?" I finally found my voice.

"They are, but we aren't up for visitors at the moment. If you want to speak with them, you will need to call and set up a meeting." The fetching creature folded her arms over her chest as she lifted a brow in challenge.

"I think your Alpha would make an exception for me and my companions." I fought the smile that wanted to surface.

"I really don't think he would."

"Who is at the door, Riv?" A man came up behind the woman.

"I'm not entirely sure." Riv cocked her head to the side as she studied me.

"I don't think she can smell us." Caspian whined. *"She can't tell we are her mate."*

"I am here to speak with the Williams." I stated again.

The man scowled at me. "My parents do not want visitors at this time. We have been dealing with family issues, and we are closed for casual visits."

I heard the lock on the car click and I immediately locked it with the key fob. I turned around to look at the SUV. "I told you to stay put." I pointed at them. I knew they could see me. They no doubt saw their brother, and wanted to come say, 'hi', but I promised to deliver them to their parents, and that is what I was going to do. I turned back to my mate and the man. "I really need to speak with the Alpha and Luna. If you do not wish to take me there, I will find my own way to see them."

"Have a good day, sir." The man pulled my mate inside and slammed the door. Caspian growled and tossed out numerous threats at the man that had touched our mate.

I returned to the car and turned to see the kids. "Why couldn't we go see our brother and cousin?" Belle asked with tears in her eyes.

"I made a promise to you that I would take you to your parents. Your brother and cousin did not want to let me in." I told them. "Do you guys want to see what I do for work?"

"Please don't kill River and Paxton!" Belle cried.

"Oh no, Belle. I didn't mean..." I ran a hand down my face. "I meant sneak in. We can surprise your parents."

"River. Such a beautiful name." Caspian commented.

"We will need to wait until it is fully dark. It should only be another twenty minutes or so. I will park out of sight, and we can move in." I started the car and drove down the lane. I pulled off around the corner and turned the vehicle off. "Can you stay here while I scout for any guards?" Both kids eagerly nodded their heads, and I got out.

I was only gone for five minutes before returning. I opened the car door and helped the kids out. I pressed a finger to my lips to tell them they needed to be quiet. I pulled a bag out from under the seat and gave them each their own pair of night vision goggles after warning them to not look into the lights with them.

They followed me wordlessly into the trees. I had counted only a handful of guards. It made sense. They had probably pulled a lot of their men to look for Belle and Nash. As we made our way to the house, we crossed paths with one of the guards. I knocked him out within seconds and the kids seemed upset.

"I just knocked him out, so he didn't ruin our surprise." I whispered quietly. Nash nodded, but Belle pouted her lips. "He will wake up soon, so we need to keep going."

I found a window that was unlocked and helped the kids climb in. I closed it before crossing to the door. I cracked it open and listened. Someone was coming down the hall. A woman came into view, and I smiled. Perfect.

As she passed the door, I opened it and grabbed her from behind, pulling her into the room. I softly closed the door and pushed the woman against the wall.

"Have I taught you nothing, Molly?" I asked close to her ear. She stopped struggling and I released her.

Molly punched my injured shoulder, causing me to wince. "You scared the life out of me, Cruz. What are you even doing here? I thought you were on assignment for another month. And why are you acting like a baby? I didn't punch you that hard."

"He got shot." Belle said from my side.

Molly looked down at the little girl with wide eyes. "I am on assignment. I am to deliver these two safely to their parents, but I couldn't get past the front door."

"Did you tell them you had their kidnapped children?"

"No, if I did that, they would have taken the kids, and I would still be on the front porch."

"We want to surprise mom and dad." Nash added and I smiled, ruffing up his hair.

Molly narrowed her eyes at me. "Seeing their kids would be surprise enough." I shrugged as I grinned. She sighed. "Dinner is almost done and then we are supposed to meet in the living room for games."

"We will be waiting." I kissed her cheek. "It's so good to see you, Molly."

"Yeah, yeah. Just don't get yourself shot." She paused at the door. "Again."

I chuckled softly as she left. We waited a minute to allow Molly time to get to wherever she was going, before exiting the room. The kids guided me to the correct room in no time. They were practically bouncing with excitement.

"Remember to stay sitting on the couch until I tell you to get up." I told them as I walked over to the window. We were on the second floor. I bet this room had a spectacular view of the forest during the day. I leaned against the wall as I watched the kids. The couch faced away from the door, so whoever entered would see me first.

The door opened and I watched Molly step into the room followed by my mate, Paxton, mom and dad, a couple I didn't know and a couple I only recognized from the file. They all stopped when they saw me.

"How did you get in here?" Paxton took an aggressive step towards me, and Caspian growled.

"It wasn't too hard. There was a window on the ground floor. I believe in a gym." I shrugged. "Sweet digs by the way, Alpha and Luna Williams."

"Cruz, we have taught you better than sneaking into a person's home." Mom scolded me as she rushed to my side, and I enveloped her in a tight hug.

"I did try to use the front door, but they wouldn't let me in." I pressed a kiss to her cheek. "It is good to see you, Mom. But unfortunately, this is not a social call. We have come on FBWHA business."

Mom's brow furrowed as she moved to allow my dad to hug me. Dad patted me on my shoulder as he stepped back, and I groaned. "Cruz was injured on his last mission." Molly supplied, and I sent her a glare. She stuck her tongue out at me.

"Who is 'we'?" River asked as she walked farther into the room.

I gestured for Belle and Nash to come to me, and they jumped off the couch before running to my side. They both had large grins on their faces as they faced those gathered. Gasps echoed through the room before everyone started for them. I stepped in front of them with a growl. "Not so fast."

"What's your angle, Cruz?" Paxton yelled angrily.

"I have no angle. I was informed that the FBWHA never reached out to you regarding Belle and Nash. I need you to be aware of a few things." I put a hand on both Nash and Belle's shoulders, keeping them in place.

"Aware of what?" Alpha Max moved forward, looking ticked.

"Nash and Belle were retrieved from a bunker two weeks ago." At that, everyone started yelling and I waited. The Alpha told everyone to be quiet. When I had all of their attention again, I continued. "Nash needed surgery because his arm had been severely broken. He is still recovering and will need to stay in the cast for a few more weeks. Belle, thank goodness, hadn't received any physical injuries. I have all their medical records in the car." I nudged the kids towards their parents now that the Alpha and his wife were calm enough to not accidentally hurt Nash's arm in their haste to hug the kids.

"Why weren't we notified when they were found?" Luna Jackie asked tearfully as she hugged her kids.

"That is a good question. One I do not have the answer to. I was part of the retrieval mission, but as soon as they were in safe hands, I was sent out on a new mission. We have someone looking into it."

"You went out again? But you were shot!" Belle turned to me with horrified eyes.

I crouched down and she ran to me. She threw her arms around my neck, careful to avoid bumping my shoulder. "Now my mom is going to be worried about me, little princess." I hugged her back. "It wasn't too bad." I leaned back and gave her a wink.

Belle pouted as she glared at me. "You had blood all over your back and you are still hurting from it. See?" She squeezed my shoulder, and I groaned as I quickly grabbed her hand.

"Please, don't do that, Belle." I said firmly.

"Must suck to be a human, and not be able to heal." Paxton commented.

Caspian roared and my head felt like it was going to explode. As gently as I could, I pushed Belle back towards her parents. The stupid jerk had ticked off Caspian, and now he was trying to shift. Pain ripped through me, and I squeezed my eyes shut. I started breathing hard as the pain grew.

Dad knelt next to me. "Caspian again?" he whispered.

"Get the kids out of here." I growled as I fisted my hands, trying to hold in my pain. They didn't need to see this.

"No, Cruz! What's wrong? No, mom, I need to stay with Cruz!" Belle cried.

She broke free of her mother's hold. I caught her at arm's reach before she could hug me. I did not want to accidently hurt her. My whole body was tense as I fought the pain. Smoothing her hair with a shaking hand, I looked her in the eye. Caspian let up just a little and my grip on her loosened slightly. He didn't want to hurt her either.

"Belle. Nash. Go with your parents." I said firmly. Dad gently pulled Belle away from me. Luna Jackie grabbed hold of her daughter. "I will see you in the morning. I promise." I gave her a ghost of a smile.

Another wave of pain hit, and I doubled over. With Belle out of the way, Caspian pushed even harder. This was going to be a long night. I looked up and met the green eyes of my mate. She bit her bottom lip as she watched me in concern. I had a strong urge to pull her close and comfort her. I growled, trying to hold back a yell. It had been a long time since Caspian had pushed this hard to shift. Usually, he only pushed enough to heal me a little or to use our hybrid ability. Not tonight though. Tonight, he was going all in.

Chapter Three

River

I watched as the man that had returned my cousins doubled over in pain after he sweetly comforted Ana. Maya began whining and pacing in my head. His dad was next to him, and a pang of envy shot through me. I wanted to be the one near him. Cruz looked up and our eyes met. My breath seemed to freeze in my lungs.

His eyes were as blue as the sea in the movies I had seen. They were filled with so much pain I could almost feel it as if it were my own. His hair was a sandy blonde that was cut short in a military style. Sweat began to bead on his forehead as his jaw clenched.

"What is going on?" Dad asked, moving closer to Alpha Maverick.

"We told you a little about Morgan's experience with shifting." Alpha Maverick said, not looking away from his son. "Cruz is in a similar boat." Cruz closed his eyes as he took a deep breath, and his jaw clenched. "Unlike his mother, Cruz has been able to communicate with Caspian since he was eighteen. Over the years, they have tried to shift multiple times, but all they can manage is the pain."

"Why is he trying to shift now?" I asked, moving closer. My heart rate picked up its rhythm as I watched Cruz's face contort in pain.

"Probably because Paxton decided to insult Caspian." Molly said as she shrugged her shoulders. "Caspian can be a bit hot tempered sometimes. Do not get me wrong, Cruz and Caspian are the sweetest, but if you piss them off, you will feel it in the morning."

"Molly, that's enough." Cruz ground out. His pain was getting worse, I could feel it. "Caspian, stop."

Suddenly I felt a wave of emotion hit me. Frustration, anger, worry. I could sense the intense pain Cruz was in, and it sent me into a panic. Maya howled in my head as she paced. "Someone needs to help him." I said desperately. I couldn't stand there and watch him like this. Someone needed to put a stop to it.

"Unfortunately, all we can do is wait. Maybe this time will be different." Alpha Maverick stood and hugged his wife as she began to cry.

I glanced over at mom and dad as they watched Cruz breathing deeply with his eyes closed. Paxton had disappeared, probably to see to Nash and Ana. Molly chewed her thumb nail as she paced. I moved to the couch and sat down. I would follow his family's lead. If they weren't panicking, I could hold myself together.

Hours passed, and the only change was Cruz's inability to remain completely quiet. It must have been his military training to deal with pain or something. Because he hardly made a sound, yet I felt like screaming for him. I could sense the level of pain he was in without actually feeling the pain itself. It was torture.

A wave of nausea washed over me. He was going to throw up. I ran and grabbed the small trash can near the fireplace and brought it to him. He looked up in surprise but then proceeded to throw up. I paced away from him as I fought the tears that stung my eyes. The pain was getting worse, but he was no closer to shifting than he had been at the beginning.

"Someone needs to do something." I looked around the room. "He can't keep going like this." Maya and I were growing desperate to make the pain stop.

"I know it is hard, but there is literally nothing we can do." Molly gave me a sad smile.

"Caspian." Cruz growled as he tried to stand up.

He stumbled for the door as more pain enveloped me. I moved in front of him and threw my arms around his neck. I needed this to stop. I couldn't handle watching him go on like this anymore. Tears slipped down my cheeks. "Caspian, please stop." I begged close to Cruz's ear.

Cruz fell to his knees, bringing me down with him. "He said not until we shift."

I looked into Cruz's eyes. They were flickering to a darker blue. I turned to look at everyone in the room, desperate for someone to help him. No one moved. Another wave of pain, and I turned back to Cruz. His skin was pale and clammy. If this didn't stop, could Caspian kill Cruz?

"What if we mark him?" Maya asked.

"What? No." I didn't even know this guy.

"River, he is our mate. We cannot let him go through this alone." Maya whined. "What if our mark could help him, like with his mom and dad?"

"Our mate? Are you sure?" I studied Cruz's face. He was handsome, I would give him that, but I had not sensed the mate bond from him.

"Caspian is buried. I get snatches of him, but he is there. Why do you think we can feel his pain?"

"Okay, so he is our mate. We can't mark him though, Maya."

"Watch me." Maya growled.

She pushed forward and took over. Before I could gain control again, she sunk her canines into Cruz's neck. His arms wrapped around me. One of his hands went to the back of my head as he rested his forehead on my shoulder. I was completely enveloped by the mountain of a man. Maya stepped back with a proud smirk on her face. I could not believe what she had just done. This man could literally snap me like a toothpick with very little effort on his part.

Pain began to fill me, and I cried out. Cruz pushed me hard enough that I went sliding across the floor, colliding with the couch with enough force to knock the wind out of me. Mom and dad moved to my side, but we all froze when Cruz yelled just before he shifted into a very large sandy blonde wolf. Suddenly the pain was gone, and I lay on the floor exhausted.

Cruz turned his dark blue eyes to me and stared. I closed my eyes and took several deep breaths. The smell of rain filled my lungs, calming me. I loved the smell of thunderstorms, but we were not expecting any storms in the next several days. My eyes flew open and met Cruz's gaze. He had shifted back to human and now he stood over me with a mask of indifference. I could feel his confusion though.

"Let's get you up off the floor, shall we?" He asked as he offered me his hand. I tentatively took it, and he pulled me to my feet. I sat on the couch, and he crouched in front of me. "I didn't hurt you, did I?" he asked.

I was acutely aware of everyone watching us, but he didn't seem to notice or care that we had an audience. I swallowed hard before shaking my head. He studied me for several minutes. I couldn't pull my eyes from him.

"You marked me." He stated.

"No! I..." I shook my head. "Maya did. She just took over, and before I could do anything, she marked you." I said quickly. "I told her we couldn't, but she wouldn't listen."

"Your wolf took over and marked Cruz?" Molly asked in surprise.

I tore my eyes from Cruz and looked at Molly. "We could feel everything. Maya was freaking out as the pain grew. No one was doing anything and she just..." I looked back at Cruz.

A cell phone rang. Cruz pulled it from his pocket without taking his eyes off me. "Storm." He listened for a minute before standing and moving to the window. "No, sir. Yes, sir. I will leave first thing in the morning. I said in the morning. If you need someone sooner, you can call someone else. Send the information over and I will take a look at it. Yes, sir." He hung up the phone and slipped it into his pocket.

I could feel his indecision and frustration. What had that been about? He still hadn't turned back around yet. He just stood there staring out the window into the blackness of the night.

"Are you really having to leave so soon?" Luna Morgan asked.

Cruz finally turned around. "I don't really have a choice, mom. I won't be far, and when I am done in a few days, I should be able to swing by one more time before heading back."

"You can't just leave." Molly stormed up to her brother.

"And why is that?" Cruz crossed his arms over his massive chest.

"Because you were just marked." Molly pointed to me, and I buried my head in my hands. "It's not just you anymore, big brother."

"She is right, Mr. Storm. Maya and River marked you. Your fate is now tied to them." Dad said.

"Not to mention that you haven't marked her yet. You will be weaker with only a partial bond." Alpha Maverick said.

"I am stronger now than when I was only human, even without marking her." He stated and I glanced up at him. His eyes were a swirl of dark and light blue. His wolf was pushing forward. "I cannot have a mate right now. It is too dangerous!" He finally yelled. His eyes flashed darker, and he took a step toward me before stopping. "Caspian, so help me." He growled as his eyes flashed again.

Molly began laughing. "I am siding with Caspian, Cruz. Regardless of whether you want a mate right now or not, you have one, and it is not anyone's fault. It is a normal part of life for us to eventually find our mates. She is part of who you are. From the moment you recognized River as your mate, Caspian would have fought for her."

"We have two Alphas here; we can do the binding ceremony." Mom laughed.

"You can't be serious?" I stood. "Maya forced our mark on him. I don't even know who he is, except that he is some sort of soldier with a bad attitude." I was desperate to get this all to stop. I wish I could go back in time and leave with Max and Jackie. None of this would have happened.

"A bad attitude, eh?" Cruz said from directly behind me and I jumped. I whirled around to face him. His eyes were so dark, and I knew Caspian had control. He took a step towards me, and I took one back. Before I knew it, I was backed against the wall. My heart was hammering in my chest as he lowered his head towards mine. His lips brushed my ear. "Cruz is a saint compared to me."

He moved so quickly that I didn't have time to react before he was marking me. I whimpered and he cradled me close. He bit down harder, and I gripped onto his shirt as pain and warmth spread through my body. He groaned in pain. I leaned more against him as he cursed, and I knew that Cruz was back in the driver's seat.

"Are you okay?" He asked me softly.

I took a step away from him and glared. "Not so fun when your wolf takes over, is it?" I tried to walk away, but my legs gave out.

Cruz caught me and helped me back to the couch. Mom and dad, Alpha Maverick, Luna Morgan and Molly all looked like they were trying to hold in their laughter as they watched me and Cruz.

"I think this is the first mate bonding I have ever seen where the humans weren't thrilled with the idea and the wolves took over." Dad laughed. "Now do you want a Binding Ceremony or are you going to leave it at just marking each other?"

"What's the difference?" Molly asked. "We don't have that kind of ceremony at home."

"Marking each other is only half of the bonding between mates. The other half is a binding ceremony performed by an Alpha that seals the mate bond. Without it, the pair are not fully connected and aren't as strong."

"I think we would need to call in Alpha Max, because I am unfamiliar with it." Alpha Maverick sat in a chair with a grin.

I looked up at Cruz. He ran a hand down his face before looking at me. He finally took a deep breath. "I leave the decision up to you, River."

My eyes widened in surprise. *"We should definitely do the Binding Ceremony. If Cruz is heading off on a mission in the morning, he needs to be at his strongest."* Maya advised.

I bit my lip as I thought. Maya was right, without the ceremony, Cruz was vulnerable. "Okay." I whispered.

Mom left to go get Uncle Max and I buried my face in my hands. I heard Alpha Maverick, Luna Morgan, and Molly talking quietly with my dad on the other side of the room. The couch dipped beside me, and I knew Cruz had sat down. "I'm so sorry." I whispered so only he could hear me.

"It's okay, River." He responded just as softly. I looked over at him. He was leaning back with his eyes closed. "I should be thanking you for helping me finally shift. It will come in handy over the next several days." He turned and looked at me.

"What do you mean that guy marked River!" Paxton yelled, just before the door burst open. He came to a stop in front of Cruz with fire blazing in his eyes.

I tried to get off the couch, but Cruz pulled me back down next to him. "You stay here. I don't want you falling over. That mark was much deeper than it had to be."

I watched as Cruz got to his feet with a tired sigh. He stood several inches taller than Paxton and he was easily twice his size. "You marked her?" Paxton asked angrily.

"To be fair, she marked me first." Cruz shrugged.

"Really? River is your wife now?" Belle came running around the couch and latched onto Cruz's leg.

"Not yet, little princess." He glanced over at me, and I felt my cheeks warm. "Could you go sit with River? I think your brother wanted to fight with me."

"But you can't!" Ana yelled as she looked anxiously between the two men. "You will hurt him."

"I promise not to hurt him. I won't even leave a bruise." Cruz crouched down to Ana's level. "I am just going to help him get a nap so he can sleep his bad attitude off."

"You promise?" Ana pressed.

"I promise. Now go keep River company for me." Cruz stood and faced Paxton. Ana crawled up into my lap and I hugged her close. I had no idea how Cruz was going to keep that promise.

Paxton raised his guard, ready for a fight. Cruz was calm as he watched his opponent. All was quiet as Paxton began throwing punches and Cruz would dodge or block them. Pax lunged and with one swift strike, Cruz hit Paxton's neck, causing him to drop like a sack of potatoes. I swear, I blinked, and it was over. Paxton was in a heap on the floor and Cruz crouched down and checked his pulse. He glanced back at us and gave a half smile. He stood and turned to Max and Jackie. He apologized for knocking out Paxton.

Dad came up to me and helped me to my feet before leading me to the other side of the room. He kissed me on the cheek before putting my hand in Cruz's. I realized what was happening and my hand tightened on Cruz's as my heart rate accelerated. Maya kept telling me to breathe, and that is what I focused on; one breath at a time. The ceremony ended and I finally looked at Cruz.

"You may kiss your bride to seal the bond." Max winked as he smiled.

I swallowed hard as Cruz slowly lowered his head. His lips were soft and warm against mine. A spark seemed to flash between us as the soft kiss turned into something more. I rose on my toes as his arms wrapped around me. I was vaguely aware of people laughing. Cruz pulled back and rested his forehead against mine.

"I thought you said they didn't really like each other and that their wolves marked each other." Max laughed.

I blushed and looked down at my feet as I lowered my hands to Cruz's chest. My mind felt like it was in a haze. All I wanted was to be close to him. Cruz blinked several times before he seemed to snap out of whatever had overcome us.

"Don't mind Max." Jackie laughed. "That weird feeling is the bond fully forming."

It wasn't a weird feeling; it was a desperate need to be close to Cruz. While we kissed, everyone and everything else disappeared. He was the only thing that mattered in that moment. I couldn't live without him. I needed him. That desperate feeling freaked me out.

I nodded and stepped away from Cruz. I ran my hand through my hair and took a deep calming breath. It had the opposite effect. His scent was everywhere. I needed to get away from it so that I could process what had just happened.

"I think I am going to go to bed." I said quietly before hugging Nash and Ana and leaving the room. Maya was pleased with herself, but I couldn't help feeling anxious. I had just marked and married a complete stranger.

Chapter Four

Cruz

I watched as River walked out of the room. Caspian was mad that I wasn't following her, but I could feel she needed space. I moved to the couch and laid down. I was completely exhausted. I hadn't had time to catch up on sleep since I made it back from the Southern Kingdom.

"Aren't you going to go with River?" Mom asked me.

"Nope." I said, closing my eyes.

"You two just got married. You are supposed to be spending time together." Alpha Max said with a chuckle.

"Not tonight." I said without opening my eyes. Not until my nightmares were not waking me up in the middle of the night. PTSD was a very real part of my life. It is one of the main reasons I stay away from home so much. I love my family, but when I sleep, I get trapped in reliving some of my missions. Miles tried waking me once, and I almost killed him before I realized he wasn't the enemy.

"Don't you think you are a little big for the couch, Cruz?" Molly asked. She plopped down on my abdomen, causing me to grunt. I grabbed her around her waist and dumped her on the floor. "Hey! That hurt."

"I'm heading out." I stood and walked out into the hall. I almost made it to the front door before my arm was grabbed.

"Your sister was just teasing you, honey. You don't need to leave." Mom said, with worry in her voice.

I sighed as I turned to face her. "I know she is just teasing. Mom, I cannot go up there. I shouldn't still be here. The only reason that I am, is because I made a promise to Belle and Nash." Hurt flashed in mom's eyes. "I love you, mom. But I am still on duty. I don't have leave for another few weeks. You know that I will always come home when I get time off." I gave her a hug and kissed her cheek. "I will be back in the morning for an hour before I have to head out."

"Cruz, might I have a word with you?" Alpha Max asked as he and Gamma Easton came down the stairs.

"Yes, sir." I followed them down a long hallway. We entered an office, and Gamma Easton closed the door.

I stood tall and waited for Alpha Max to speak. He cleared his throat a few times. "I want to thank you for saving my kids and bringing them home."

"You are welcome, sir. Nash and Belle are incredibly brave."

"Just so you are aware, this office is soundproof and secure. We brought the kids here after you asked us to take them out of the family room." Alpha Max eyed me up and down. "Nash and Belle told us that you killed several men in order to save them."

"I...Uh...I tried to limit what they saw."

"Nash told us that you threw a knife into the man holding onto Belle and asked them to close their eyes before shooting another man. He said he peeked and saw you moving the bodies out of the room."

I swallowed but said nothing. I should have never told them that I was Shadow. But then again, they are smart kids, and they would have figured it out. Who knows who they would have told if I hadn't issued the warning to keep it to themselves.

"They didn't say much else, but I wanted to thank you for doing what you could to save them and protect them from the men that took them."

"You are a soldier and the son of Maverick and Morgan. Other than those two facts, we know nothing about you." Gamma Easton studied me. "Now, my daughter is married to you. So, what kind of man are you, Cruz?"

I knew this was why they had pulled me into the room. They wanted to learn more about me. If I were them, I would be doing the same thing. But I was tired, and I was not in the mood to be interrogated. "I am a kitten of a man." I smiled at them. "Just a ball full of cuddles and I get along with everyone."

Max's lips twitched and Easton crossed his arms over his chest. "From what Ana and Nash have said, a kitten isn't how I would describe you." Max commented.

"Marshmallow? Fluffy cloud? A feather pillow?" I asked shrugging my shoulders.

"I think we can add jester to the facts we know about him." Max chuckled.

"Cruz, my daughter marked you. I have to know that she will be well cared for." Easton said in frustration. A knock sounded on the door and Easton pulled it open.

"Daddy, I need to talk to you about...Oh!" River stepped into the room and froze when she saw me. She blinked a few times before looking at her father and then Alpha Max. "Please tell me you two aren't..."

"Oh, they sure are." I said, crossing my arms over my chest. "But don't worry, we have discussed how big of a teddy bear I am."

"You, a teddy bear? Are you also the size of a dwarf?" River looked me up and down.

I placed my hand over my heart. "You wound me, River. How dare you say I'm tall."

"I just don't know which is bigger, your height or your ego." She crossed her arms over her chest.

"Hmm, do you have a measuring stick? I don't think I have compared the two in a while." I smirked back at her. Caspian was chuckling. I rather liked verbally sparring with River.

Easton and Max started laughing and I eyed them. "Do you still think that they are ill suited?" Max asked.

"No, I think my worries are put to rest." Easton shook his head.

"Good. Am I free to go to my car?" I asked as I headed for the door.

"Car?" River watched me approach her and the door with concern.

"Cruz has decided to sleep in the car tonight." Easton commented.

"You do not have to sleep in the car. I mean, you could...we have guest rooms at our house if you don't want to stay in the packhouse." River's face turned a pretty shade of pink.

I stopped beside her and leaned close to her ear. "It's safer this way." I let my fingers barely brush hers as I passed.

I could feel her confusion as I headed outside. I jogged back to the car and climbed in. I entered in my security code on the dash and visors slid up the windows. They created a soundproof barrier and made it impossible for anyone to see inside. They even blocked heat signatures. I twisted around and grabbed my bag from behind the seat. I needed to look at the information that Miles sent me on my new mission.

As soon as the sun started to lighten the sky, I headed back to the packhouse. The door was locked. I quickly picked the lock and slipped inside. The house was completely silent. I explored the ground floor as I looked for a dining room. I didn't find one. I made my way to the gym that I had entered through the night before. I could use a little training to help clear my mind. Thoughts of River had plagued me all night, making it impossible to focus on the information I was supposed to be going over.

I had moved from machine to machine as I worked up a sweat. My shirt was soaked so I pulled it off before laying on the bench. Shaking out my hands, I grabbed hold of the bar. I was halfway through my third set of thirty when I heard a slight noise near the door. Caspian stepped up, allowing me to use our ability. It was weird not having the pain with it. I saw River and Nash standing just inside the door. I finished my set before racking the weights.

I sat up and looked over at them. "Are you here to be my spotter, Nash?"

"Can I?" he asked excitedly as he ran over to me. "No one else is up and Riv said I could come watch her run."

"It's a good thing you showed up. I need someone to sit on my back." I stood from the bench. "If it is okay with you, River. Can I steal your running buddy?"

She had a confused look on her face as she stared at the ground. She didn't respond and she wouldn't look at me. I walked over to her, and I could feel her nervousness increase. I stopped right in front of her, and she took a deep breath.

"Is that okay?" I asked again.

"How did you get in here?" she finally asked.

I chuckled. "The lock was easy to pick."

"Do you always break into other people's homes?" River still hadn't looked at me.

I hooked my finger under her chin, applying just enough pressure for her to lift her head to look at me. "That depends on what is inside."

"You should kiss her." Nash hugged my leg. "Dad always kisses mom to say good morning."

"I'm sure your mom likes that, but I'm not sure if River would appreciate me doing that." I smiled.

"But she told that Molly girl that you were good at it." Nash said in confusion. "I heard them talking last night before she went back home."

River's face turned bright red as her eyes widened. I could feel her embarrassment through our bond. "Did she now?" I gave her a crooked grin.

"That's not exactly what I said." River said quickly. "And yes, you can have Nash help you." She brushed past me as she moved quickly to the treadmills.

I watched her for a minute before turning to Nash. I explained how I needed him to sit on my back while I did pushups. The six-year-old wasn't nearly the weight I normally added, but the kid was having fun. I caught River watching me several times and whenever our gazes met, I would wink at her. She blushed easily and I found it fun to get her flustered. I completed my workout and stood.

"What next?" Nash asked.

"Time for a shower. I need to start getting ready to leave." I ruffed up his hair.

"You're leaving? But we just got back." Nash complained.

"I am still on the clock, buddy. I will stop by as soon as I can."

"How long will you be gone?"

"That is a tough question. Anywhere between a few days and a few weeks. This time is supposed to be shorter. Usually, I am gone for months at a time." A started yelp came from the treadmills, and I looked over in time to see River fall hard before getting swept off the belt. I ran over to her and pulled her into my arms. "Are you okay?" I asked desperately.

She was shaking and breathing hard. I quickly scanned her body for any injuries. She had road rash on her right leg from being caught against the belt. I pulled up her shirt to check her side. "Hey!" She swatted my hand and pulled her shirt back down. "I'm fine." She snapped.

I took a deep breath to try to calm the worry filling me. I smoothed the hair out of her face as I watched for any sign of pain. *"She is not fine. Her leg is all scratched up."* Caspian growled. *"And I saw some on her side before she pulled her shirt down."*

"Cruz, I promise I am okay." River said softly as she grabbed the wrist of my hand that held her head. "Maya can heal us within a few hours." I let out a tense breath as I rested my forehead against hers. This woman is going to be the death of me. I couldn't believe the effect she had on me, and I had known her for less than twenty-four hours. "Cruz, you really stink. You should go get a shower or something."

I chuckled as I straightened up. I was still holding River in my lap with my arms around her. "I thought mates were supposed to smell good?"

"I guess not all mates do." She retorted as she scrunched her nose.

"He stinks because he is all sweaty, not because he is your mate." Nash laughed.

I grinned as I got to my feet and set River on hers. I didn't release her though. She leaned against me, and I grew worried. "Be honest with me, how bad is it?" I asked quietly.

"I am a little banged up, but like I said, I will be healed by tonight." She straightened and took a step back. "But seriously, you stink."

I pressed a kiss to her forehead before releasing her. I was halfway to the locker room when I realized what I had done. I had kissed River. I stopped walking and glanced back at her. She was watching me with a curious expression. She shook her head before turning and walking out the door with a slight limp.

I watched her go before continuing to the locker room. Nash followed me inside. He took a seat on a bench while I jumped in the shower. I had just finished rinsing the soap off my body when I heard a soft noise on the other side of the curtain. I paused to listen.

"Cruz?" Nash said quietly.

"I'm almost done, buddy, and then we can go find something to eat." I told him.

"We didn't tell you everything." His voice was softer, and I barely heard him.

I shut the water off and wrapped a towel around my waist before pulling the curtain back. Nash looked nervous and scared. "What is it, Nash?" I knelt down, and he stepped closer to me.

"I had my dad's phone. Ana wanted to send a video to mom with her dancing in the garden. I was recording her when I heard them talking. The men got really angry when they saw I was making a video. Ana told me to run, but I tripped and fell. I hid the phone before the man grabbed me." Nash's eyes were wide with fear.

"Where were you, Nash?" I asked. The phone's location had to be what they were trying to get out of him the night I rescued the kids.

"We were in the North Wind Pack."

"Do you remember where you hid the phone?" I kept my voice gentle, even though I was ready to bolt from the house to retrieve it. Nash looked down as he wrung his hands. "Do you trust me, Nash?" He nodded. "If I can get that phone, you and your sister will no longer be in danger."

Nash looked back at me. He chewed his bottom lip a few times before he moved even closer to me to whisper in my ear. "I fell at the base of a fountain that looked like a dragon. There was a small crack along the base, and I shoved it in there. I put a rock over the hole so no one would see it."

I lifted Nash into my arms as I stood. I grabbed my phone and quickly moved to the front lobby of the pack house. "Belle! Molly! Alpha Max!" I yelled. I didn't have to wait long before the whole household came running, including River and her parents. I set Nash down. "Alpha, I need you to keep everyone inside the packhouse. I am sending a security team to help keep the property secure. Molls, I need the keys to your bike."

"Cruz, what is going on?" Mom asked in alarm.

"Just some precautions while I am gone." I glanced at her.

"Why are you only in a towel?" Molly asked.

"I took a shower. Apparently, I stink." I turned my attention to Belle. "I need to leave now, little princess."

"Where are you going?" Belle asked.

"I need to go get something before I have to catch a plane."

"Is your plane going to blow up, too?" Nash asked, tugging on my hand.

I looked down at him. "I thought you said it was only going to go down?"

"Yeah, in a ball of fire after the explosion." Belle clarified.

"If I do my job right, everything will be fine." I shrugged, trying to put the kids at ease.

"What?" Mom practically screeched. "You are going to fly on a plane that you know is going to explode?

I closed my eyes briefly before turning to her. "Mom..."

"Don't you mom me, young man. You cannot get on a plane that is set to blow up." Her eyes darkened and I felt her push her aura out.

Everyone, including the Alphas, all ducked their heads at the strength she was putting out. Caspian whined, but I stood tall, resisting the urge to cave. "Nice try, mom, but I have learned to resist auras. This is nothing I haven't done before." I hadn't even told Molly about that mission. I had lost my entire team that day. The bomb killed everyone and damaged the plane to the point it crashed. I was the only survivor and had been found by the enemy. I was their prisoner for two weeks before Caspian healed us enough for me to escape. That was the mission that haunted me.

"But you can't." Belle cried as she ran to me.

I scooped her up and held her close. I caught River's eye, and she looked concerned. This is why I didn't want a mate. What I did was dangerous and leaving behind a family, not knowing if I would see them again, was a different level of torture. "Can you do something for me, Belle?" I whispered close to her ear. She nodded as her arms tightened around me. "I need you to look after River for me. Do you think you can do that?" She nodded again and I set her down.

"Please tell me you are going to get dressed before you leave." Molly said.

I gave her a crooked grin. "I was thinking on going like this. You know the whole element of surprise and all."

"Do the world a favor and get dressed. No one wants to see that." Molly teased.

"*I kinda like the way River is looking at us.*" Caspian commented, and I glanced over at her. Her emerald, green eyes were flickering from their normal color to a darker hue as her gaze traveled slowly over me.

"You aren't getting on my bike like that." Molly continued.

"Have the keys ready. I am going to run out to the SUV to grab my tactical bag and then I need to leave."

Without waiting for a response, I pulled open the door and stepped outside. I held the towel up as I jogged down the lane until I reached the SUV that was still parked in the trees. I scanned my fingerprint, and the vehicle unlocked. I climbed in and typed in my code, securing the vehicle. I quickly changed into my gear as I mentally went over the information from last night and what Nash had said this morning.

My mission was to get into the royal palace and find out all of their flight plans for the next several months. We needed to narrow down what flight was being targeted. That was the first step. After the royals were secure, we needed to figure out why they were suddenly being targeted.

I got out of the vehicle and strapped on my belt. I transferred the rest of my gear from the duffle bag to a backpack. I sent a message to Miles to get a team here to protect the family within the next couple of hours and headed back to the packhouse.

When I stepped inside, River was the only one in the lobby. She was pacing anxiously but stopped when she saw me. We stood there for a minute, just watching each other. I could feel how upset she was, but I wasn't sure why she was feeling that way.

"Do I smell okay?" I asked as I sniffed myself, trying to lighten her mood. She growled as she turned away from me and started to walk away. I grabbed her arm to stop her. "Hey, what's wrong, River?"

Her entire body was tense as she glared up at me. "I don't know." she finally said, looking down at the ground. "I am so mad, and I don't know why." She whispered.

I hugged her and she buried her face in my chest. She took several deep breaths before she began to relax. I rested my chin on her head and closed my eyes. "River, I need to go." I whispered after several minutes.

Her arms tightened around my waist briefly before she looked up at me. "Be safe, Cruz."

I smiled down at her. "I didn't think you would miss me."

"Missing you and not wanting to feel you die through the mate bond, are two separate things." River scowled at me as she tried to take a step back.

"Good to know where I stand with you." I couldn't help my smile from growing. River was full of fire, and I loved it. Most women I had met just giggled and threw themselves at me. I had zero interest in them. She tried again to pull away from me, but I only tightened my arms around her. I pressed my face into her neck as I took a deep breath of her heavenly sent.

"Let go of me, Cruz." She growled. I pressed a long kiss to my mark, and she shivered. "I thought you said you needed to leave." Her voice came out airy. I smiled when she stopped trying to push me away.

"I do." I straightened back up. "As much as I like my job, I find I rather enjoy getting under your skin more." She huffed and shoved against me again.

"Don't take it personally, River. Cruz is a world-class butthead." Molly said as she descended the stairs. "You might need to top it off soon if you are planning on going far." She tossed the keys at me, and I caught them.

"Butthead?" I gasped in mock horror.

"And you still stink. Do you not have any clean clothes or is that your natural musk?" River glared at me, but I could feel her anxiety rising again.

"I haven't had time to do laundry. I thought that is what a wife was for." I asked her with a straight face.

Her mouth fell open in surprise. "Is it also a wife's duty to put arsenic in her husband's food?"

I laughed but stopped when my phone rang. I pulled it from my pocket. "Storm."

"Security team is three hours out." Miles said. "When do you expect to get to the palace?"

"I have to make a detour before I can go to the palace." I glanced down at River as I spoke.

"How long is this detour going to take?"

"Why do you need to go to the palace?" she asked quietly.

"I need to know the flight schedules of the royals." I whispered in her ear. "I will get the information, sir. I always do." I told Miles.

"Whatever is going on with you, kid, sort it out. I need your head in the game. I don't want to have to leave you behind with a bullet hole again. That had been too close, and you know it. You were missing for a week and a half. For all we knew, you bled out somewhere."

River tensed as she laid her head on my chest. "I understand, sir." I ended the call and put my phone back in my pocket.

"I have an easier way of getting the flight information." River whispered.

Chapter Five

River

I closed and locked the door of my dad's office. Cruz watched me as I crossed the room. "All right, you got me alone in a locked room, what's your plan now?" Cruz smirked at me.

I rolled my eyes as I reached my dad's desk. "Do you have a knife on you?" I asked as I took a seat.

"Always. Why?" Cruz's eyes twinkled, even though he looked confused. He was so stinking cute when we bantered. Most guys I tried to talk like this with couldn't keep up.

"I think we need to cut off your legs." I said seriously.

His eyes widened, but his lips twitched as he fought a smile. "Why is that?"

"There is no hope for shrinking that ego of yours, so we might as well cut you down to a normal size." I smirked as I picked up the phone on the desk. It was a secure line and the only one we used to call Papa Toren and Papa Jet.

Cruz chuckled as he walked towards me. "Hello." Papa Toren answered before Cruz could respond.

"Hey, Papa Toren. How are you?" I smiled as I met Cruz's surprised gaze.

"River! I am doing good. How are you?"

"I'm fine. Just working and training. The usual." I sat back in the chair. Cruz took a seat as he watched me intently. "You sound busy."

"Unfortunately, I am. I'm glad you called though, can you let your parents know that the meeting with the Southern Kingdom and the human president was moved up. We need to leave first thing in the morning." Paper rustled on the other side of the phone.

I tensed. I forgot about the upcoming meeting of all the leaders to discuss trade. "I don't know if mom and dad will be going. Nash and Ana were rescued, and just got home. I can have them call you later to let you know what they decide."

"I hate to cut our call short, sweetheart, but I need to get some last-minute things together for the meeting. I also have to get everyone packed and ready to leave by five."

"Everyone?" I asked, trying to mask my alarm.

"Yeah, Jet and his family will also be coming. It's not very often we all get to go on vacation together, so we are going to make the most of it."

"That sounds like a lot of fun." I started playing with a pen on the desk.

"You should come with us. Maybe you will find your mate." Papa Toren said, and my eyes snapped up to meet Cruz's.

"About that," I said slowly, and I could feel my cheeks heat. Cruz lifted a brow in question. "I don't need you guys forcing me to find my mate."

"You should not be alone, River. You are too special of a girl to waste your life taking care of everyone else." Papa Toren said firmly. I looked down at the desk again as my cheeks heated even more.

Cruz took the phone from me, and I gasped. I tried to get it back, but he put it up to his ear. "I agree that River is one of a kind." He grinned down at me. "Yes, sir. I am her mate."

"Cruz, give me back the phone." I reached for it again, but he blocked me.

"What I like most about her? Well, she smells nice." He grinned at me. "I like the way she compliments me, too. You should have heard her going on about how great of a kisser I am."

"Cruz!" I yelled, causing him to laugh. I punched him in the gut, surprising him enough that I was able to get the phone back.

"I didn't say he was a good kisser." I corrected, causing Papa Toren to chuckle. Cruz grabbed me around my waist, careful of my right side as he pulled me back to him.

"I have a six-year-old's eyewitness that can even confirm that she did." He said loudly.

Papa Toren started laughing harder. "I'm glad you have found your mate, River. It's nice to know there is someone out there that can keep up with you. But I need to get going, kiddo. And Cruz?"

"Yes, sir?"

"Treat River right or there won't be a place on earth you can hide from us."

I hung up the phone and turned to face Cruz. "You are impossible." I growled. "Even after I got you your information."

Cruz's teasing smile faded as his arms tightened around me. "What did you find out?"

"There is a meeting with the human president and the Southern Kingdom's ruler. Mom and all the royal family were planning on going to talk about trade and a bunch of other stuff. The meeting was moved up, and they are leaving at five tomorrow morning." I told him.

Cruz leaned forward and kissed me. "You are a life saver, River." He released me and moved to the door. He stopped just shy of opening it. He turned back to me. "Tell your parents to stay here. I have a security team that will be here in a few hours."

I stood and ran to Cruz and threw my arms around his neck. "You are still leaving?"

"River, I have to. I am the pilot for the plane the Alpha King is going to be on." He said quietly as he cradled the back of my head.

"The plane that is going to explode." I stated.

Cruz leaned back and looked into my eyes. "We don't know that for certain. My team and I will check the plane before we let anyone on board." He tucked my hair behind my ear.

"But..." Fear and anxiety had my stomach knotting. I just found my mate. I couldn't lose him, even if I barely knew him and he was a pain in the butt.

He pressed his lips to mine, and I clung to him. He slowly pulled back after I relaxed against him. He rested his forehead against mine. "I will be back as soon as I can." He kissed my forehead and stepped back. "I really do need my laundry done."

"Are you saying I have to do it?" I quirked an eyebrow as I fought the desire to beg him to stay.

"Walk me out, River." Cruz extended his hand to me. I slowly put my hand in his. I was amazed at the warmth that spread up my arm at the simple contact.

We walked outside and there was a motorcycle parked out front. Molly must have brought it out. Cruz paused at the bottom of the porch steps. I was two steps up, which made me eye level with him. "I'm not doing your laundry." I told him.

He gave me a forced smile. "I wouldn't force you to. I usually have to wash them a certain way." He started to turn but hesitated. My heart was breaking watching him go, and I cursed Maya again for marking a complete stranger. He turned back to me and kissed me again.

I moaned as he deepened the kiss. I slid my hands up his chest and ran my fingers through his short blonde hair at the back of his head. His hand moved up my back until he cupped my face. He pulled back, barely breaking the kiss. "I need to go." He whispered.

"You keep saying that." I pressed a light kiss to his lips.

"This is your fault, you know." Cruz muttered.

"What is?" I asked looking into his blue eyes.

"Stay inside and don't go anywhere alone." Cruz took a step back as he continued to watch me.

"Be careful." I whispered.

"Does he really have to go? He shouldn't have to leave. And why on earth would he get on a plane with a bomb on it?" Maya complained.

I knew why, he was a soldier. Soldiers put their lives on the line in order to protect the innocent. It wasn't just a job for Cruz, it was a calling. From the tiny bit I have heard from Molly and his parents, Cruz worked with his uncle at the FBWHA. They worked to keep a balance between werewolves and humans. In the country just south of our kingdom, humans and werewolves lived side by side. I had always wanted to visit the country and see the ocean.

Cruz's jaw clenched as he turned away from me. I wrapped my arms around my waist as I watched him get on the bike and start the engine. He glanced over at me one more time before he nodded and rode off. Maya howled as we watched him go.

He stopped just before the turn and twisted around. I held my breath. What was he doing? I couldn't see the details of his face, and after a long minute, he continued down the road.

"I have never seen Cruz so reluctant to leave on a mission. Usually, he gets a call, and he is gone within thirty minutes or less." Molly said from behind me.

"He is worried about the twins still." I said as I stared at the empty driveway.

"That is why he ordered a security team. And he wasn't out on the front porch kissing them." Molly bumped my shoulder with hers as she came to stand beside me.

I turned to her. "It was probably Caspian."

"It wasn't Caspian not wanting to go. Caspian lives for missions."

I shrugged. "It doesn't matter because he is gone, and that is that." I started to walk back inside when the roar of an engine sounded. A motorcycle came flying down the driveway. Gravel sprayed as the rider came to a stop. "Cruz?"

"Sorry for spraying you guys." He called over his shoulder as he sprinted inside. Molly and I followed him, but he was nowhere in sight when we reached the lobby. A minute later he came running back toward us. "I forgot my bag."

"When do you forget anything?" Molly asked.

"Since someone started distracting me." He paused long enough to give me one more quick kiss. He winked before running out the door. We watched as he hopped back on the bike. "I will see you in a few days, ladies." He gave us a nod and was off again.

"Yeah, it was definitely Cruz kissing you because Caspian would never have forgotten his tactical bag." Molly laughed.

*   *   *

Cruz had been gone for two days. Yesterday, I had felt a moment of anxiety and worry but it went away after a while. I was curled up on the couch reading a book when mom burst into the room and grabbed the remote. She had tears in her eyes as she flipped through the channels. She finally stopped on a news report. Dad wrapped his arms around her as mom turned up the volume.

A newscaster was telling how the whole royal family was going on a vacation as the camera zoomed in on an airplane. Toren and Jet shook hands with two huge men in all black. My heart hammered as the camera zoomed in. One of the men looked similar to Cruz, but the man had jet black hair instead of blonde. The man also wore a formfitting mask that covered everything but his eyes. The second man in black wore the exact same things.

"Hey! That's Shadow." Ana called as she pointed at the screen.

"Who is Shadow?" I asked without taking my eyes off the TV.

"He was the one that saved us. He works with Cruz." Nash said as he sat down.

Jet and Toren stood to the side as their families boarded the plane. After everyone boarded except for the two men in black, a blonde man walked up to Shadow. The blonde man kept his back to the camera, and I couldn't be certain if it was Cruz or not. The two men in black shook hands with the blonde man before they, too, boarded the plane.

The blonde man walked backwards as the plane began to taxi out onto the airstrip. The newscaster was explaining the videoclip. "The plane seemed to be in perfect working order during takeoff. The crew did a thorough walkthrough before the royal family arrived, yet we are still faced with this terrible tragedy."

I closed my book and leaned forward. The newscaster continued to explain how the pilot radioed for permission to make an emergency landing. There was something wrong with the left engine, and when the crew tried to land, it exploded. My heart stuttered and my stomach knotted.

A video of an airplane with black smoke billowing out of the engine as it nosedived toward the ground filled the screen. The plane started to level off as an explosion tore the left wing off. Next, images of the mangled airplane on the ground with fire engines trying to put out the flames were shone. My hand flew over my mouth and Molly moved to my side.

"No survivors have been found so far, but the fire crews are still trying to put out the flames. Our thoughts and prayers go out to the family of the Northern Kingdom's Royals. The name of the pilot and co-pilot have not been released at this time."

I couldn't listen anymore. I stood and walked out of the room. Had I felt Cruz's anxiety before the plane crashed yesterday? He said he would be careful. I made my way to the gym and got on the treadmill. Like my mom, I ran when I needed to think or was stressed.

Over the next hour, I increased the speed of the machine until I was sprinting. A hand reached over and hit the stop button. I slowed with the machine and looked over to see mom standing there with concern in her eyes.

"Why don't we go for a walk." Mom said softly as she grabbed my hand.

I wordlessly followed mom as we left the packhouse. Immediately a large man stepped out in front of us. "I am under orders to keep everyone in the house until Storm checks in."

"When was the last time he checked in?" I asked.

"Yesterday morning."

"You are more than welcome to join us, but we are going for a walk." Mom said as she pushed her aura out. The man grunted and eventually, his head dipped. It paid having a mom with royal blood. She was stronger than any Alpha I had met. The only person with a stronger aura was Luna Morgan.

Mom started walking again and the man fell into step behind us. We took the fork to the waterfall, and I smiled. This place was special. It had been where my parents first met, and where dad had realized mom was his mate. Mom still came here when she needed to recenter. We took off our shoes and slowly walked into the natural pool that the waterfall drained into.

Once we were thigh deep, mom turned to me. This close to the falls, you had to be right next to each other in order to hear what the other said. "Cruz was on the plane, wasn't he?" she said softly.

"He said he was going to be the pilot of the plane." I felt the sting of unshed tears. "He said if he did his job right that everything would be fine. He said he would be careful."

"He doesn't seem like a careless man." Mom put her arms around me.

"I don't even know him, but I don't want to lose him either." A tear leaked from my eye. "This is all Maya's fault. She should never have marked him."

"We had to mark him, River, and you know it." Maya scoffed. *"Caspian wasn't going to stop trying to shift. He could have killed them."*

"But now we have to deal with losing him." I sniffled.

"If he did die, so help me, I will bring him back to life so I can kill him myself." I smiled at Maya's comment.

Mom talked me into diving into the deep end. She said the shock of the water would help clear my head. She was right, I felt a little better.

When we got back to the packhouse, I went straight up to my guest room to change into dry clothes. My phone was ringing when I walked in. "Hello?" I answered as I kicked my shoes off.

"Reject your mate, River." A male voice said. It was digitalized so I couldn't tell who it was.

I pulled the phone from my ear and looked at the number: Unknown. "Who is this?"

"Reject your mate or you both will share their fate." The man threatened.

"Who's?" My heart was pounding so hard that I thought it would break out of my chest.

"I am sure your mom doesn't want to lose a daughter the same way she lost her parents." The line went dead, and my blood ran cold.

I ran from the room and only made it halfway down the hall before colliding with someone. "River? Are you alright?" Molly's worried voice broke through my panic.

I looked around desperately searching for a safe place to go. "Follow me." I grabbed her hand as I ran down the stairs to the second floor and to my dad's office. I pushed the secure button as I locked the door.

"Why are you all wet?" Molly asked. "River, talk to me."

"I need to call someone, anyone that you and Cruz trust. Please." I begged.

Molly studied my face for only a moment before pulling a black phone out of her pocket. She pressed the number one and it started ringing.

"Hello?" A male voice answered the phone.

"Uncle Miles? Why do you have Cruz's phone?" Molly asked in surprise.

"Molly? He asked me to hold onto it while he flew the royals to the meeting."

"He was on the plane?" Molly gasped.

"Molly, you know Cruz. He is always ahead of everyone and keeps his cards close to his chest. I know what the news looks like, but I have to believe he and everyone on board are fine." Even though this Miles guy sounded reassuring, there was a note of worry in his voice.

"Uncle Miles, I have someone here who needs to tell you something. If Cruz trusts you enough to give you his phone, then I trust you."

Molly gave a nod, and I took a deep breath. "I just got a call. The voice was male but digitalized, so I do not know who he is." I said quickly.

"What did this man tell you?" Miles asked.

"He told me to reject my mate. If I didn't, both my mate and I would end up like my grandparents." I started to shake, and Molly wrapped her arms around me.

"Who is your mate?"

"Cruz." I whispered.

Miles remained quiet for a long moment. "Cruz has a mate?"

"They met when he brought back Ana and Nash." Molly said. "Caspian tried to shift again, and River marked him. They were married that night."

"That would explain why he was being extra cautious and called in the security team for the Silver Moon Pack and airstrip. He usually does things on his own, not caring about the risks." Miles said. "River, has this happened before? Have you received any threats in the past? Or met anyone seeming to be overly interested in you?"

I sniffled as I thought. "A few months ago, I had a man approach me. We talked for a while before he asked me if I had found my mate yet. I told him 'No'. He became more...insistent. Before I left, he asked if I would choose a chosen mate. I told him it depended on the man. He winked at me and told me that I could stop looking. I was creeped out."

"What did he look like?" Miles asked.

"He was my height and athletically built. He had dark brown hair and brown eyes. There was a burn scar on his neck. Most of it went down past his collar, so I don't know how big it was." I ran my hands up and down my arms.

"River, is there a reason why someone would target you like that man did?" Miles asked.

"I don't know." I stammered.

"If the royal family and your mom died, who is the next in line?" Molly asked softly.

"I am, and then Kyson." I answered confused.

"Cruz told you to make sure your parents didn't go on that trip." Molly whispered.

"Miles, Gin just called in." A male voice said quickly.

"What about Shadow?"

"Gin said that Shadow beat the snot out of him before strapping the only parachute on him and kicking him out the side of the plane."

"Only parachute? When we checked there were at least twenty." Miles said.

"The explosion left only one. He came back with a message for you."

"What's the message?" Miles growled.

"A promise is a promise, and he always keeps his promises."

There was a muffled conversation before Miles came back on the line. "Molly, River, you still there?"

"Yes." Molly wiped tears off her cheeks. I didn't care anymore and let my tears fall. "Do not leave the packhouse for any reason. River, if you get any more threats, call this number again. Neither one of you should be alone. If you can, bunk together. I am on my way."

The line went dead, and we sat in silence. Was Mom's family alive? Was Cruz on the plane when it went down? I wanted to scream. I wanted to hit something. I wanted Cruz.

Chapter Six

Cruz

I finished my third examination of the plane. Everything looked fine, but something still nagged at the back of my brain. Caspian, too, felt like something was off.

"What are you thinking, Shadow? I have never seen you so unsettled." Gin asked me as we took our positions at the base of the ramp.

"Coconuts." I said, and I received a collective 'yes, sir' from all six of my men.

Spur came up with the plan's name. He said it reminded him of the coconut shell game. The one where you hide an object under one shell and mix it around with several others in order to confuse the observer.

Something didn't feel right, so I was calling for a change in plans. The royals would be seen boarding the plane but not leaving it. My team would offload them and hide them until the coast was clear. From the outside, it would appear as if Gin and I were flying the royals as scheduled.

News crews were setting up on the other side of the airport fence. They were far enough away that they wouldn't be able to get very good shots of the plane. I took a deep breath and let it out slowly. After this business with the royals was settled, I was going to take an extended leave of absence. I needed to figure out what was going to happen now that I had River to look after.

A line of vehicles slowly made their way down the road, heading for us. "Let's go to work, boys." I said over the coms.

The vehicles unloaded and Martinez led fifteen passengers towards us. The group was a mix of men, women, and children. Alpha King Toren and

Beta Jet shook our hands before they stepped aside. They waited for the rest of their family to board before they followed them onto the plane.

Miles approached me. "Everything okay, Shadow?"

"You are putting me back on a plane." I stated.

"I know how you feel about plane missions, but we need you on this." Miles extended his hand. As I shook it, I handed him the phone that is used only for Molly.

"I made you a promise when I got back from the last one. I always keep my promises, Miles." I said quietly and Miles tightened his grip on my hand. "It's a bird's song." I said in order to explain the phone. A 'bird song' was code for emergency line.

He nodded and stepped back as Gin and I boarded the plane. We closed the door, and I glanced into the cabin. Marco and Tango were assisting the royals into the hatch where Fox, Spur, and Cheese waited to stow them into a gutted fuel truck. The five of them were to take the royals to my beach house and wait for further orders.

Marco was a seven-foot giant of a man. His hair was normally fiery red, but like all my men, his hair was currently jet black, and he had on a mask. Tango was five-ten and looked skinny. His size was very misleading, the man was lethal.

I found Gin passed out drunk on homemade gin a few years ago. Even being completely hammered, he fought off the police, and SWAT was called in. The man had broken into a secure military base and barricaded himself in their security room. They assumed he was stealing sensitive information, but the opposite was true. He had warned them several times about a hole in their system. No one took him seriously, so he broke in to fix it himself. I paid for his bail and took him to Miles. Now, he is our technical expert.

Fox could con himself in and out of anything. Spur was raised in a tiny town on a cattle ranch. He kept trying to convince us to add horses to our list of getaway vehicles. Then there was Cheese. Cheese usually sat behind a desk. He was barely eighteen, but the kid was a genius when it came to finding weaknesses in buildings and security systems.

The Alpha King looked back at me, and I gave him a nod before I walked into the cockpit. Gin and I began the process to get this bird in the air. Marco gave us the green light, and we taxied out onto the runway. Minutes later, we were airborne. We had been in the air for two hours, and so far, everything was going smoothly.

"Can I ask you something?" Gin asked as he glanced at me.

"You can always ask, but that doesn't mean I will answer." I said as I checked the instruments.

"You don't seem like yourself." He said slowly.

"That's not a question." I glanced over at him.

"I guess my question is, what is wrong?"

"Nothing is wrong, Gin."

"And I am supposed to believe that?" Gin scoffed. "I have known you for two years, Shadow. We have gone on more than thirty missions together. I have never seen you so..." he gestured up and down me. "And don't think for a second that we missed that mate mark on your neck."

My jaw clenched and Caspian growled. So help me, if he speaks a single crude word about River. "What are you getting at, Gin?" I looked at him.

"I get it, man. I have a wife and baby waiting at home for me, too. I wish that I was with them instead of sitting here with you." Gin chuckled.

"How do you balance work and family?" I asked.

"I'm retiring from the field, Shadow. This is my last mission. I want to see my kid grow up." Gin smiled at me.

"I had no idea you were leaving."

"I let Miles know earlier tonight." Gin turned back to the console in front of him. "Don't get me wrong, I love this, but I need to be able to return home every night, you know? Having to say good-bye before missions has to be the hardest thing I have ever had to do."

"So, it doesn't get any easier?" I almost turned around so many times it was ridiculous. Kissing River had only added to my desire to stay.

"Nope, and it shouldn't. If you love and care for her, you should always have a hard time leaving her behind."

I opened my mouth to ask him something, but a beeping sound filled the cabin. We both turned toward the instrument panel. "Engine one is down."

"We checked each of the engines before takeoff. What is going on?" Gin yelled as the plane began to nosedive.

It was like someone had taken over our controls. I pulled back on the stick, trying to straighten us out to give us a little more time. "Get in the back and get a chute on." I yelled.

Gin jumped from his seat and scrambled to the door that connected the cockpit with the cabin. My adrenaline was pumping as I finally straightened out the plane. I radioed for permission to make an emergency landing at the nearest airstrip. I got the confirmation before I ran for the back. I could see black smoke coming from the left wing. This was not good. I sprinted for the back of the plane as the engine exploded. The force of the blast threw me against the opposite wall.

My ears were ringing, and I blinked slowly. Gin was suddenly standing over me. I could see his mouth moving but I could not hear what he was saying. He pulled me to my feet, and I looked around. The left wing was missing and there was a hole in the side of the plane. Gin was shaking one parachute.

"There is only one!" I read Gin's lips.

"You take it!" I yelled back, but he shook his head as he shoved it at me. I tried to put it on him, but he backed away. I growled. No way was I leaving him. I made a promise that if a plane was going down with my team on it again, I would get each of my men out of the plane safely, even if it cost me my life. An image of River flashed in my mind, but I forced it away. We had only minutes left before we hit the ground. He needed to leave now. "I'm sorry, Gin!"

I threw my fist into his face. He stumbled back a step. He looked at me with wide eyes. I tried to slip the chute on him again, but he moved away. I kicked him in his chest, sending him falling onto his back. I jumped on him as I forced one of his arms through the strap. He started fighting me again. I punched him three times in the side of the head. His eyes got a dazed look, and I finished putting the parachute on him.

"You get to the safe house!" I told him. "Tell Miles, a promise is a promise, and I always keep my promises!"

I hauled him up and dragged him toward the rear door of the plane. I released the lever and pushed him towards the opening. He caught himself and turned to face me. I gave him a salute before kicking him again. He fell out of the plane.

Now that I kept my promise to Miles, I needed to figure out a way to keep my promise to River. I moved to the furthest seat in the back and strapped in.

"This is a bad idea." I muttered, just as the plane hit the ground.

*   *   *

I groaned as I blinked my eyes open. I looked around. Flames and smoke were all around me. I unhooked my seatbelt and tried to move. Pain slashed up my leg. It was pinned between two seats. I coughed as I looked around again, this time searching for something that I could use to get my leg free.

"Caspian." I coughed.

"I can't heal us until we get the metal out of your leg. It's also broken. You have several cracked ribs and a concussion."

"Is that all?" I pushed on the seat in front of me. It moved a little and I cried out in pain. Oh man, this is going to suck.

It took me way too long to get myself out of the plane. My arm and chest got burned in the process and I could not put weight on my leg. My leg wasn't just broken, part of the tibia was sticking through the skin. I dragged myself out of the wreckage. I needed to put as much distance between me and the crash as possible. No one could know that I survived.

I managed to find a space under a rock. I wedged myself under it as much as I could, before passing out. I woke sometime later. It was dark and I was in a tremendous amount of pain. Caspian said my injuries would take time to heal. I listened to the noises around me. I could hear sirens and people shouting not too far away. I guess I hadn't gotten as far away as I had thought.

With my uninjured arm, I carefully dug in my vest pocket. I found my S.O.S. transmitter and pressed the button. Not once in six years had I been forced to activate it. Usually, I would have waited until I could travel on my own, but not now. Not when I needed to get back to River. I told her I would see her in a few days, and I prayed I wouldn't break my word to her. I closed my eyes and allowed the darkness to claim me again.

Chapter Seven

River

Cruz had been gone for two weeks and I was beginning to feel frantic. I needed to find him. Especially with the nightly phone calls from my robotic psychopath. I needed Cruz. Miles had arrived at the pack within a couple of hours after the phone call to him. He brought several more men with him. All were very intimidating and seemed a lot like Cruz in the way they held themselves.

It was getting late. I had an hour left until the phone call from Mr. Robo would happen. Each time he would tell me to reject my mate or face the same fate as my grandparents. I was growing more and more concerned.

Molly was taking a shower, and I was laying on the bed. My phone dinged with a text message. It was a picture of Cruz holding me in the gym after I fell off the treadmill. Another message came in. 'We know who he is, and you have not rejected him yet. My patience is growing thin, River.'

I ran from the room and down to the first-floor offices. Dad had loaned Miles his office while he was here. I knocked quickly and waited anxiously. The door cracked open, and Martinez stood there.

"Is Miles in there?" I asked breathlessly. "I really need to talk to him."

"Let her in." Miles called and Martinez opened the door. I slipped past him.

"Oh. I did not mean to interrupt." I said when I saw two large men dressed in all black standing near the desk. A third man was laying on the couch against the wall. All three had jet-black hair and wore masks that covered the lower half of their faces.

"It's okay, River. They can wait a minute or two. What is it?" Miles gestured for me to move closer.

I took a hesitant step forward but stopped when the scent of rain filled my lungs. Cruz. I glanced between the three men again. All of them were of similar build. The only thing that was different was their eyes. My phone went off again and I began to shake as I read the new message. It was an image of Cruz on the motorcycle looking back at me as I stood on the porch. 'Time is ticking.'

I crossed to the desk and handed my phone to Miles. He looked at me sharply after reading the messages. "Has he called?" I shook my head. "What are your orders?" Miles turned to the two men standing near the desk.

"Shadow hit the distress signal. We quickly located him but he has been in and out of consciousness since."

"Gin, why weren't you with Shadow?" Martinez growled.

"Have you fought Shadow lately? He literally kicked me out of an airplane after beating me senseless." Gin shot back.

"And where were you, Spur?" Miles asked.

I slowly walked over to the man on the couch. The smell of rain grew stronger. I blinked back tears. Now that I was closer, I could see the bruising and cuts on his face. His leg was splinted, and his eyes were closed. I took a seat next to the couch. He was lucky he was so banged up or I would pummel him myself for causing me to worry so much.

I combed my fingers through his black hair softly. His eyes fluttered open and found me quickly. He let out a sigh as his eyes closed again. "Hey, babe." He whispered.

"You are lucky you look like you can't even stand, because if you didn't, I would be knocking you senseless myself." I said softly.

He chuckled, then coughed. "I take it my laundry didn't get done while I was away."

"Not even close." I ran my hand through his hair again. "I think I like you better as a blonde."

"River?" Miles called.

"Yes?" I pulled my eyes from Cruz and looked across the room. All four men were watching me.

"Do you know, Shadow?" Gin asked in surprise.

"No. All I know is he is a soldier, and by the looks of him, he is terrible at it." Cruz's chuckle ended in a groan of pain.

"Watch how you talk about Shadow, Miss." Spur growled.

I cocked my head to the side. He was human. That fact alone gave me the upper hand. I may only be five foot six, but I was much stronger than I looked. All my pent-up anger and anxiety over the last several days rose to the surface. "All I said was he must not be very good at being a soldier because of his current physical state. Anyone could draw the same conclusion if they didn't know him." The man took a step towards me, and Miles stood when I did. "I can also easily draw other conclusions. He smells. He is egotistical. A jerk. A Sexist."

Spur took a swing at me, and I dodged. Maya and I needed a release from all of these emotions. I was ready for a good fight. Mom and dad had been training me since I could walk. I was a werewolf with royal blood in my veins, making me stronger and faster than most.

Spur took another swing at me. I heard a growl behind me but ignored it. I rolled and ended up behind Spur after he attempted to kick me. I quickly kicked the back of his knee, causing him to fall. I wrapped my arm around his neck, placing my hand in the crook of my arm. I placed my other hand on the back of his head. I squeezed my elbows together while pushing his head forward. I kept up the pressure until he went limp.

I released him and he slumped to the floor. Cruz was sitting up with pride and admiration in his eyes. I glanced over at Miles, Martinez, and Gin. They were watching me with shocked expressions. "So, what are we going to do about the phone calls and texts?" I asked Miles.

"What phone calls and texts?" Cruz asked as he laid back down with a groan.

I returned to my seat next to him. "The night we saw the news report on the plane crash, I got a phone call. A digitalized male voice told me to reject my mate or share the same fate as my grandparents."

"Who is your mate and what happened to your grandparents?" Gin asked.

Since the men all wore masks, I figure they were trying to keep their identity hidden from someone, so I ignored the first question. "My grandparents were attacked, and the packhouse was set on fire. No one knows if they were killed before the fire was set, or if they were burned alive."

"Why would someone be targeting you?" Martinez asked.

"My mother is the niece of the Alpha King. I am technically in line for the throne. Toren's family, Jet's family, Mom, and then me and by extension, my mate." I chanced a glance over at Cruz. His eyes were glued to me. "I have received three calls threatening me to reject my mate. Tonight, he sent me a few texts."

"Can I see the texts?" Cruz asked. Miles brought the phone over and handed it to him. I could feel Cruz's anger flowing through the mate bond. "Miles, can we get Gin and Spur a place to sleep and some food? Looks like we are staying for a while."

I sat silently as the men left the office, leaving me and Cruz alone. As soon as the door closed, I turned back to Cruz. "You are seriously so lucky you are injured right now." I snapped at him.

He scooted a little farther back. He reached over and grabbed my hand. He pulled on it and I stood up. "Come sit for a second before you start yelling at me." He sounded tired. I sat and rotated to face him. "Can you pull this mask off?" I did as he asked, and he gave me a tired smile. "How is your side and leg?"

"My side and leg?" I asked confused. I was feeling so tired. I laid down and he draped his arm over my waist.

"From the treadmill."

"Oh. That was healed days ago." I carefully rolled to face him. "What happened, Cruz?"

He pressed a kiss to my forehead. "Can I tell you all about it in the morning? I need some sleep." Pain filled his voice.

"Do you need me to get up? I don't want to hurt you." I said through a yawn.

"No. You stay where you are." he said firmly.

*   *   *

Cruz mumbled before he jerked a little and my heart started to race. We were still lying on the couch in my dad's office. The room was dark, and a blanket had been draped over us. "Cruz?" I asked softly. He didn't respond to me, but his breathing increased as he moved again. "Cruz?" I said louder. I reached up and stroked his cheek. His jaw was clenched, and his skin was damp with sweat.

Suddenly, I was under him as he grabbed my wrist. His eyes were open and there was a wild look about them. "Cruz, look at me." I said calmly. He tucked me more under him as if shielding me from something. "Cruz." I tried again to get his attention. He stared down at me, but didn't seem to be seeing me. I had read about this in my medical books. Soldiers dealing with PTSD. "Look at me, Cruz." I said again.

He blinked rapidly and his eyes cleared. He lowered his head to my shoulder as he took several deep breaths. "I'm so sorry, River. I shouldn't have let you stay." He said quietly. He lifted his head. "I didn't hurt you, did I?"

I smiled at him. "This is what you meant when you said it would be safer if you slept in your car?"

He slowly lowered himself back down next to me and I put my head on his shoulder. "You should go up to bed, River."

"I would like to see you make me." I smiled.

"Don't tempt me." He kissed my forehead. "Please, go. It is not safe here with me and I don't want to hurt you."

"I don't know who you thought I was, but you were protecting me, not attacking me. I think I am quite safe where I am. Plus, I don't want to be alone."

"Are you worried about your mystery caller?" Cruz repositioned and I could feel his whole-body tense.

"He took pictures of us through the window and again while we were on the porch. He is close by, Cruz. So, yes. I am scared." I admitted.

He pulled me closer to him and I sighed. "We will figure out who he is, River. I promise, we will sort it all out."

I nodded and pressed closer to him. The smell of rain filled me, and I started to relax. My phone rang on the desk and my heart rate accelerated. I shook my head as I squeezed my eyes closed. Not tonight. Not again.

"River?"

"I don't want to answer it." I whispered as I started to shake.

Cruz tightened his arms around me. "River, you are safe." He whispered. I didn't respond. I knew with Cruz nearby I was safe, but I couldn't help the fear coursing through me. After a few minutes, he started to stroke my hair. I snuggled closer to him as I began to relax. Maybe Cruz really was a teddy bear, even though he was the size of a mountain.

"It's weird seeing you without your mask." Gin's quiet voice woke me from a deep sleep. "You are uglier than I thought you would be."

"I didn't see a need to wear it in here." Cruz replied.

"For not knowing each other, you two seem awfully cozy."

"She is my mate."

"I figured that much out, Shadow." Gin chuckled. "But she said she doesn't know you and I didn't get the impression she was lying."

"She wasn't. We met the evening before I left."

"You just found your mate, yet you refused to take the last parachute. What were you thinking?" Gin growled out.

"You have a wife and baby, Gin. This is your last mission before getting out of the game. I wasn't about to leave you on that plane. River would have been fine. She is strong and capable. Your wife and kid need you." Cruz pulled me a little closer.

"She does seem like a fighter. Not many people can drop Spur like that." There was a pause. "How are you feeling?"

"Like I was dropped out of the sky."

"I would think so. This is the first time I have seen you fully conscious since we found you under that rock. Has Caspian been able to heal the leg after we set it?"

"As a hybrid, I don't heal as fast as a full-blooded werewolf. He has managed healing the ribs and fractured skull but not much else."

"I might have something that can help with that." I mumbled. Cruz tensed and I looked up at him. "Morning." I smiled.

"How long have you been awake?" Cruz narrowed his eyes at me.

"Long enough to know that you go by Shadow when working, Gin is married with a baby, and you are hurt because you were stupid enough to get on that plane." I stood up and stretched.

"You should have said something earlier." Cruz commented.

"Oh, where is the fun in that. People tend to talk more when they think you can't hear them." I smirked at him before walking over to the desk and picking up the phone.

"Who are you calling?" Cruz asked as he tried to sit up but groaned and laid back down.

"Gin, do you have a knife on you?" I looked at the man. He still had on all his black gear, including the mask. He gave me a nod. "If Shadow cannot get his shirt and pants off, cut them. I need to have access to all the wounds and injuries." I said, as I dialed my mom's number.

"Hello."

"Hey, mom, can you bring me our big med kit? I am in dad's office." I ignored Gin and Cruz as they tried to tell me that Cruz had already been treated.

"I will have your father bring it to you in a few minutes." Mom said, and didn't press for details.

"Thanks, mom."

I hung up the phone and went to the minifridge in the corner. I grabbed three water bottles and walked back to the couch. I handed one to each of the men. Cruz still had his clothes on, and he was scowling at me.

"I have already been treated, River. There is no need for this." Cruz said firmly.

I reached over and grabbed the knife out of Gin's hand. "I don't believe I asked if you were treated before." I spun the knife in my hand. "There is a lot you don't know about me, Shadow. Are you sure you want to test me on this?"

Gin laughed and stepped back. Cruz continued to glare at me for a few minutes. I sagged my shoulders and sat down next to him, acting defeated. "River, I will be fine in a few weeks." He wrapped his arm around my back. I looked up at him and his eyes dipped to my lips. His head started to descend, and I closed my eyes.

Slowly, I slid the knife under the hem of his shirt. Just before his lips touched mine, I leaned back and slid the knife up quickly, stopping with the tip against his throat. There was a clean slice all the way up the shirt. "Don't test me, Shadow." I said sweetly. His eyes were wide in surprise. Gin was laughing so hard he was doubled over.

A knock came at the door just before it opened. Dad stepped into the room and paused when he saw me holding the knife to Cruz's throat. "Ticked her off, did you?" Dad continued to walk towards us.

I pulled the knife away from Cruz and set it on the floor. "Thanks for bringing this, dad." I gave him a smile as I slid onto the floor next to where dad put the med kit.

"I still don't know how you and your mother keep all this straight." Dad shook his head.

I lifted the lid and scanned all the jars and pouches inside. Everything was here. I glanced back at Cruz. His chest had burns all over it, along with bruises and cuts. I glared at him. Why didn't he say anything? I was cuddled up against him all night. I was probably causing him a tremendous amount of pain.

"It is going to be incredibly painful to use the creams to take care of the broken bones and burns. We can't do that to him." Maya whined.

"We can't just let him deal with this either." I told her as I looked back at the contents of the kit. I grabbed a long thin vial. The contents were dark purple and thick.

I took a deep breath and sat back on the couch. "Drink only half of this." I passed the vial to Cruz.

"What is it?" he asked with his brows furrowed in confusion.

"Drink half of it." I said again.

Cruz hesitated before putting the vial to his lips. He passed it back to me and I drank the second half. A shudder shook me, and I gagged. I had never tasted anything so disgusting before. I returned to the kit and pulled out a red jar and a glove.

"River, what was that purple stuff. Your mom has never touched it before." Dad asked. "I remember her telling me once what it was, but I can't remember."

"She never had cause to use it." I didn't look at him. "Which bones are broken?" I asked looking at Gin.

"He has a compound fracture of his tibia, and his ankle is shattered. I'm not sure what else."

"Take the pants off, Shadow." I glanced at him over my shoulder.

He looked ready to protest, but dad spoke up. "Trust her. These creams help accelerate healing, even for humans."

It took a couple of minutes for dad and Gin to help get Cruz's pants off and for him to be laid back down. He was breathing hard, and his face was twisted in pain. I took the time to mentally prepare for what was to come. The purple ooze was a transference potion. Whatever magic was dealt to Cruz, I would feel instead.

I put the glove on and unscrewed the lid of the red jar. "Are you familiar with witches?"

"No." Cruz said through clenched teeth.

"All of these are healing potions created by one. They can heal you within hours."

"But there is a drawback to using them. All magic has a price. The price for accelerated healing is pain. Pain more intense than what you are currently feeling. For example, if you get a papercut and decide to use a cream, the pain would be worse than a papercut but bearable." Dad explained. I wasn't planning on telling Cruz this part. "My wife had a dislocated elbow, and she nearly passed out."

"Perfect." Cruz muttered.

I pressed a kiss to his forehead. "Don't worry. You won't feel a thing." I gave him a forced smile.

"Don't lie to him, River." Dad scolded me.

I scooped a large amount of cream out of the jar as I sat next to Cruz's legs. His ankle was severely swollen and purple. The bandage had been removed from his shin. There was a long gash about halfway up. I swallowed hard. This was going to hurt. I glanced at my dad. "I didn't lie." Dad looked confused and then worried as my hand moved closer to Cruz's ankle.

Chapter Eight

Cruz

"River, stop!" Gamma Easton yelled as he lunged for River.

I looked at her as she pressed her hand to my ankle. She sucked in a quick breath and squeezed her eyes closed. She was incredibly tense, and her breathing was ragged. Gamma Easton reached River's side and pulled her hand from me.

"Dad," her voice sounded weak. "I'm not done."

"Yes, you are." Gamma Easton said firmly.

"What's going on?" I asked as I tried to sit up. River's head lolled to the side, and she swayed where she sat.

"She gave you a transference potion, then took the second half. The price of using the creams is now hers to bare." Gamma Easton said as he stripped the glove off her hand. She made a feeble attempt to stop him. He picked her up and laid her next to me and I wrapped my arms around her. She whimpered as she shook.

"Daddy." River's voice was soft. "I need...to finish." She slowly blinked. Her eyes were unfocused, and my anxiety rose.

"What are you doing?" I asked in alarm, as I watched Gamma Easton put an exam glove on and reach for the red jar. "I won't put her through anymore." I growled, holding her tighter.

"Do you really want to face her when she is fully back." Gamma Easton gave me an apologetic look. "At least you don't have to be the one putting it on. I had to do that for her mother."

"No, but I now have to live with the fact that she is experiencing the pain meant for me." I looked down at her.

Her green eyes were watching me. They seemed more focused than before. I felt someone touch my ankle again and pain flashed in her eyes. She whimpered as she squeezed her eyes closed. Gamma Easton worked quickly as he spread the cream all the way up to my knee. River's breathing became erratic. She screamed out in agony, and I held her close.

"We need to stop this!" Caspian yelled.

"River would kill us if we did." I snapped back. I wasn't any happier having to watch her go through this. I rested my forehead against the side of her head. I prayed this would be over soon.

"I am going to give you a bit of a rest, Riv. And then I need you to tell me what to use on the burns." Gamma Easton said.

She turned more into me, and I bit the inside of my cheek. My chest was burned, and she was pressing into it, but there was no way I was going to let her go. Last night had been rough, but I was able to keep her from touching the burns too much. I wiped the tears off her cheeks with my thumb. She was so pale.

Twenty minutes past and River was still shaking and tense. She took a deep breath and let it out slowly. She opened her eyes and looked at me. "You are in so much trouble, River." I whispered in her ear. "I can't believe you would do this."

"And I can't believe how much you stink." She wrinkled her nose.

I chuckled and pressed a kiss to her temple. "I would have showered before getting here, but I don't really remember the journey."

"That's because you let yourself get blown up, knowing full well that it was going to happen." She retorted.

"River, honey. Which cream do I use for the burns?" Gamma Easton put his hand gently on River's head.

"The blue square jar with the silver lid. Dad, this cream is more potent than the red jar." River said softly. "You will need to use two or three gloves."

"River, I don't think you should do this." I told her. "I don't want you to do this."

"Do what? All I am doing is laying here." She glared at me.

Caspian surged forward. "You are not doing this." He growled firmly.

River's eyes flickered to a darker green before settling back to their normal hue. "Fine, can I get a drink of water?" she said through clenched teeth. Caspian stepped back as he continued to pace.

Gamma Easton helped River sit up and handed her a bottle of water. Gin was watching her with concern. She leaned forward and I saw a spark of amusement in Gin's eyes.

When River turned around, she had a syringe in her hand. I immediately tensed. "Then at least have some pain killers." Her voice was stronger and filled with anger. "It will feel like a bee sting and will burn, but you should be able to handle it."

She moved quickly to stick the needle in my arm, and I caught her wrist. "Nice try, babe. I'm not letting you put anything in me unless I know exactly what it is." A sharp pain stabbed into my leg followed by a burning sensation. "River." I growled.

"Nice try, babe. You need to be smarter than that." She smirked at me. Warmth spread through my body and my mind started to feel fuzzy. "Sweet dreams, Shadow."

"You little..." My voice trailed off as blackness claimed me.

* * *

I groaned as I opened my eyes and sat up. My whole body felt like it was in a fog. I looked around the room a little disoriented. Gamma Easton, Miles, Gin, and Martinez were looking at me from a group of chairs on the other side of the room. I ran a hand down my face as I tried to get my thoughts in order.

"How do you feel?" Miles smiled at me.

"Like I got hit over the head with a sludge hammer." I shook my head slowly.

"Close enough." Gin chuckled. "A five and a half foot sludge hammer to be exact."

"It's probably best if you do not tick off River." Gamma Easton grinned at me. "She is too much like her mother."

River. I got to my feet with only a small amount of pain in my leg. I looked down. I was in nothing but my underwear. Memories of her asking me to drink that purple ooze and then stabbing me with a syringe came back to me. "Where is she?" I growled as I headed for the door.

"I think she and Molly went to the waterfall with Spur and a few other guys." Miles called after me with a laugh.

I ripped open the front door as I stormed outside. Caspian surged forward as he took a deep breath, catching River's scent. I followed it at a jog. It took me down a path that led into the forest. I came to a fork and paused. Her scent was stronger on the left path, so I took that one.

I heard the waterfall before I saw it. I saw Spur standing by a tree. He gave me a nod as he tried to hide his smile before turning back to scanning the clearing. I spotted River and Molly easily. They were fully clothed and standing thigh deep in the water, facing away from me. I approached slowly as I tried to calm my frustration.

I stood at the water's edge for a long moment before stepping in. The water was freezing, but I remained quiet. I moved slowly enough that I didn't create a wave. I stopped once River was within arm's reach. I grabbed her by the waist and tossed her into the water. She let out a scream before her head went under the surface.

Molly whirled on me, but I was already heading back to shore. "Cruz!" Molly and River called after me, but I didn't slow down.

Spur watched me approach with a grin. "Get those two back to the packhouse, now!" I yelled before walking back down the path.

I clenched and unclenched my hands. I was nearly completely healed. I was a little achy but that was it, which meant River went ahead with her magic creams. I was beyond furious. I went to the only shower I knew the location of.

I turned on the water and stepped in. I hung my head as I let the water run over me. A small noise near the door had Caspian perking up, and I used our hybrid ability. River was moving slowly toward the shower I was in. She reached in and tried to turn the temperature knob to cold. I grabbed her wrist and pulled her in.

She let out a startled squeak. "Let go of me, Cruz." She said as she squeezed her eyes closed.

"You are the one that came in here and tried to turn the water to cold." I couldn't help the smile that curved my lips. Her scent filled the small shower, calming my irritation.

"You threw me in the pool." She tried to pull away from me, but I held her upper arms, keeping her in place. "Do you realize how cold that water is?"

"You drugged me." I scoffed.

"You are impossible, you know that?" River snapped. Her eyes were still closed, and she was shivering.

I took a step back, pulling her into the warm water. "I didn't want you hurt, River. I'm not worth it." I said firmly.

Her eyes popped open as she cocked her head to the side. "Everyone is worth something, Cruz." Her eyes darted up to the top of my head. "I thought it was going to be somewhat permanent."

"My hair?" I ran a hand through it. "No, after twenty-four hours, it's no longer waterproof and rinses out without a trace."

"Can you tell me what happened now?" she asked softly.

"Not here, River. We need to be in a more secure location than a locker room shower." River's eyes widened and her cheeks turned pink. She again tried to move away, but I didn't let her. "Why are you suddenly so shy? You were the one who came in here."

"Cruz, let go. I need to leave." She looked almost panicked. Her eyes were squeezed shut again.

I smiled down at her. "Look at me, River." She shook her head. "River,"

"It was a mistake to come in here. I'm sorry." She said over me.

"River, you need to warm up after that dunking." I chuckled.

"I can go to my own shower."

"What if I told you that I had a feeling you or Molly would come in here and try something, so I didn't get undressed?" I reached around her and turned the warm water up a little.

River let out a shaky breath, but she relaxed a little. I pulled her head to my chest and wrapped my arms around her. "Thank you for healing me. I am not happy with the way you went about doing it but thank you. Next time leave the potion out of it, I can deal with the pain."

"You're welcome and I hope there isn't a next time. Plus, I won't need to give you the potion again, its permanent." She leaned back and put her arms around my neck.

"Do you have a knife on you?" I asked.

"Not currently." Her brows drew together in confusion.

"Good." I pressed my lips to hers.

River pulled back and laughed. "Not in the mood to get stabbed today?"

"Not particularly." I kissed her again. "I'm sorry, River." I whispered against her lips. "I should have been more careful."

River leaned back as she studied my face. "I know we are practically strangers, but..." she chewed her bottom lip. "I can't handle seeing you in pain."

Caspian tried to push forward, but I managed to keep him back. "We should probably get out." I swallowed hard. At her questioning look, I kissed the tip of her nose. "You are proving to be a hard temptation to resist."

River rose on her toes as she pulled me down to her. Her lips met mine briefly before she stepped away from me. I resisted the urge to pull her back. She looked at me over her shoulder one more time before getting out of the shower. I took a deep breath and let it out slowly. I washed quickly before turning off the water.

I reached out and grabbed my towel. I pulled my wet boxers off and wrapped the towel around my waist before drawing back the curtain. River's back was to me as she wrapped a towel around herself. Her shoulders were bare, and I quickly spotted a pile of wet clothes on the floor near her feet. I had thought she would have left by now.

I was on the verge of telling her to get out of here and get up to her room, but Caspian brought up the fact that my men were all over the place. River took a step towards the door, and I grabbed her arm to stop her. "I can't let you go out there like that." I told her.

River smirked. "You went running outside in nothing but a towel, I'm not even going outside."

"My men are all over the place. You are not going out there in a towel." I said as my frustration began to rise.

"I haven't seen a single guard in the house except for in my dad's office." River turned her amused eyes on me.

"If you saw them, then they aren't doing their job right and I would be forced to retire them early." I glared at her.

"What do you suggest we do, Cruz?" River laughed in exasperation.

I thought about it for a minute. I moved to the door and stuck my head out and let out a soft whistle that sounded like a bird call. Within seconds, a man appeared. He worked directly under Miles. I had been keeping my eyes on the kid. He had potential and I was thinking of recruiting him. "Storm. Is everything okay, sir?"

"Cameron, I need my tactical bag. I am sure Miles or Martinez have it."

"Yes, sir." Cameron disappeared and I closed the door.

I turned around to see River watching me. "That's great for you, but what about me?"

I smiled at her. "Don't worry, I have you covered." A knock on the door had me pulling it open just a crack. "Thank you, Cameron." I said as I accepted the duffle bag.

I dropped the bag on the bench and unzipped it. I pulled out a shirt and tossed it to River before grabbing a change of clothes for me. River stepped into the shower and pulled the curtain closed and I quickly pulled on my pants. When she finally stepped back out, her gaze remained on the floor.

My shirt reached almost to her knees, and I couldn't help thinking she never looked so beautiful. I tugged my shirt over my head and closed the bag. "Ready to go?"

"I can't go out in this." River's face turned pink. "What would everyone think?"

"You were going to walk out in just a towel." I pointed out.

"Okay, so not the best idea. Cruz, I'm serious. I cannot go out like this." River's face was so red, and she wouldn't look at me.

"I really don't care what they think." I shrugged my shoulders as I grabbed her hand. "What they think has nothing to do with what happens between us." I stopped and pulled her close. I gave her a quick kiss. "Plus, you are my wife. You are supposed to be wearing my shirts."

I pulled her out into the hallway as I headed for the stairs. "My room is on the third floor." she said quietly.

We made it to her room a few minutes later. I stopped at the door as she walked in. She turned back to me and bit her lip. She looked like she wanted to say something, so I waited. Her phone rang and she ran to her bed and answered it. Her face went pale, and I rushed to her side.

Chapter Nine

River

"Hello?" I said into the phone as I turned to look at Cruz. He stood in the doorway. He watched me closely and I couldn't help thinking he looked really cute standing there with one arm on the doorframe watching me like that.

"You were supposed to reject him, not marry him. Now he will pay the price for your disobedience." I felt the blood drain from my face. "Say your good-byes soon, River. I don't want you feeling any regrets over him."

Cruz was at my side by the time the line went dead. The phone dinged and I looked down. A picture of Cruz kissing me in the locker room minutes ago filled the screen. Cruz took the phone from my hand. I stood frozen as I struggled to remain calm.

"We can't let them hurt Cruz. We cannot lose him." Maya began to pace in my head. Her anxiety mixed with mine and I started to feel lightheaded.

"River, look at me." Cruz's voice commanded and my eyes snapped up to his. His were filled with anger and his eyes flickered to a darker blue several times. "Everything will be okay."

"That's what you said before you left and got blown up." I whispered.

Cruz pulled me into his arms, and I started to cry. I just wanted this nightmare to end. After several minutes, I pulled myself together. "He said I was supposed to reject you, not marry you. Now you were going to have to pay the price for my disobedience." I sniffled.

"Thankfully, Maya didn't give us much choice in the matter. He will never have you, River." Cruz kissed my temple.

I stepped out of his arms. "He is going to try to kill you, Cruz!" Why was he being so calm about this?

"I got that from the text message." Cruz just stood there watching me. "The royal family is presumed to be dead. The only other person standing in your way of being placed on the throne is your mother. We need to get your parents to a safe house. Then we can figure out who is targeting you."

"Did you hear me? They are going to try to kill you." I was shaking. He wasn't getting it. He needed to go to a safe house as well.

"I get it, River. I am a primary target." The corner of Cruz's lips twitched, and amusement flashed in his eyes.

I turned away from him and walked into the bathroom, slamming the door. I moved into the walk-in closet and quickly got dressed. I heard Cruz's voice in the other room. He sounded like he was making a phone call. I was so mad at him. He was the one person that stood in the way of my stalker using me to get the throne, and he was laughing about it.

I paced the small space wrapped up in my own thoughts and speaking with Maya. I jumped when arms came around me. I whirled around to see Cruz looking down at me. "Why did I ever think a locked door would send the message that I didn't want to see you?" I asked in irritation.

"I got the message and chose to ignore it." Cruz grinned. I glared at him as I tried to push him away. "River, I don't think this guy knows who he is dealing with. Come with me and I will explain further."

Cruz extended his hand to me, and I took it. He led me to my father's office and opened the door. Gin, Spur, and Miles were inside. Cruz didn't even acknowledge the other people in the room as he locked the door and took me to the couch where he pulled me down beside him. I tried to scoot away from him, but he kept his arm around me. I was frustrated that I was so mad at him, yet I wanted him to never let me go. Stupid mate bond.

"What do you know about what Cruz Storm does?" he asked me, and my brows furrowed in confusion. "What have my parents told you I do?" he clarified.

"They said you work with your uncle at the FBWHA. You help keep the peace between the werewolf and human population." I answered.

"That is what I did for the first six months of my career. I was scouted for a special program. Gin and Spur are the second generation of that program. The training lasted a full year and was intense. I was trained for any and every situation."

"Cruz excelled in his training to the point that we had to create a cover for him. He became Shadow. After his first three missions, it became obvious that he was a one-of-a-kind soldier." Miles said from the desk. "I alone knew his real name and what he looked like. Martinez was eventually brought into the loop, and we became his handlers. We pass mission details to him from the higher ups."

I looked between the four men. That would make sense as to why Cruz had been sent to pilot the plane. Gin and Spur still had on their masks and their hair was black. I turned back to Cruz. How did he manage to keep up his persona as Cruz Storm, FBWHA Agent, while going on missions as Shadow?

"I was sent on a mission with the other four men that Miles had put through the program with me. We were shot out of the sky. I was the pilot and was far enough away from the blast that killed everyone else. I barely survived the crash. Long story short, I became the only asset our government had that could take out whole camps by myself and leave without anyone knowing I was there." Cruz ran his hand down my arm.

"For the next four years, Cruz was sent where we couldn't send in a team or where other teams had failed. Your cousins, for example, ended up being one of those missions. We sent in two previous teams where seven men had been killed. They asked for Shadow, and he managed to get the kids out within twelve hours of receiving the call." Miles said.

"Two years ago, he started bringing in strays that he told Miles to train. We are his B-team for when he is feeling cautious." Gin added. "Though the rest of us are always sent together, Shadow is more of a solo assassin."

"I'm not an assassin." Cruz scoffed. "River, what I want you to understand is that I am not someone to mess with. Miles, Martinez, and now these two, are the only ones who know that Cruz Storm and Shadow are the same person. So, whoever is threatening you is messing with one of the most dangerous men in the world."

"I find that hard to believe. You are not exactly a normal sized wolf or human. You would stand out." I shook my head.

"Miles, where are the guard rosters? Both yours and mine?" Cruz asked. Miles brought over two pieces of paper and handed them to him. He passed them to me. "Pick five names from each list. My men will tell you they work for Shadow, and they will not realize that I am him. They know me as Cruz Storm, FBWHA Agent. The men under Miles will be just as clueless."

"It's true. We had no idea that Agent Storm and Shadow were the same person, and we worked with both of them for years." Spur spoke up.

I was really having a hard time believing that not one person figured it out. I pointed out five random names from each list, and Miles called them to the office. Fifteen minutes later, the ten men stood around the room. All of them became uncomfortable when they saw Gin and Spur.

"Be at ease gentlemen, we just have a few questions for you." Miles leaned back against the desk. "River?" he gestured to me.

I stood and walked over to them. "Do any of you know Shadow?" I asked. "Met him in person?" Looks were exchanged before they all nodded. "Who is he?"

"Ma'am?" A man asked in confusion.

"Who is Shadow?" I repeated.

No one spoke and I felt a large presence move up behind me. Cruz put a hand on my waist. "Answer the question."

"Agent Storm, we don't know who he is. I only know him as Shadow." A younger man said quickly. "I have met him a few times when he issued orders but that's all."

"Who are these two?" I pointed to Gin and Spur.

The first man glanced nervously at them. "Gin and Spur, Ma'am. They are part of Shadow's strike team."

"What are their real names?" I asked, leaning back and Cruz wrapped his arms around me from behind.

It was quiet for several long moments before the young man spoke up again. "Is this some sort of test? No one knows the real identity of Shadow or his strike team. The Board has asked us several times already."

I felt Cruz tense. "They have?" I asked with a raised brow.

"Yes, ma'am. They feel like they are too dangerous to keep active." The young man said nervously as he glanced over at Gin and Spur.

"What were you offered?" I asked.

"Promotions, money, protection." A third man spoke up.

"Not all of you work directly for Shadow, yet all of you seem to be privy to this deal from The Board." I said stiffly.

"It's no secret that Agent O'Brien is Shadow's contact." A man at the end spoke up.

"Do you see that wooden box over there?"

"Yes, Ma'am."

"Could you bring it here for me?" The man nodded, and I moved away from Cruz. Not a single man was a werewolf, so auras were of no use. I directed the man to set it on the desk. I opened the lid and grabbed a small pouch out of the first row before closing it. "Are any of you familiar with Terror Roots?"

There was a collective 'No, ma'am'. Cruz watched me with a curious expression. I dumped the dried root out into my hand. Mom had used one on me once when I was about ten years old. For five minutes I could say nothing but the truth. It wasn't magic, so there wasn't any price attached to it, but the plants were extremely rare and only found near the North Wind Pack in a cave that was hidden.

"Despite its name, it is delicious. I grew up with it as a special treat. You cannot find it anywhere else. I would like you all to have one for your honesty." I lifted my hand to Cruz.

"I think I will pass." He smirked at me.

"How are the men supposed to trust me if you don't? I can only imagine the thoughts going through their minds right now, wondering if I am trying to poison them." I smiled sweetly at him. "You too, Miles. They are really good."

Cruz grudgingly took one from my hand and popped it into his mouth. His eyebrows raised in surprise as he chewed and swallowed. The roots had to be prepared in a certain way to make them edible, and the process made them sweet. He reached for another one, but I shook my head and closed my hand. "Why can't I have another one, babe?"

"Because I have a very limited amount, and I wanted to share." I laughed as I offered one to Miles. I knew I was taking a chance having them eat one. I really didn't want them to blurt out that Cruz was Shadow. While my back was turned, I made eye contact with Miles as he put one in his mouth. "Don't speak." I mouthed. He nodded.

I offered the roots to the ten men in front of me again, and they each took one. While they ate, I returned the bag to the box. I took an extra root out of the bag, just in case. Cruz came up to me and pressed a kiss to my cheek. "What did you have me eat?" he whispered.

"On a scale between zero and ten, how cute do you think I am?" I asked with a smile.

"You break the scale." He said without hesitation.

"What is going through your mind right now?"

"How incredibly hot you are when you are being mischievous." He clenched his jaw as his eyes narrowed.

"If you could do anything to me, what..." My question was cut off by him kissing me. I laughed when he pulled back. "You didn't let me finish my question."

"A truth pill?" he shook his head. "I can't believe you gave me a truth pill."

"I thought you found it hot?" I said, but he just shook his head and walked over to the couch and sat down. I grinned at him. I turned my attention back to the ten guards. "Have any of you taken The Board up on their offer?"

"No, ma'am." All of them answered.

"I don't know anyone stupid enough to cross Shadow. The Board is afraid of him enough to want to eliminate him, imagine what he would do to someone who betrayed him?" The man that brought me the box said.

"Do you know of anyone who would take The Board up on the offer?"

Most of the men responded in the negative, but one of the young men cleared his throat. "Darius Wood. He has been asking questions."

"Miles, send these men back to their rooms for the night." I said without looking away from the young man. Darius Wood? Did he have a connection to Dax Wood? Mom and Dad had told me and Kyson all about mom's abduction and Dax. But they said he was dead. "Except for you." I waited for the room to clear. "What is your name?"

"Cameron Stewart."

"Cameron, what do you know about Mr. Wood?"

"Ma'am, no offense, but I don't answer to you, and I don't think I should be talking about this." Cameron said nervously.

"The root is wearing off. He needs more." Maya pointed out.

"Here." I offered him the root. He shook his head. "You either eat it willingly, or I will help you." The man swallowed hard but made no move to take it. "If you don't believe I can, just ask Spur what happened to him the other night when he tried to take me on."

Gin laughed. "He dropped like a sack of potatoes in less than two minutes."

Cameron took the root and ate it. I gave him a smile. "Good choice. Now tell me what you know of Darius Wood."

Cameron looked like he tried to resist the effects of the terror root but failed, and his words came out in a rush. "Darius is always gloating about how his dad knew the royal family of the Northern Kingdom and how he is engaged to a royal descendant, or something like that. He said she was drop dead gorgeous with green eyes. From his description, you could fit the build of his girl. Said she needed to be tamed a bit. Said she was like a wildfire."

I swallowed hard. "What does Darius look like?" I asked softly.

"Blonde hair, six-foot, brown eyes. He is not as thick as most of the guards, but he sure packs a punch. He is one of the better fighters on the team. He has a burn on his neck and chest that he tries to keep hidden."

"Thank you, Cameron. That will be all." I said as I sat on the desk. Cruz crouched in front of me. "I know him. I met him. He was the guy that hit on me a few months ago. The one that asked if I was open to having a chosen mate."

"River, Gin and Spur have already gone to bring him here." Cruz put his hand on my knee.

"I don't want to be here." I whispered as my anxiety flared. I needed to tell Cruz about the history between Dax and my parents.

Cruz grabbed my hand, and we went back to my room. There was a piece of paper on the bed. I stopped walking when I saw it. Cruz closed and locked the door before releasing my hand and picking it up. He broke the seal and read it quietly.

"What does it say?" I asked nervously. Cruz shook his head, and I could tell he was fighting against himself.

"What do you think Shadow will do if the identity of one of his men is compromised? We know your soon-to-be late husband is on his strike team." He said, and then growled. "What did you give me, River?"

"The root only lasts five minutes. It should be out of your system by now." I said as I walked up to him and looked at the note.

"I am a hybrid, River, things affect me differently." Cruz muttered.

"How worried are you about Darius?" I asked.

"I'm not worried about what he will do to me." Cruz answered.

"Are you worried about what he will do to me if he gets his hands on me?" I looked up at Cruz's face.

A muscle ticked in his jaw. "He isn't going to get you."

"That wasn't my question, Cruz. They have access to witches. They can mask their scent, and who knows what else. A man named Dax Wood kidnapped my mom from her house when she was eighteen." I ran a hand through my hair in agitation. "If you aren't going to be honest, I will. I am terrified."

Cruz cupped my face, forcing me to look at him. "I am being as honest as I can, River."

"Can we sleep somewhere else tonight? I don't want to be in here." I asked as a tear slid down my cheek.

"Where will you feel safest?" Cruz brushed the tear away.

"In the Alpha's room." I grabbed his hand and quickly left the guest room. I moved five doors down and turned the knob. "Wait. Where is everyone?"

"I will tell you later. Right now, I think you need some rest, so let's get you settled." Cruz pulled me further into the room.

It was not lost on me that he only referred to me staying here. I walked into the closet and pushed Uncle Max's shirts aside. I found the hidden switch and pressed it. The wall panel opened up to reveal an elevator. I stepped inside with Cruz close behind. I clicked the bottom button, and the doors slid closed.

When the doors opened again, we were in an underground safety shelter. The space looked like a giant hotel suite with multiple bedrooms that branched off a common area. "My room is over here." I said quietly as I crossed the room and pushed open the fourth door on the right.

I was so exhausted and just wanted to lay in bed and not think. Thoughts kept swirling around in my head. Where were my parents? What would happen to me if they took me? Not only was Cruz being targeted by the man after me, but also by his own government. I walked to the dresser as I pulled off my shirt and dug out a clean pajama shirt. Next, I swapped out my jeans for shorts. I turned around to find Cruz watching me from the doorway.

"What?" I asked.

"It's just...Did you forget I was here?" He smiled at me.

My cheeks flushed as I realized I had forgotten he was there and totally got dressed in front of him. Maya laughed. "I guess that's what happens when you are forgettable." I shrugged and climbed into the bed. Praying he thought I was unconcerned with what I had just done .

"Forgettable? River, please. I have seen you checking me out several times." Cruz's teasing tone was back.

"And yet I forgot you were in the room." I shot back. "Is this where you tell me you have to go now?" I asked, unable to help myself.

"River, I can't stay with you. It's too dangerous." Cruz said regretfully.

"You were fine last night. I honestly do not see you hurting me, but if that is how you feel, just go." I closed my eyes and willed my tears to stay in check.

Chapter Ten

Cruz

I watched River as she curled into a ball. I could still feel her fear and anxiety. She had been absolutely terrified when she heard about Darius Wood.

"*I don't want to hurt our mate. We can't stay.*" Caspian whined.

I kicked off my shoes and pulled my shirt off. I was taking a risk, but she was right, I hadn't hurt her when we slept on the couch. I grabbed my phone before sliding under the covers. She scooted away from me, and I dragged her back.

"*You are an idiot, Cruz. If you hurt her because of a nightmare, I will never help you again. I will find a way to leave you.*" Caspian growled.

"Nice try, babe." I whispered in her ear. She remained tense, even though I could feel her relief through our bond. I hadn't realized how scared she was to be alone. I pressed a kiss to her shoulder. "If you didn't want to be alone, you should have just said so."

"Cruz, I am terrified, and I do not feel safe in my own home. Let's go to a secret underground bunker so I don't have a panic attack. Oh, and while we are down there, I will probably still not feel safe and be so lost in my own head that I will get changed without a second thought as to whom is in the room with me." She took a breath. "Caspian, give Cruz back control so you guys can go do whatever it is you need to do."

"I get it, River. I wasn't thinking." I rolled her over to face me. She was glaring at me. I smoothed her hair out of her face. "And I am here despite Caspian telling me it's too dangerous. He is even threatening that if I hurt you, he will abandon me."

"I just want this to end." She whispered.

"I know." I kissed her forehead. She moved her head to my shoulder and cuddled close. I pulled my phone out and sent Miles a quick message letting him know that River and I were safe, but unreachable except through my phone.

We laid there for a while, and I was almost asleep when River's hand moved to my chest. "Cruz?" River said sleepily.

"Hmm?"

"I'm not strong enough."

"Strong enough for what?" I asked quietly as I ran my hand through her hair. I loved how silky smooth it was.

"Losing you." She didn't say anymore and within a few minutes, her breathing deepened, and her body completely relaxed.

I held her closer as I breathed in her scent. I had managed to evade her question about being worried about what would happen to her if she was taken. The truth is nothing scared me more. I would do everything in my power to make sure no one touched her.

My phone rang and River groaned as she buried her face in my chest. It took me a minute to find the blasted device. "Storm." I said, once I got it to my ear.

"Where are you? I thought you just wanted time with your wife, but no one can find you two." Miles asked.

"What time is it?" I asked, trying to wake myself up.

"Six. Are you sleeping? Since when do you sleep?" Miles asked in surprise.

River took the phone from me. "Miles, is this an emergency?"

"Not really." Miles said slowly.

"Is there a pressing matter that requires Cruz to be there?"

"No, it's just he is usually..." River hung up the phone and dropped it on the mattress before she buried her face against me. I chuckled and placed a kiss on her head. "I just want a few more minutes. I haven't been sleeping well."

I ran my fingers through her hair, and she sighed. "I think I like having you answer my phone."

"Does that mean we are making this a habit?" she asked sleepily.

"Are you referring to answering my phone or sleeping in?" I asked.

"All of it. Now shush so I can go back to sleep."

I smiled as I closed my eyes. I must have dozed off because the next thing I knew, my phone was ringing again. I quickly answered it, grateful that River hadn't stirred. "Storm." I said quietly.

"Okay, we need you to come to the office, immediately." Miles said quickly. "Darius is nowhere to be found. He didn't report for his shift and all of his gear is missing. We have a lead on where he might be. I will have your tactical bag ready for you." I hung up the phone.

I kissed River's forehead. "Hey, babe, time to get up." River groaned and hardly stirred. "Sweetheart, we need to get dressed. I have to go to work." Her head snapped up and her green eyes momentarily filled with panic. She blinked several times, and her expression cleared. "I just got a call; Darius has gone AWOL."

I waited for River in the common room while she got dressed. When she came out, she was pale. We stepped onto a second elevator, and she pressed the first button. "River, what's the matter?" I asked as the door slid closed.

She threw her arms around me, and I hugged her tight. "You have to be careful." She whispered.

I leaned back and looked into her eyes. "River Storm, you and I will be just fine. I happen to know Shadow and he is as fearsome as everyone thinks he is."

River took a step back and looked me up and down. "Is he better than you in a fight?"

"Definitely." I tried to keep a straight face as my lips fought to break into a smile.

"Let's hope so, because from what I have seen, you are easily distracted, which isn't the best practice to have in a fight." River's eyes sparked with amusement.

"The only reason I have been distracted lately is because of you." I cupped the back of her head as I took a step closer to her. Before I could kiss her, the doors slid open, and I took a quick step back. Miles, Gin, and Spur whirled around in surprise.

"What the...?" Spur said as River and I stepped off the elevator. I looked back as the doors closed. It looked like a normal part of the wall.

"I hear a single word about this, and I will end you myself." River said as she moved to the minifridge. "No one except for the Alpha, Beta, and Gamma families know about it."

"What is going on, Miles?" I asked.

I watched River bend over to grab a water out of a mini fridge in the corner. She unscrewed the lid as she straightened and took a long drink of the chilled liquid. Her long hair fell in soft curls around her shoulders. The shirt she wore barely reached the waistband of her low riding jeans. As she drank, the shirt lifted just enough to show a small amount of skin. My eyes continued downward, admiring how her jeans hugged her every curve.

"Cruz!" Miles snapped.

"What?" I returned my eyes to him.

"Did you hear what I said?"

"Uh..."

"I think he was too busy checking out his wife." Gin laughed. "I had heard that a werewolf mate bond was strong, but I didn't realize how much it affected someone. I don't think I have ever seen Shadow give a woman so much as a second glance, yet he can't seem to take his eyes off of her."

"I wasn't..." I tried to deny that I was, once again, distracted by River, but the lie fell from my lips. "Just tell me what I need to do."

"We unlocked the phone that you retrieved. A woman and two men met in the garden that day. One of the men was Darius. We got a lead on where their base is. We need you to infiltrate it and figure out what their plan is without letting them know you were there." Miles crossed his arms over his chest.

"Do we know how many men are stationed inside the base?" I asked as I moved to the desk where a map was laid out.

"Intelligence has the count around sixty." Spur said.

"That's a lot of people." River said, coming up beside me.

Gin and Spur laughed. "When this is over, we could tell you stories about Shadow taking out bases with more than a hundred men inside." Gin commented.

"No, you won't." I growled.

"I know where to get plenty of Terror Root, why don't we have him retell it." River smiled.

I pinched the bridge of my nose and took a deep breath. The last thing I wanted was for River to know about my previous missions. What I did was dangerous, and I knew she wasn't going to be happy if she knew how much danger I was in every time I went out. I looked at Miles, who seemed amused. "Do you have a knife?"

"Always. Why?" Miles asked in confusion.

"You might as well kill me now. I'm sure it will be far less painful if you do it instead of River doing it." I said, causing Caspian to laugh.

River punched me in the stomach. It wasn't hard, but I knew she was mad at me. I looked down at her. "When does he leave?" she asked as she glared at me.

"As soon as he gets dressed." Miles chuckled. "Your bag is on the couch."

I moved to the couch and pulled out my gear. The pants were made of a special material that couldn't be cut. The long-sleeved shirt was a spandex-type material that hugged the wearer's body so there was nothing for an enemy to grab onto in a fight. I quickly changed into them, ignoring the chuckles behind me. I could feel River's embarrassment through our bond, and I smiled. I put on my vest and belt before reaching back into the bag, grabbing the oil and blackening my hair.

I checked my firearms and holstered them. I grabbed out my burner phones, an extra S.O.S device, and my mask before turning around. River was watching me as I approached the desk. "Checking me out while I'm dressing?" I asked her with a smirk.

"Wow, I see your ego is back. Maybe we should drop you out of the sky again to bring it back down." She crossed her arms over her chest as a blush colored her cheeks.

"You planning on nursing me back to health, Babe?"

"No, I think I will let you be. You are far easier to be around when you are delirious with pain."

"How did you two ever agree to mark each other when you are like this?" Miles asked.

"My wolf took over and marked him. I didn't get a say." River turned her back to me.

"I'm guessing Caspian did the same."

"Yup." I said as I leaned over the map. "Where am I going?"

We talked more about the location of the base and how I was going to get in. River had moved over to the couch. My eyes kept straying over to her during the last hour. She was currently curled up against the arm of the couch and her eyes were closed, but I had a feeling she was listening to every word we said.

"You ready to go, Shadow?" Gin asked.

"We have one more thing to discuss before I can leave." I said, looking back at the men around me. "River needs to be taken somewhere off the map."

"What?" River yelled from the couch, and I smiled. I knew she hadn't been asleep. "I'm not going."

I ignored her as I looked at Spur. "I am trusting her safety to you."

"She took me out, and Gin said she stabbed you with enough drugs to knock you out for more than twenty-four hours. Do you really think I alone can handle her?" Spur shot a concerned look over at the couch.

"He is right, Shadow. Your little wife will not be easy to keep under lock and key." Gin lowered his voice.

"I can still hear you, little human." River snapped as she came to stand next to me.

I twisted her so she was facing me and pressed her against the desk. I leaned forward causing her to lean back. I caged her in with my arms, my face inches from hers. "You will not take out my men. You will not drug them. You will not leave their sides." I said firmly. "Miles, Gin, and Spur will be your security detail."

"And if I refuse to be babysat?" River cocked an eyebrow.

"I am trying to keep you safe." I snapped.

"You don't have to. I can take care of myself." She tried to shove me away, but I didn't budge. Panic flowed through the mate bond.

"Cruz." Caspian called and an image of River reaching around me, her hand inching towards my knife filled my mind. I grabbed her wrist, and her eyes widened in surprise.

"Everyone out." I said through clenched teeth. When I saw the door close behind Miles, Caspian laid back down and yawned. He was thoroughly enjoying River's fight, but I wasn't. The blasted woman was terrified, yet she was refusing to let me protect her. "I told you we would be fine, River, and I will not break that promise to you."

River scowled at me. "How did you know I was going for your knife?"

"There are things you don't know about me, River. And you will not distract me from this." I said firmly.

She ran her hands up my chest until they were around my neck. Her eyes flicked to my lips before returning to my eyes. I narrowed mine. She wasn't going to fool me again. The last time she stabbed me with a needle. I unhooked her arms from around my neck as I stood to my full height. River's smile grew as she sat on the desk.

"Maybe you have learned a thing or two." She muttered as she watched me.

"I need you to go with Miles while I am gone. I won't be able to focus if I am worried about you." I grabbed her hand and put the S.O.S. device in her palm. "This will send out a distress signal. The signal will transmit to the receiver that only my team has access to. If anything were to happen, press and hold for five seconds."

"But..."

"This is yours." I placed the phone in her hand. "It can only dial out to one number, and that is mine. Keep both items with you at all times."

"No weapon?" River teased, but her voice was filled with tension.

I reached around my waist and pulled an arrow off my belt. "You can have an arrow."

"That is not an arrow." River laughed.

I took back the first two items I gave her and placed them on the desk before spinning her around, so her back was to my chest. I grabbed her hand, placing her fingers in the right places and squeezed. The arrow extended and River jumped as she gasped. I showed her how to retract it. "It has enough force that it can impale someone, so don't hurt yourself." I whispered.

River turned around to face me. "I don't think you should go." She searched my face.

"I have to, River. That is why I need you to stay with Miles." I tucked her hair behind her ear. "I should be back within a week."

River wrapped her arms around my neck, pulling me down to her as she rose on her toes. I returned her kiss, desperate to convince her to stay with Miles and my men. I needed her safe. A throat cleared loudly, and River jumped with a squeak of surprise. Her cheeks were red, and she looked mortified as she glanced over my shoulder.

I pulled her back to me as I turned us to face the others. River buried her face in my chest as she tried to hide. "Makes you wonder who initiated it." Spur stage whispered.

"Considering her wolf was the one to mark Shadow first, my money is on Finley." Gin smiled.

"Finley?" Miles asked.

"Yup, Irish for 'fair hero'." Gin shrugged. "A fitting name."

"You three will be looking after Finley." I said, and I felt River tense. "For my sanity, please stay with them." I tilted her face up, so she was forced to meet my eyes.

"Fine." River huffed.

"Thank you." I breathed out and rested my forehead against hers.

"So, you are going alone now?" Spur asked.

"That's been the plan from the beginning." I said as I pressed a kiss to River's forehead. "Getting information is easy, protecting my wife is proving to be another story entirely."

"Did you just call me difficult?" River smacked my chest.

I put my mask on and gave River a pointed look. "Those three items go with you everywhere." I turned to leave. I stopped just before opening the door. I turned around and River was there. She jumped and I caught her. She wrapped her legs around my waist, and I buried my face in her neck. "River," I lifted my head to look at her.

She pulled my mask off and kissed me. "You come home like you did a few days ago and I will slip Terror Root in your food for days."

I chuckled. "Yes, ma'am." I kissed her one more time before she unwrapped her legs from my waist, and I set her down. I grabbed my mask from her and replaced it over my face. I gave her a wink before leaving.

Chapter Eleven

River

I watched Cruz as he walked out of the office and a knot of dread settled in my stomach. I could feel how worried he was, but I wasn't sure if he was worried about me or his mission. How was he going to infiltrate a base with so many men?

"He will be fine, River. He has done this kind of mission too many times to count." Miles came up to my side and put a hand on my shoulder.

I pulled my eyes away from the closed door. "Do you have a mate?" I asked him.

"I do." He smiled at me.

"Is it like this when you leave?" I asked quietly.

"No. I mean it is hard going on assignments, yes, but never like what I just saw. Especially from Cruz. You mentioned your wolf marking him, why did she do it?" Miles asked.

"When he first knocked on the door, I didn't recognize him as my mate. He appeared later that night in the family room, and I learned his name and that he was the son of the Storms. He started to shift right after explaining that Nash had a broken arm. I could sense his pain. He was like that for hours. Maya said she could sense his wolf periodically and recognized him as our mate. Watching and feeling his pain became too much. Maya wanted to mark him like his dad did to his mom, I told her no."

"She marked him anyway." Miles said softly.

"Yeah, and he shifted. He got a call a minute or two later. I was still trying to process what my wolf did. She has never once taken over. Everyone kept telling him that he was weaker with only a partial bond and couldn't leave without marking me in return. He grew mad. Said he didn't want a mate right now. Molly told him that now that he recognized me as his mate, Caspian would fight for me. I told everyone they were insane. I had no idea who he was, save his name and bad attitude. That's when Caspian took over. He backed me against a wall and told me Cruz was a saint compared to him, then he marked me. The jerk bit down so hard I almost passed out. Cruz groaned and swore before he apologized for hurting me."

Miles chuckled. "I could see Caspian doing that. There are differences in werewolves depending on what country you come from. Are you familiar with the different depths of a mark?"

"No." I said quietly.

"It is rare, but some barely mark one another. It seals the bond, but not enough to tie emotions. Most marks are deep enough to allow their mate to feel their emotions as a symbol of trust and openness. Then there is a deep mark like what Caspian gave you. It is a sign of complete devotion. It is incredibly painful to give and receive, but the bond formed is stronger. I have even heard of some mates being able to mind-link in human form."

"My parents can do that. Communicate through a mind-link as humans. They had been able to feel some of their bond since they were kids, and the bond continued to grow until they marked each other." I turned away from him. "But Cruz is the biggest pain in the butt I have ever known. Kyson and Paxton don't even come close. I hate that I feel like I can't breathe without him. I don't even know him."

"You seemed to be enjoying each other's company well enough when we came back in." Gin commented.

I clenched my hands into fists as I glared at him. "They can't help it." Miles explained. "It would be hard enough to stay away from each other with a normal mark, but thanks to Caspian, they are dealing with a stronger pull towards one another."

"Don't both mates need to have deep marks in order for it to work?" Gin asked.

"No. Cruz felt the pain of the mark, so I'm guessing Caspian was able to create the bond."

"In the Northern Kingdom, our Alphas perform a ceremony to complete the bonding between mates." I said.

Miles looked surprised. "Did you...?"

I nodded. "It is part of the wedding ceremony. Afterward, it was like my mind went into a fog where only Cruz existed. Aunt Jackie said it was the bond forming."

"Caspian's mark had already created the bond. I wonder if the ceremony magnified it?" Miles mused.

"Great. Just what I want and need." I grumbled. "At least when he isn't here, I can think again. I swear it's like my brain turns to mush whenever he is nearby." I plopped down on the couch. "So, what now? We just sit around for the next week?"

"We should probably move you to a different location." Gin said.

"That will leave us vulnerable." I shook my head.

"How so?" Spur asked.

"They are obviously keeping eyes on the packhouse. If I leave, they will know about it. They would probably follow us and attack us when they see an opportunity." I fiddled with the phone Cruz had given me.

"What are you suggesting?" Miles asked studying me.

"We stay here. This room is secure. I will stay either here or in the bunker. The bunker is not even on the blueprints for the packhouse, so literally, no one knows about it. It is the most secure place for me."

"She is right, you are at your most vulnerable when on the move." Gin agreed. "We already know the layout of this location and have already set up security around the place."

"I don't think that is what..." Miles said as he shook his head, but I interrupted him.

"He said off the maps. The bunker is off the maps." I said as I walked over to the desk. "This phone, and the one in the Alpha's office are the only ways to communicate with the bunker. There is a control panel down there that changes colors depending on what is dialed up here. "1# sends the signal that everything is secure up here. 2# is for whoever is down there, to come up. 3# is to stay down there until further notice. 5# locks the elevator, preventing anyone from coming or going." I explained.

"How do you access the elevator?" Spur asked.

"That information is classified." I smirked at them over the desk. I opened the desk drawer and pulled out a file. If I was stuck here while my parents, Uncle Max, and Uncle Mike are all away, I might as well keep up with pack business.

"What are you doing?" Miles asked as he moved closer.

"Since the Alpha, Beta, and Gamma are not available, I need to keep the pack running smoothly." I glanced up and saw his eyebrows raised in surprise. "How much do you know about my family, Miles?" I sat back in the chair.

"Your mother is the niece of the Alpha King, and your family is the Gammas of the pack."

"Did you know that my father, even though born to the Gamma family, has an Alpha's aura? My parents were supposed to be the Alpha and Luna of the North Wind Pack but refused, choosing instead to stay near family. My mother's cousin is the current Alpha of the North Wind Pack, but he only has daughters. None of them want to be Luna, so the pack is being passed down to my brother, Kyson, who is also an Alpha."

"Shouldn't you be next in line for Luna then?" Gin asked.

"I was." I shrugged.

"You rejected it as well." Spur sounded surprised.

"I am no Luna." I laughed. "After graduating, I went to spend the summer with Uncle Kion. I ended up finding the witch that had saved my mom's life when she was little. She focused on healing and helping others. I found I enjoyed working with her. I stayed for an additional year, learning all I could. Then I came home and got my nursing degree online. Both on the human and werewolf side."

"Yet you are planning on spending your time going over pack business?" Spur asked.

"I was practically raised in this office. I have been taught everything a Luna would need to know in order to run a pack. As the daughter of a royal and an Alpha, it was presumed I would be mated to an Alpha." I shook my head as I looked back down at the file again. "I guess everyone was right. I am mated to an Alpha." I sighed.

"*Alphas aren't all that bad. And being a Luna doesn't mean we have to give up on what we love to do.*" Maya said softly.

"*Being a Luna means having to be the leader of a pack. Taking care of everyone and everything.*" I sounded so selfish, and shame filled me.

"*It isn't selfish to want to live a quiet life, raising a family and helping those less fortunate.*" Maya tried to console me.

"Why do I get the impression that you aren't exactly thrilled with that fact?" Miles asked.

I looked up at him. "You are an Alpha's son, are you not?"

"I am."

"Then you understand the responsibilities heaped on those of such a position. Try magnifying that just because you have royal blood in your veins. I have responsibilities to the royal family, obligations I am required to fill. A Gamma's daughter was bad enough." I glared down at the pages in front of me."

"You should talk with Cruz about this." Miles said calmly.

"Yeah, good idea." I said sarcastically. I stacked the pages in a nice pile and returned them to the drawer. "I am going to go to the gym. Who thinks they are up to being my punching bag?"

*   *   *

"I'm so sorry." I said for the hundredth time.

"You hit almost as hard as Shadow." Miles groaned as he held his nose. "This is the fifth time you have broken my nose."

"I don't know what happened. I was being careful this time." I said in a rush.

I had been trying to keep my frustration under control while I sparred. Being a royal, I was stronger than other werewolves, and I didn't want to hurt anyone. But over the last three days, I couldn't seem to stay in control. I hurt Gin and Spur pretty bad on accident that first day. I had been so frustrated over the mate bond and my inability to resist Cruz, that I lost my head. Both men had put up a challenge for me. It surprised me that humans could fight like that. Miles was the only one to spar with me now. Being a werewolf, he could heal from the fights.

"Are you working through something again?" Miles asked as I helped him slowly lower onto the couch in my dad's office.

"No. I mean, I don't think so. We were doing fine, exchanging blows, then I felt so frustrated all of a sudden. Then angry. Red hot anger and I kicked you. I don't know what happened. I am so sorry." I felt so guilty.

"How are you feeling now?" Miles closed his eyes.

"Like I am a complete jerk. I feel bad. I didn't mean to kick you so hard." I ducked my head.

"No more anger or frustration?"

"No. As quickly as it came, it was gone."

"I wonder if..." Miles was cut off by his phone ringing. "O'Brien. What do you mean there is a vehicle approaching? River, bring me my laptop."

I ran to the desk to retrieve the computer. I handed it to him as I sat down next to him. He opened the laptop and typed in a crazy long password. Within a few clicks, a video feed popped up. A dark blue sedan was pulling up in front of the packhouse.

"Stay in position, but don't fire until we know they are a threat." Miles said as he watched the screen.

My heart was pounding as the vehicle pulled to a stop. The driver's door opened, and a man stepped out. I sucked in a quick breath. "Don't shoot!" I yelled. "Bring him here."

"That is not a good idea." Miles said.

"You bring him here unharmed, or I will go out there." I watched as the man jogged up the steps and opened the front door.

"You heard Finley, bring the man to the office." Miles said angrily before ending the call. "If he shows the slightest hint of hostility, I will shoot him."

I jumped to my feet as the door opened and I was across the room by the time he entered. Miles yelled at me, but I didn't care. I slammed into him, and his arms wrapped around me tightly. "River." He breathed out. "Where is everyone? Who are these guys? Have they hurt you?" Kyson asked, holding me protectively.

"I'm okay." I managed to force out through my tears. Kyson stroked my hair until I stopped crying. I looked up at him. His blue eyes were filled with worry as he looked at me. "Everyone is okay."

"Where are they, and who are these guys? They grabbed me as soon as I stepped inside." Kyson glanced around the room. "Are you being held here?"

I laughed as I wiped my cheeks. "They are..."

"Wait, are they part of Shadow's strike team? We heard rumors that they were in the area, but nothing could be confirmed." Kyson pulled me closer.

"We are." Spur cocked his head as he studied us. "Now, the question is, who are you?"

"This is Kyson, my little brother." I took a small step away from him. "What are you doing here, Ky? You aren't supposed to be back for another month."

"Are you serious?" Ky gave me a look that told me I had lost my mind. "The royal family's plane went down with our parents on board. I have been trying to call the house and the packhouse all week trying to get ahold of someone, anyone. Last I talked with mom, she said that they were going to ask you to go with them." He pulled me back to him. "I thought you were dead." He whispered.

I held my brother for several minutes without saying anything. When he finally pulled back again, anger was in his eyes. His attention focused on the men around us. "Did you do it? Did you kill them?" He was shaking with his rising anger.

"Ky, look at me." I said, grabbing the sides of his face and forcing him to look at me. "They are not responsible for the plane going down."

"What the heck is the most feared strike team doing here with you?" Kyson's eyes shifted down to my neck and he grabbed my jaw, tilting it up. "You are marked?"

"Kyson, it's a long story. Why don't we go to the Alpha's Room and talk?" I suggested. I had a feeling Kyson was going to flip a lid when I told him that I had found my mate and never called him.

After a heated discussion with Miles, Kyson and I were able to go to the bunker alone. Kyson was currently pacing in front of me while I sat on the couch. I told him that I had found my mate. He was the FBWHA Agent that brought home Ana and Nash. I explained that Maya had marked him, and we were married before everyone left. Kyson was relieved that our family was safe but ticked that I had gotten married without him meeting the guy.

"You don't seem to know much about him, Riv." Kyson finally said.

I shrugged. "I don't right now. I am sure that we will get to know each other eventually."

"Why did Maya do it? She has never taken control. She isn't one to be impulsive. It doesn't make sense. You have experienced the pains of a shift before, and you even helped me through mine. Why would she do it?"

"You will understand once you find your mate." I got to my feet. It was getting late, and I still needed to go upstairs and speak with Miles. "You are now under the protection of the FBWHA. You will need to stay down here until whoever is trying to kill our family is caught. I need to go check on Miles, we sparred earlier, and he got banged up."

"This conversation isn't over with, River. In the morning, you are going to tell me more about this mate of yours, because I know you know more than you are telling me."

It was late and I was not in the mood to talk with anymore overprotective males. My talk with Miles went relatively well, considering I broke all their protocols to keep me safe. After my lecture, I came back down to the bunker. Kyson was going over several files from dad's desk. I went to my room and closed the door, feeling exhausted. I showered and laid in bed with a sigh.

Chapter Twelve

Cruz

It was completely dark. The moon provided hardly any light. I crouched near a rock as I scanned the clearing below me. There were men milling around the perimeter fencing. The building I needed to get into was in the center of it all. I let my eyes slowly move over the area again. Something was off, but I couldn't put my finger on it.

I continued to observe the compound for another two hours, hoping to figure out what was bothering me. *"What do you think, Caspian?"*

"The sooner we get this over with, the better." Caspian said as he paced restlessly in my head.

"You are no help tonight." I told him.

"Thank that little she-wolf of ours. Now stop acting like a sissy and get down there so we can get back to her." Caspian growled.

I moved to my right, slipping into the shadows. I picked my way down the steep hill but paused at the bottom. Using my hybrid ability, I closed my eyes and saw all around me. I cocked my head to the side.

"If you were protecting information, where would you place guards?" I asked Caspian.

"The perimeter, directly outside where I was storing the information, and inside with the information. I would have several men watching security cameras." Caspian answered.

"The only guards we have seen have been around the perimeter. None have gone within a hundred yards of the building." I commented.

"An ambush?"

"Let's find out."

I silently made my way along the fence until I found a spot to climb over. When I dropped down on the other side, I found a stack of crates near a truck. I moved behind them for cover. A man about my size walked by and I grabbed him from behind, one hand over his mouth and the other pressing a knife to his throat.

"What is inside the building?" I growled into his ear. He tried to fight me, and I stabbed his shoulder before bringing the knife back to his throat. "What is inside the building?" I asked again. "I can do this all night. Where would you like your next hole?"

The man nodded his head, and I removed my hand enough for him to speak. "Explosives. It's just a storehouse." He ground out through his pain.

"I believe that." Caspian rolled his eyes. *"It is most likely a gift for us."*

I thought over my options. If I didn't show up, then they would know I was tipped off somehow. If I let the man go, he was going to raise the alarm. If I went inside, I was dead.

"You are going to enter the building." I told the man, and he shook his head. "I either kill you here, or you enter the building and pray that what you just told me is correct. If you try to run away, if you try to talk to anyone, you will get an arrow through your heart before you can even utter a word or take two steps."

The man moved slowly toward the building. He glanced back once and saw me with my bow at the ready. His eyes were wide with fear. I felt a little bad sending this man to his death, but he wasn't going to live much longer anyway. I shot the security camera over the door before he made it into the frame. He paused at the door for a brief second before entering. Thirty seconds later the whole place exploded.

*   *   *

River

I was standing on the top of a hill. It was completely dark with the sliver of moon providing barely any light. I saw Cruz crouching down near a large boulder observing the scene below him. A building sat in a small clearing, and I recognized it as the building that Cruz was supposed to go into to gather information. Men were all over the place. They seemed to be watching the fence line.

Cruz moved to the right and disappeared into the shadows. I sat in the place where he had just been. There was no way I was going down there with him. It felt like an eternity before I saw a large shadowy figure approaching the door of the building. From this distance, he looked to be Cruz's size. I watched him go into the building. Thirty seconds later, there was a massive explosion.

"Cruz!" I screamed as I bolted upright in bed. I was drenched in sweat, and I was shaking. The scent of rain filled my lungs as my door burst open and I screamed.

"River!" Kyson was at my side in seconds. I was shaking as the explosion kept replaying in my head. "What's wrong?"

"I'm okay. It was just a dream." I told him. My voice was even trembling.

"You don't look okay." Kyson looked at me. "Maybe you should sleep with me tonight."

"I'm fine, Ky. I will just take a shower before I try to go back to sleep. You go back to bed." I said, and he gave me a hard look. "Go, I'm fine."

Kyson grudgingly got up and left. I covered my face with my shaking hands and took a deep breath. "Dreaming about me?" Cruz's quiet voice reached me. I didn't respond. Warm hands touched my knees, and I slowly removed my hands from my face. Cruz was crouched in front of me. "That guy was right; you do not look fine."

I threw my arms around his neck as I slid off the edge of the bed. He put a hand to the back of my head, and I buried my face in his neck. My shaking increased as I saw Cruz enter the building and then the explosion flashed into my mind again.

"River, what's wrong?" Cruz whispered. I shook my head and took a deep breath. Cruz was fine. He was alive. Cruz stood, lifting me with him. He lay on the bed with me in his arms. I curled into him as I fought the fear trying to take over. "Babe, I need you to take a deep breath for me." I took several. After a few minutes, his scent began to calm me. "What happened, River?" Cruz asked again.

"We were on a hill looking down on a compound. You moved into the trees, but I stayed up top. I watched the clearing where the building stood that Miles had shown you. Someone that looked like you went inside, and then there was a huge explosion." I took a shuddering breath. "I felt the explosion."

Cruz pulled me closer and placed a kiss on my forehead. "I'm here, River. Everything is okay." He whispered.

"It felt so real." I clung to him.

"I know but everything is fine." He kissed the top of my head. "Try to get some sleep and we can talk more in the morning." I nodded and closed my eyes. I have never been more scared in my life.

I woke up with a start. I was still cuddled up to Cruz. His breathing was deep and even. Maya was pacing as she whined. I sighed as I sat up and scooted to the edge of the bed. I was shaking again. I kept seeing the explosion over and over. I ran my hand through my hair as I brought one of my knees up to my chest.

Cruz kissed my shoulder. "Hey." He said softly.

"I just keep seeing it. You going inside. The explosion." I whispered.

Cruz scooted to my side and wrapped his arms around me. I leaned against his chest. "I never went inside the building, River."

"Are you saying there was an explosion though?" I turned my face up to look at him.

"I have no idea how you saw what you did. It is pretty accurate to what happened, except I wasn't the one that went into the building. I wasn't even in the blast radius." Cruz tucked my hair behind my ear. "I need to figure out where the lead came from in the morning. But tonight, I think we both could use some sleep."

"Okay." I nodded.

Cruz scooted back and laid down. I crawled over to him and settled next to him, letting him pull me close. He started combing his fingers through my hair. Maya's restless pacing stopped, and she laid down. My breathing started to deepen as I felt myself growing closer to sleep.

"Who is that guy that came in here earlier? The one that asked if you wanted to sleep with him." Cruz asked. There was a hint of irritation in his voice.

I laughed. "Careful, you almost sound jealous."

"I don't get jealous." Cruz said with a growl.

"Mmhmm." I mumbled.

*   *   *

Cruz

I held River as she fell asleep. Thankfully, she was no longer shaking. She had been so pale and completely freaked out after she had screamed my name. Then that man had come in here, asking for her to sleep with him. I was ready to strangle the man. River had clung to me after he left. I could feel her fear. It had been consuming her.

I had woken up when she moved away from me. I managed to get her to come back to bed. She was curled up against me now. She was asleep, but she still fisted my shirt. I kissed her head, and she snuggled closer.

How did she see what had happened on my mission? The woman was baffling. And who was the guy down the hall? Caspian growled just thinking about him touching River.

Hours passed, but I couldn't fall asleep. River would periodically grow restless, and I would whisper close to her ear until she settled back to sleep.

The handle jiggled before someone knocked on the door. "Riv, why is your door locked?" The man from last night called.

River groaned as she rolled to her back. "What do you want?"

"I want to know if you are okay. Last night you were upset. Now there is someone else's scent down here."

"Don't worry about it. The stench goes away after a while." She called back.

I pulled her back to me. "Back to saying I stink, are we?" I whispered in her ear.

She smiled at me. "I think it is the oil. You should really go take a shower."

"River, open the door." The man called again.

"I'm fine, Ky."

"If you are fine, then open the door. Time for you to tell me more about this mate of yours."

"Not now." River's face went red as she turned away from me.

"Why not now?" I asked her in a whisper. "I would love to hear what you have to say." I held her against my chest as she continued to try to wiggle out of my arms.

She let out a huff of frustration. "He is a pain in the butt!" River yelled. "Oh, so full of himself." She tried again to break my hold on her. "It's a wonder why Maya would even mark him." I chuckled as I pulled her closer to me.

"Well, you weren't exactly looking for your mate last time we were together." The man said. "Can you please open the door? It is really weird talking to you like this."

"Give me a few minutes and then I will be out." River scowled at me even though her voice was pleasant. I heard the man move away from the door and my attention focused back on River. "You are the biggest pain, you know that?" she pushed my arm again.

I released her and she quickly got out of the bed. I watched her grab a change of clothes before stomping into the bathroom and slamming the door. I chuckled. It was so fun to rile her up. I loved seeing that fire in her eyes. I also found I liked holding her.

I gave myself a mental shake. I sat up and pulled my shirt off. I ran my fingers over the spot where some shrapnel from the explosion had hit me. Now that I had Caspian fully with me, I was healed. How had River seen the explosion. The bathroom door opened, and River stepped back into the room. I dropped my hand from my side, but I didn't look up at her. She stopped just shy of opening the bedroom door.

"Hurry up and shower. Kyson isn't known for his patience, and he loves to cook. So, food is most likely already on the table." River pulled open the door and left.

I stared at the closed door for another minute before getting up. The shower felt good after six days of not getting one. My mind wondered back to the mission. It had been a trap. Someone had wanted to kill Shadow. The question was, who?

"We need to figure out who gave Miles the tip off about Darius." Caspian growled.

"Before we go talk with Miles, I want to know who this Kyson is and make sure River is okay. Last night was not normal." I said as I got dressed. "A nightmare fine, but she had described what had happened that night."

"She is still upset about the dream. Maya is too." Caspian pointed out.

I could feel it also, the fear and worry coming through the mate bond. I couldn't blame her. If I had seen her go into a building, only for it to blow up within a minute, I would be going out of my mind.

I opened the bedroom door and stepped out quietly. River was sitting on a barstool leaning on the counter as she talked with a man. He was several inches shorter than me with brown hair. He was athletically built and moved around the kitchen with confidence. His back was currently to me.

"Is he an Alpha?" Kyson asked. I stayed back and listened.

"Yes." River said slowly. "But I really don't want to talk about this right now."

"River, I love you. More than anyone in the world. I want to know you are going to be well cared for." Caspian growled at the man's comment.

"I will be cared for." River pulled her hair into a high ponytail.

"You said he was full of himself and a pain in the butt." Kyson set a plate in front of her. "I want you to be happy, to have love in your life like Mom and Dad." Siblings? My hatred for the man melted away as I continued to watch the two of them.

"All Alphas are full of themselves. It is hardwired into their DNA or something. And you are a pain in the butt, and I still love you." River took a bite. My eyes widened at her statement. Love?

"So, you love him?" Kyson stopped what he was doing and turned to face River.

River choked. "I didn't say that. He is my husband and mate. I'm sure love will come eventually. Isn't that how it works?"

Kyson chuckled as he put his arms around River, pressing a kiss to her temple. "No, usually a couple fall in love and then they mark each other."

"It was Maya." River groaned as she put her hands over her face. "And she is beyond proud of herself. When I told her that we couldn't mark him, she said, 'watch me'."

Cruz smiled at that. Caspian was beyond happy about our mate, but I had to agree with River, we shouldn't have marked each other. At least not yet. We should have gotten to know each other first.

"You could make a life together. Maybe not the one you were wanting, since he is an Alpha, but who knows. I can't really say much, I haven't even met the guy yet." Kyson kissed the top of River's head again. "So, what does he look like? If Maya is happy with him, he must be a looker."

River laughed. "Wow, what are we, a couple of sixteen-year-old girls?"

"So, that is a yes." Kyson smirked at her.

"I didn't say that." River said in exasperation.

"Is he ugly with a sweet spirit, then?"

"No, I didn't...Ky...Ugh...this conversation is over. He is going to be out here any minute." River said quickly.

"I don't think I have seen you blush before. Dang! You must really think he is hot." Kyson's grin widened. "Does he have a chiseled jaw? Sculpted abs? Is he a great kisser?"

"Ky, stop." River said desperately.

"I don't know, I was kind of enjoying the conversation." I said as I walked closer to them.

Chapter Thirteen

River

My lungs ceased to work as Cruz took the stool two spots over from me. I couldn't look at him. How long had he been standing there? Maya was laughing as her tail wagged. I could not believe this was my life right now. First that stupid nightmare that I couldn't seem to shake, and now Cruz overhearing that conversation.

"Hi, I'm Cruz Storm." Cruz extended his hand and Kyson shook it.

"I'm Kyson Shepherd, River's brother." Kyson gave Cruz the smile he reserved for when he needed to be diplomatic.

"River said you enjoy cooking." Cruz said as he looked around the kitchen. "What do you enjoy about it?"

Was Cruz serious? What was he trying to do? I stared at him, trying to understand what was going on. I looked over at Kyson and he glanced at me. His dimple appeared as he fought his smile. They talked for several minutes.

"That depends on who I'm cooking for." Kyson crossed his arms over his chest. "River loves it when I make waffles." He gestured to my half-eaten breakfast. "Would you like to try some?"

"If there are extras." Cruz gave Kyson a friendly smile. "What do you typically put on it?"

"River likes fresh fruit and whipped cream, but for you, I think a dash of arsenic."

Cruz burst out laughing. "You are the second person to tell me that arsenic would be a good additive to my food."

"River tends to enjoy that threat. I think I have been hearing it since the day I was born." Kyson laughed, putting a plate in front of Cruz. "She is a healer at heart, so I wouldn't put too much stock in the threat."

My mouth fell open as I stared at my brother. Was he really getting all buddy-buddy with Cruz. What was going on?

"I wasn't worried." Cruz took a bite of his food.

"So, you are my sister's mate?"

"I am." Cruz didn't look up from his plate.

"How do you feel about that?" Kyson asked.

Cruz glanced up. He set his fork down and sat back. "I didn't want a mate. I didn't come here looking for one. I came to drop off Nash and Belle before being shipped out on my next mission. I didn't have time for a mate. I am in a dangerous line of work. The last thing I want is to have someone waiting at home for me when there is a very real possibility that I might not come back." Cruz's attention remained focused on Kyson. "Even though my wolf recognized River as our mate, she didn't seem to recognize us. I was hoping to finish dropping the kids off and leaving. I don't have leave for another several weeks. After I had time off, I was planning on coming back here."

"I thought you were an FBWHA Agent? Is it really all that dangerous of a job?" Kyson's brows furrowed in worry as he glanced at me.

"Dangerous enough." Cruz picked up his fork. The explosion flashed in my mind again.

Kyson looked between us several times. I could see the gears in his head turning. He was bright and knew something wasn't adding up. I looked back down at my plate as I began messing with a strawberry. My appetite was completely gone.

"Dangerous enough that River had a nightmare that upset her enough that she called out your name, was pale, and shaking?"

"Drop it, Ky." I stood up and walked away. I went back into my bedroom and pulled on my shoes. When I came back out. Kyson was sitting next to Cruz as they ate. I got on the elevator to Alpha's office instead of dad's. I needed some time alone and I needed a good run.

As I ran on one of the treadmills, images from my nightmare kept coming back. I pushed myself faster and faster until I was sprinting. I had been at this speed for a good hour when the smell of rain filled my lungs. I pushed the stop button and slowed with the machine. I laced my fingers behind my head as I took deep breaths to try to slow my heart rate.

"I haven't seen many who can keep up that speed for so long." Cruz commented. I glanced in his direction but didn't say anything. "Your brother seems nice."

I stepped off the machine and walked toward the girls' locker room. I locked it before moving away from the door and window to get changed into clean clothes. I was paranoid someone would be looking through the window, and I didn't trust Cruz to not pick the lock. There was no way I was getting in a shower here.

When I walked out of the locker room, Cruz was waiting for me. "What do you want?" I asked as I stepped out into the hall with Cruz right behind me.

"You are still in danger, River. Someone needs to keep an eye on you." Cruz said.

I ignored him as I headed for dad's office. I went directly to the minifridge and grabbed a bottle of water before sitting on the couch. Miles looked surprised to see Cruz.

"When did you get in?" Miles asked.

"Last night." Cruz answered as he closed the door.

"Why didn't you let me know?"

"Caspian needed some time to cool off before talking to you, Gin, and Spur." Cruz took a chair near the desk.

Just then the door opened, and Gin and Spur walked in. "How did things go?" Gin asked as he took the chair next to Cruz.

"Not exactly how we thought it would." Cruz said as he tightened his fist.

"That's an understatement." I muttered. Everyone turned to look at me, and I glared at them. "It was a complete set up. Not only were there not nearly as many men as you had thought there would be, but they were also positioned weird."

Cruz straightened up as he turned to look at me. "How do you know that?"

I stood and began pacing. "There was a clear barrier between the men guarding the building and the building itself. There weren't even powerlines anywhere near the meadow. I guess there could have been generators or something, but I didn't see any."

Cruz was suddenly in front of me, and I stopped. "You talked with her about your mission?" Miles asked, surprised.

"I didn't." Cruz said, studying my face.

"I'm confused." Gin said slowly. "If you didn't talk to her about it and she was here, how does she know what happened?"

I raised the back of my hand to my forehead. "It was a dream." I whispered. "Just a dream, right?" I looked up at Cruz, hoping he would tell me that it was only in my mind. Last night he said he wasn't in the building.

"River had a dream last night that is accurate to what happened." Cruz touched my elbow. "I don't know how though."

"River, what did you see?" Miles asked. I explained about being up on the hill, Cruz slipping into the shadows, watching the movement of the men, a large man entering the building, the explosion. Miles sat there staring at me as if surprised. "Cruz, your turn." Cruz glanced down at me before giving his account. He hesitantly added that he had come across a man, was told the building was storage for explosives, and then of sending the man into the building first.

"Is it some sort of werewolf thing to see what each other are doing through dreams?" Spur asked.

"No. River didn't just have a dream about Cruz. The dream happened several days after it occurred. After Cruz came back." Miles said thoughtfully.

"Are you saying that I gave her the dream somehow?" Cruz asked.

"You said that Caspian's mark was deep enough to create a stronger bond." I said as I took a seat on the couch again. "Is it possible that Cruz's thoughts came out in my dreams?" I shook my head. "No, because it was like I was there. I saw Cruz move into the trees. Almost like I was reviewing what had happened." I furrowed my brows as I tried to puzzle this out.

"We could have experienced a sort of mind-link." Maya suggested. *"You should try to reach out to him."*

"I am not going to do that, Maya." I told her firmly.

"Why not? Are you scared of our bond with him?" Maya challenged.

"Of course I am." I snapped at her.

I stood and stormed out of the office. I didn't want this bond. I didn't want a mate. I still didn't know how to interact with Cruz on a normal basis, now I have to contend with our minds linking while I slept. When I finally looked up, I was at the waterfall. I jumped into the water. When my head broke the surface, Cruz was standing on the shore.

"Interesting place to go when you are upset." He commented. His eyes scanned the area. I noticed Spur and Gin were near the path.

"It's a good place to cool off." I said as my teeth started to chatter.

"I bet." Cruz's gaze returned to me. "Are you ready to head back or do you need more time?"

I swam towards the falls and dove under, coming up on the backside. I climbed up to the cave mom had shown me when I was eight. I definitely needed more time. I curled into a ball and watched the water distort the thick forest that surrounded this little clearing. When I couldn't stand the cold anymore, I sighed and scooted to the edge. I knew Cruz was going to still be down there.

I sucked in my breath and jumped. I slowly swam to the surface. When I broke the surface, arms circled me. Cruz was there with a worried look on his face. "Where did you go?" He asked.

I gave him a small smile. "That is classified."

"Come on, let's get you to dry land and warmed up." Cruz began swimming to the shore. I slowly followed him. He grabbed my hand as soon as I was standing. Gin and Spur fell into step behind us. I kept my head down and didn't say anything. Cruz pulled me up the stairs and into Uncle Max's room. I let him pull me onto the elevator.

"Went for a swim at the falls again?" Kyson asked. "Nothing like a quick dip to center yourself."

"She was in there for forty minutes." Cruz practically growled.

"River!" Kyson snapped. "Why would you do that?"

I pulled free of Cruz and headed for my room. I went straight to the shower and stepped into the hot water. As I warmed up, I slowly pulled my soaked clothes off. I wrapped a towel around myself and opened the bathroom door. Cruz sat on the edge of the bed. He was in clean clothes, and he looked like he had showered.

"Get out." I said.

"Mind telling me what is going on?" Cruz asked, showing no sign of getting up. He looked at me like dad did when I did something wrong.

"I want to get dressed. Get out." I walked to the dresser.

"Why would you intentionally stay in freezing water for more than forty minutes? That was reckless. What were you thinking?"

"Why would you intentionally fly a plane you knew was going to blow up?" I shot back. I grabbed my clothes and headed for the door.

Cruz was right behind me. "It was my job, River. You nearly freezing to death serves no purpose." He growled. Kyson's eyes widened when he saw me in my towel and Cruz following behind me.

"Just because you don't know what it is, doesn't mean I didn't have a purpose for my actions." I turned to face him. My anger was back in full swing. "I don't have to tell you why either, Cruz. I am not one of your soldiers who will fall in line behind you."

Cruz turned around and took several steps away from me. I took the opportunity to get on the elevator. When Cruz turned back around, the doors completely closed. I pressed the fourth button and waited. I got off in my parents' room. I pressed the button to return the elevator to the bunker before moving into the closet. There were no windows in here. I hated that I was becoming paranoid. I dressed quickly before running down the stairs and outside.

I shifted into my wolf. Maya let out a howl as she paced the back lawn. We wanted to run, but knew how reckless that would be, so we settled for growling at the blades of grass as we flattened them under our large paws. My mystery caller hadn't reached back out since Cruz left. Our growling increased at the thought of him and his threats. I let Maya have full control. I needed to not think.

At least we were on the same page about a few things. Cruz's reaction to a swim in the falls ticked us off. Maya may like having him as our mate, but he wasn't the boss of us. He didn't have the right to treat us like a child. Kyson's scent hit me, and I whirled around to face him. My lips curled back over my teeth and my hackles rose. I was not in the mood for a brotherly lecture, either. Cruz stood next to him on the back porch. Both looked ticked.

My hackles rose as I growled at them. Miles came out next and looked between us. He walked slowly down the stairs. I moved away from him. Gin and Spur came around the side of the building but stopped when they saw me.

"River, you might need to take control, I might hurt one of them if they tell us to calm down." Maya growled.

I shifted back to human, but I turned my back to everyone. I was still furious. Kyson had even taken on his 'I can't believe you would be so stupid' tone.

I felt someone moving closer and I balled my hands into fists. "River, I know you are working through a lot right now, but can we take this inside?" Miles said softly.

"No one said you had to come out here." I snapped back.

"River, I think you need to calm down." Kyson said.

I took two running steps, but my wrist was caught in a large hand. I turned to see Cruz. My momentary surprise gave way to anger. His eyes darkened. I tried to punch him, but he seemed to know what I was thinking and blocked it. How did he do that?

I remembered Molly saying that as hybrids, they had special abilities. Could Cruz anticipate someone's moves? I tried to twist away from him, but he **stopped** me. I pressed my lips to his and I could feel his surprise. I punched him in the gut, and he groaned as he bent forward. I tried to run again, but he grabbed me.

Maya growled as she surged forward. Suddenly, I could see all around me. Cruz's arm was moving slowly around my waist, and I spun out of the way. I jumped and kicked my feet into his chest. He went stumbling backwards several steps before falling. Everything sped up and I couldn't catch myself. I hit the ground hard. The wind was knocked from my lungs, and a loud snap filled the air. Maya yelped and retreated. I rolled to my side coughing. Pain flashed through my head, and I curled into a ball.

"River!" Cruz was at my side. "I'm so sorry." He said franticly. "Where are you hurt?" He smoothed my hair back from my face with a shaky hand. "Oh gosh, what did I do?" He muttered.

I swallowed hard. "I think I broke my arm." I whispered.

Cruz scooped me up and ran inside. My mind felt sluggish, like I couldn't keep up with the world around me. Everyone was moving so fast it was making me dizzy. Voices were even speaking in rapid fire, and I couldn't understand them. Cruz's face was suddenly looking down on me. He was the only thing not moving at hyper speed at the moment.

I closed my eyes. When I managed to get them open again, Kyson was pacing near dad's desk. Miles was working on his laptop and Cruz was sitting on the floor next to the couch I was laying on. The world was moving normally again. I sat up and winced. Cruz spun around to face me. I looked down at my arm. It ached a bit, but it wasn't hurting like it had before.

"River." Cruz breathed out as he sat beside me on the couch. He pulled me into his lap as he buried his face in my neck. "I'm so sorry." He whispered.

I was feeling so tired, and I curled into him. *"Maya, are you okay?"* I asked her. She had never yelped like that before, even when I had broken bones.

"I think I'm okay." Maya said softly. *"What was that? What happened to us?"*

"Cruz?" I whispered.

He pulled back and looked down at me. His eyes were filled with guilt and concern. "Yes?"

"Is that how you do it?" I asked. His brows drew down in confusion. "Slow down time, or whatever that was?"

"You figured out my secret." He stroked my cheek with his thumb.

I shook my head. "I saw it." I closed my eyes. "You were reaching around me; everything was moving so slowly. As soon as I kicked you, everything sped back up."

"How did you...?" Cruz sounded confused.

"It's your bond. You and River are connecting on a deeper level. First, her being able to see your memory of your mission. Now, using a bit of your hybrid ability." Miles said.

"How is your head, Babe?" Cruz asked softly. "After my first couple times, I had a splitting headache. And Caspian was weak for a few days."

"All of the above." I turned more into his chest. I felt him kiss my head as he held me tighter. "I'm still mad at you." I said softly.

"I'm mad at me, too." Cruz whispered back.

"I get first dibs at ripping you apart." Cruz's chuckle reverberated through his chest.

"Deal."

"Are they always like this?" Kyson asked.

"The whole love-hate thing? Pretty much. Though this was the first physical altercation." Miles said with a laugh. "I would love to see them have an actual sparring match instead of Cruz just trying to stop her from running off. She broke my nose several times in the last couple of days."

"That's why I quit sparring with her. It's embarrassing for a future Alpha to get his butt kicked by his older sister." Kyson laughed.

I leaned more against Cruz and kept my eyes closed. I could feel an intense amount of guilt and worry flowing through the bond. He held me protectively and I felt safe and comforted with him close. Today, I got to see a side of Cruz I hadn't seen before. He cares for me.

Looking back, his anger was out of concern with me spending too much time in the icy water. He wasn't trying to hurt me, even though I took the first swing. His only concern was keeping me safe. He was even now blaming himself for my actions, while I had been acting out of anger.

Chapter Fourteen

Cruz

I cradled River in my arms. No matter how many times the guys told me that it wasn't my fault, I still felt the crushing weight of guilt. Caspian whined in my head. He was beating himself up, too. I had felt strong for a few seconds before River had kicked me and gone down. If she had tapped into my ability, had I tapped into her royal blood, becoming stronger?

It didn't matter, River was hurt. Kyson had used some of the cream on her arm in order to help it heal. The pain had been worse than if I had broken my own arm. I was glad I was the one to feel it. My guilt would have been much worse if I had to listen to her screaming in agony again.

I looked across the room as Gin and Spur walked into the office. "How did you receive the tip about the building?" I asked. I had been worried that I would lose my temper when I had this conversation. Holding River would prevent me from getting up and hurting someone. I might as well do it now.

"Harrison found a folded-up map with the location circled on it under the mattress Darius used." Gin answered. "It was a sound lead, Cruz."

"What happened is they played us." I said as my frustration began to build. River whimpered and I looked down at her. Her brow was furrowed. I ran my finger along her jaw and her expression smoothed. "That map was left intentionally. River received another threat, this one claiming they knew I was part of Shadow's strike team. They threatened to expose my identity and let Shadow take care of me."

"I knew there was more to what you did." Kyson spoke up. "Shadow's strike team? And what threats?"

"River has been getting calls and texts from an unknown number. The caller has digitalized his voice, so it is unrecognizable. The gist of it is, she needs to reject her mate or end up like your grandparents. The threats went onto say that Cruz would pay the price for her disobedience, once the man found out Cruz and River were married." Miles explained.

"We believe that whoever these threats are coming from are the same people who tried to kill the royal family and your parents." I added. "At first, I thought the explosion was meant to kill Shadow, but now I'm thinking it was probably their attempt to get rid of me."

"Why are they not trying to kill me and River?" Kyson took a seat behind the desk.

"They want to use River to ascend to the throne. You are below her in the pecking order, so you aren't in the way." Gin said.

"They want to force her to be their mate?" Kyson looked over at River. "She would never stand for it. Even if she hadn't found Cruz. She and Maya aren't ones to roll over and take orders, hint, this afternoon's display."

"So, what do we do now?" Spur asked.

"Have there been any more calls or texts?" I asked.

"Not since you left." Miles answered.

Just then the phone on the corner of the desk rang. All of us froze. It rang again, and River bolted upright. Her face drained of color as her eyes focused on the phone. She began to tremble, and she shook her head. Miles picked it up before walking over to us. River pressed herself more into me as Miles drew closer.

"I don't want to answer it." she said desperately.

"Babe, we need to know what he wants. Please answer it. I am right here with you." I whispered in her ear.

She hesitantly grabbed the phone and answered it, slowly raising it to her ear. Her eyes met mine. "Hello." Her voice trembled.

"My condolences, my dear River. Did you get to say your good-byes?" The man's voice was almost gleeful.

"You did it?" River breathed out. Her eyes never left mine and I could see her fear. Caspian growled in my head, and I shoved him farther into my mind. I didn't need his anger mixing with mine. I needed to stay calm for River's sake.

I touched my forehead to hers and breathed in her calming scent. "You forced me to. You were the one who refused to reject him. You are the one who sealed his fate. His death is on you, River."

I moved my mouth close to her other ear. "You are doing great, Baby. Ask him what he wants." I whispered.

"What do you want from me?" River pressed her face into my neck as her trembling increased.

"I know you are feeling weak right now from the breaking of your bond with him, but I promise you will feel much better once I mark you. Together we can raise this mourning kingdom higher."

"That future will never happen." River said firmly.

"Play nice, my River, and we might just find someone other than your brother to frame all the murders on. After all, with you gone, he would take over." The line went dead, and River dropped the phone on the floor.

I pulled back and looked into River's eyes. They were filled with unshed tears. I pressed my lips to hers. "You did great, Babe." I told her.

"What did he say?" Miles asked.

"He was gloating about killing me, told River that he was going to mark her, and he is planning on framing Kyson for the deaths of the royals." I said, and a tear escaped River's eye, rolling down her cheek. I brushed it away. "River, he will never have you."

River closed her eyes briefly before looking back at me. "What if he succeeds? What if he kills you? What if he takes me?" River's fear slammed into me through our bond. I could feel her panic.

"You are mine, River, and I am yours. You can't separate two sides of a single coin. You are my wife, and as such, I will protect you with my last breath. I will always be here for you." I told her firmly. She closed her eyes and took in a shuddering breath. She nodded her head before laying it on my shoulder. "Always remember that."

River had fallen asleep. It didn't surprise me. After the rough night she had, our fight, and then the phone call, she had to be exhausted. I laid her carefully on the couch and slowly stood. She turned so she was facing the back of the couch. I kissed her temple before draping a blanket over her. When I turned around, everyone was watching me.

"What?" I asked, glaring at my men while I walked over to them.

"Nothing. It's just we haven't seen you be so...soft with anyone before. It's as weird as seeing your face." Spur commented.

"Don't push him too far, Spur." Miles warned. "I bet his soft side only extends to River."

"If you are done teasing the poor guy, I have the location of where the call came from." Gin spoke up. I moved to his side, standing over his shoulder as I stared at the computer screen. "It is just outside the North Wind Pack's territory."

"Is there anyone there that would want to hurt the royal family?" Miles asked.

"No. The North Wind Pack is loyal to Toren and Jet. My grandmother was their sister, and she had been a fair and kind Luna. The pack adored her." Kyson shook his head.

"Nash said that the woman couldn't wait to get revenge on *her*. One of the men told the woman to be patient and wait for the plane to go down." I began to pace. "Nash also mentioned that the second man couldn't wait to have *her* warming his bed."

"Are you thinking they are seeking revenge on River?" Gin asked.

"I think they were talking about two different people." I said. "What kind of revenge would put a target on a throne?"

"You didn't say she would be on a throne, just warming the guy's bed." Spur pointed out.

I clenched my jaw to try to rein in my anger. River wasn't going to be in anyone's bed but mine. "River is the only woman in connection with the plane crash that wasn't killed. The question is, who were they seeking revenge on?"

"Do we know any names?" Kyson asked.

"Just a Darius Wood. He worked for Miles for a number of years. He was here for a little while before disappearing." Gin said in frustration. "We thought we knew where he ran off to, but it was a trap to kill Cruz."

"Wood. Wood. Where have I heard that name before?" Kyson muttered as he began to pace.

"Dax Wood was the man that kidnapped mom and took her to the North Wind Pack. She was forced to be marked by Alpha Kion. The only reason Dax was successful at capturing mom was because he and his men had the support of witches. They had no scent, and powerful drugs that kept her out for days." River's soft voice sounded from the couch.

"How long have you been awake?" Spur asked. "I thought you would be out for a while."

"As soon as Cruz put me on the couch." She muttered. She didn't turn around or try to get up.

"Do we know of any connection between Dax and Darius?" Miles asked.

Gin smacked me and gestured toward River with a pointed look. "I can look into it." He said.

I walked to the couch and crouched down. "Do you know anything else about Dax?" I asked her. Gin coughed, and when I glanced in his direction, he was glaring at me. Apparently, that wasn't what he wanted me to do.

"Dax is thought to be dead." Kyson said. "Mom punched him for touching her. After he handed mom over to Alpha Kane, he demanded more money for his troubles. He was escorted out to get his payment, but mom assumed he had been killed."

"Cruz," River's voice was soft.

"Yeah, Babe?" I pulled the blanket higher up on her shoulder.

"Who was the woman?"

"What woman?"

"The one in the video."

"We aren't sure yet." I smoothed her hair back. "Try to sleep, River. You need rest."

"You weren't kidding about the headache." River turned her head into the couch cushion.

"Do you have a cream or something we can use?" I asked her in concern.

She shook her head then groaned. "Even if I did, I wouldn't use it."

"Why not?" Kyson asked.

River shook her head again but didn't say anything. I could hear Miles, Spur, and Gin talking quietly over at the desk. I rested my hand on River's hip as I turned to look at Kyson. "Get whatever you want out of this office. You are going to be spending the rest of 'this' in the bunker."

Kyson nodded and turned towards the far wall where there were filing cabinets. He began pulling files from the drawers and stacking them. I turned back to River. She was a little pale. She had been that way since her nightmare.

"River, Babe." I whispered.

"Hmm?"

"Scoot over." I laid down beside her. I slid my arm under her head as my other went over her waist. River sighed as she ran her hand along my arm. "Better?" I asked, placing a kiss on her neck. She nodded as her body began to relax.

"You are leaving soon, aren't you?" she asked softly.

"Probably in a few hours. I will leave Gin and Miles here with you and your brother. Spur and I will go see if we can find the caller." I laced my fingers through hers.

The lights clicked off and I heard the door close. Using my ability, I saw that River and I were alone. I pulled her closer. "Cruz?"

"Yeah?"

River rolled over and put her hand on the side of my face. "Don't ever treat me like a child again."

I smiled. "Yes, ma'am." I kissed the tip of her nose.

River pressed her lips to mine. My hand went to the back of her head as I deepened the kiss. This woman was driving me mad. I pulled back, needing to put distance between us before I lost all my control. "Get some rest, River. I will wake you before I leave."

"Where are you going now?" River asked.

"I can't stay, right now." I started to get up when River let out a frustrated sigh. "I really can't."

"What's your excuse this time?" River huffed.

"You are too big of a temptation." I kissed her forehead. I stood and looked down at her.

"Your excuses are terrible." She scowled at me.

I caged her in with my arms as I leaned over her. "You don't think you are a temptation?" I asked her.

"I didn't say that. But I also wasn't complaining. The only one who was, was you." River looked into my eyes. A range of emotions swirled in their depths.

"What are you saying, River?" I asked as my head dipped down towards hers.

"I'm not saying anything." River shrugged. I pressed my lips to hers. She responded by wrapping her arms around my neck and pulling me closer. I allowed her to lead, just enjoying the feeling of her in my arms.

Chapter Fifteen

River

I watched Cruz as he got dressed. He had several scars on his back. He reached into his bag and pulled out the tin of oil. He blackened his hair and took an inventory of his weapons. When he was finally done, he turned and looked at me. "Checking me out while I get dressed?" he smiled.

"No…I wasn't…" My face turned bright red.

Cruz walked over to the couch and grabbed my hand, pulling me to my feet. I squeaked in surprise as I struggled to keep the blanket around me. I tried to pull away from him, but his hold on me only tightened. I couldn't look at him. I couldn't believe what we had just done. I don't know what had come over me.

"River…" Cruz's voice was soft.

My heart rate accelerated as my hand gripped the blanket tighter. Cruz put his arms around me, and I leaned into him. Even though I was feeling a little self-conscious about what had just happened, I didn't regret it. I just didn't know what Cruz was going to do. Miles called us a few minutes ago. We had been lying together. Cruz had been slowly running his fingers through my hair and I was almost asleep.

"Cruz?" I took a deep breath for courage before looking up at him.

He kissed me before I could say anything more. "Babe, I need you to get dressed. The guys will be coming back in a few minutes. We can talk after the meeting."

I nodded and got dressed quickly. Cruz watched me with a soft smile on his face. When I finished, he pulled me down next to him on the couch. His mouth was back on mine. He groaned as he pulled back. "You are definitely a temptation." He murmured against my lips.

I smiled. "Hmm. I don't think I care."

Cruz chuckled. "So, I am a great kisser?"

I pulled back and glared at him. "I never said that."

Cruz's grin widened. "What did you say then?"

"I...Molly...She was just asking about the whole brain fog thing." I explained. "All I said was it was like everything faded but you. It was weird. Leave it to a six-year-old to read into a simple comment."

"What did Molly say?" Cruz asked as he ran his nose along my jaw to my ear. He began pressing light kisses to my neck.

"She made the comment that she never would have thought her brother would even know how to kiss, since you never had a girlfriend before." I whispered. What was Cruz doing to me?

"And you said..."

The door opened and I jumped. Cruz sat up but kept his arms around me as Miles, Spur, and Gin walked in. "How are you feeling, Finley?"

"I am feeling much better, thank you." I said, fighting my blush.

"You ready to go, Cruz?" Spur asked.

"Yeah." Cruz stood and offered me his hand. I took it and got to my feet. He turned to look at me. "You still have those things I gave you?"

I nodded. "You said to make sure I always had them."

"Good." He pressed a kiss to my forehead. "This room and the bunker are the only rooms I want you to be in. Miles and Gin will be staying with you. Please, River, don't run off or fight them."

"I can't guarantee anything if they treat me like a child." I responded.

Cruz cupped my face with both hands. "No jokes, not right now. I need you to promise me that you will follow their orders." The intensity in Cruz's eyes scared me. I wasn't worried that he would hurt me, but it made me feel like something bad was going to happen.

"I promise." I whispered. He rested his forehead against mine and took a deep breath.

"What happened between you two?" Gin asked. "You two have been at odds every time you are in the same room. Now you are acting like she is the most precious thing in the world."

"To be fair, she always has been, he is just showing it now." Spur crossed his arms over his chest. "It only took her breaking her arm while fighting with him to see it."

Cruz growled and I kissed him. "Be safe." I stepped away from him and he glared at me.

"I wasn't done with you." He took a step forward, closing the distance between us.

I wrapped my arms around his neck and buried my face in his neck. "You need to go, Cruz. I will be fine until you get back." He released me slowly and gave me a quick kiss.

A muscle ticked in his jaw as he paused at the door and looked at me. I walked up to him, took the mask from his hand, gave him a quick kiss, and put it on his face. "I'm really starting to hate this thing." He muttered before walking out of the room, slamming the door.

"I think it has gotten worse." Gin shook his head. "Never thought I would see the day when Shadow had to be forced out the door to go on a mission."

"I have already started on his retirement papers. All that is left is his signature." Miles commented. "After seeing them together, I knew it was a matter of time."

"What do you mean?" I asked. "Caspian and Cruz love their job."

"Of course they do. They thrive in this field. But they have found something to live for. You can't have anything to lose when you do what he has been doing for six years. I am sure once the dust settles, Shadow will be a thing of the past. Cruz will most likely still want to stay on as an FBWHA Agent." Miles looked at me with a smile.

"I'm going to go to the bunker and see if I can help Kyson with dad's paperwork." I said, and they left so I could access the elevator.

Kyson and I were managing to run the pack from the bunker. We caught up on the paperwork that had piled up over the last couple of weeks. Cruz and Spur had been gone for a week now, and I was restless. I wanted Cruz to come back. I hadn't been sleeping well. I tossed and turned as the explosion kept replaying in my head. I knew Cruz wasn't the one going into the building, but my mind kept seeing it that way.

Kyson had stayed up late speaking with another pack about a deal dad and Uncle Max had been working on. He was still sleeping, so I decided to read a book until he woke up. We had talked about working on an expansion project for the school to include some additional classes.

A beeping near the elevator had my head snapping up. The light was flashing purple. What did Miles want? The purple light indicated that the person in the office was calling the people in the bunker to come up. I closed my book and stood. I stretched before checking to make sure I had the S.O.S.

transmitter, phone, and arrow. I was just about to step on the elevator but hesitated.

If anyone checked my pockets, they would find all three items, and then where would I be? I went back to the kitchen and pulled open the drawer that housed a bunch of miscellaneous items. I searched through the chaos until I found the super glue. I set the transmitter on the counter before pulling my shirt off. I added a good amount of super glue to the back of the quarter-sized device. I tugged down the side of my bra and pressed the transmitter to the area of my ribs just below my armpit.

Once the glue dried, I pulled my shirt back on and got on the elevator. Maya grew unsettled as the elevator rose. By the time the doors opened, I was ready to return to the bunker. Something didn't feel right. The room looked empty. On my second scan of the room, the toe of a shoe caught my eye.

I ran to the other side of the desk. Miles lay in a pool of blood. I dropped to my knees beside him, and when I rolled him over, he groaned. I ran to where I had stashed my medical box and brought it back to Miles. Opening the lid, I pulled out several different powders. I cut his shirt open to expose the wound. After applying the powders to the hole in his abdomen, I put a clean bandage over the wound. I pressed firmly, trying to stop the bleeding. It would take a few hours for the powders to kick in. They would seal the wound and heal any internal damage.

Miles's eyes flew open, and he stared at me with concern. "Run, River." Miles groaned out. "Run."

My heart started racing faster as I watched Miles close his eyes again. What had happened to him? I scanned the room again but no one else was there. The door suddenly opened. A large man walked into the room. He had blonde hair and blue eyes. He smiled when he saw me. He slowly walked along the wall as he studied me.

"You, River, are a hard woman to get to." The man said.

I slowly got to my feet, my eyes flickering to the open door. It was my only escape. This stranger was currently between me and the elevator, not that I would risk him finding out about it. I inched my way closer to the door as I watched him.

"You seem tense. I'm sure your mate can help put you at ease." The man's grin widened. He may have been a little shorter than Cruz, but he was just as wide. I couldn't tell if he was a werewolf or not. He had no scent.

"My mate? You know very well that my mate can't comfort me right now." I was almost close enough to the door now that if I ran, whoever this guy was, wouldn't be able to stop me.

"The man you killed? Yeah, he won't be able to help you. I was referring to your true mate."

I shook my head. Maya sniffed the air, trying to see how many bad guys were nearby, but couldn't smell anyone but Miles. "I will never be with anyone but Cruz."

I bolted through the door. I pressed the button on the phone to call Cruz. Where was Gin? I needed to get out of here. If I was gone, the threat to everyone would be as well.

I ran around the corner as I heard Cruz answer the phone. "Babe?"

Something hit me with such force that I flew against the opposite wall before I could respond to him. I cried out in pain as I fell to the floor. I scrambled to my feet and looked around me. The man from the office was blocking that hallway, while a man that looked similar to him, blocked the other one. I was trapped in a corner.

The second guy had brown eyes and a burn scar that ran along his neck. Darius. "When I first saw you, you took my breath away."

"You already used that line on me." I snapped at him. "After getting shot down the first time, you would think you would come up with better material."

"I am going to enjoy taming you, River." His eyes narrowed as he smiled. He took a deep breath, and his smile turned to a scowl. "I can still smell him on her."

"It takes time for a mate bond to fully break. He died not long ago. Give it time, his scent will fade." The man from the office took a step closer.

"Do you really think two against one is fair?" I asked as the first man took a step towards me.

"Who said anything about fighting fair? Your mom was quite a fighter. Are you like her? She chose to make things hard for me. Are you going to do the same?"

"Who are you?" I asked, widening my stance. He better believe I wasn't going to go quietly.

"Your parents didn't talk about me? Now that is insulting." The man clicked his tongue. "Dax Wood, at your service, my queen."

"I am not the queen." I said.

Darius lunged for me, and I twisted out of the way. He slammed into the wall behind me as I dodged a fist from Dax. I managed to deflect most of their blows. I kicked Darius in the chest, causing him to crash against the wall. A picture fell to the ground along with him. I turned my attention to Dax. After dodging his fists, I glanced back to where Darius had fallen. He wasn't there. He seemed to have disappeared. Dax's level of aggression grew, and I focused on him. I only needed to get him down long enough so that I could make a run for it. I jumped back when Dax tried to kick me.

Pain exploded in my head as I was struck from behind. I fell to the ground in a heap. My vision was going in and out as two figures stood over me. "We don't want to kill her, Darius. You shouldn't have hit her so hard."

"Got her to stop fighting, didn't I?" Darius commented.

"That is what this was for." Dax held up a syringe. "We just needed to get close enough to inject her with it. Hitting her in the head with a bat wasn't necessary."

"Whatever. Let's just get her in the car. Mom can't wait to meet her." Darius said as he went to grab me.

I tried to fight again, but my body wasn't doing what I was telling it to do. A sharp sting in my arm had me cursing. Blackness closed in around me. My last thought was about Gin and what they had done to him.

Chapter Sixteen

Cruz

Spur and I had been observing the cabin for the last week. We had seen dozens of people moving in and out of the small structure, but there was no sign of Dax, Darius, or the woman from the video. We had agreed that we would wait until one of the three known suspects showed up before we moved in. We were alternating keeping watch. I just finished my shift and was laying down in our shelter. My frustration over the situation grew with each passing day. Caspian was becoming hard to keep under control. He wanted to tear apart everyone in the cabin so we could get back to River.

My pocket vibrated and I froze for a second before scrambling to pull the phone from my pocket. Why was River calling? "Babe?" I said as I brought the phone to my ear.

A loud thumb followed by River's cry of pain came through the line. River was talking to two men. Dax introduced himself and a fight broke out. I listened as I sat frozen. I didn't know what to do. My worst nightmare was coming to life, and I could only sit and listen to it. I clenched my fists when I heard one of the men say they had hit River in the head with a bat. I heard shuffling around but then all was quiet. The silence pulled me out of my shock. I hung up the phone and ran outside. I hurried over to Spur.

"River was just attacked. I need to leave." I said quickly. I was trying to rien in my panic but failing.

"Where were Miles and Gin?" Spur looked surprised. "Is River okay?"

"I plan to find out where those two went off to. There was no sign of them." I felt Caspian pushing for control. "The men that attacked took her."

Spur cursed. "Stay here. I'm going back. Call if there are any new developments."

I shifted into my wolf and let Caspian have control. We ran into the forest with no intention of stopping until we got back to the Silver Moon Pack.

Caspian crashed through the front door of the packhouse. We sniffed the air. It had been two days since River had called, and her scent was faint. I followed it down the hallway heading for the offices. I came across a broken table, baseball bat, and blood on the carpet. After shifting into human, I continued to look around. I found River's phone up against the wall by a broken picture.

I picked it up and ran to Gamma Easton's office. Blood was splattered across the surface of the desk and a dark spot was on the ground. Someone had been shot. I left the office and ran upstairs to the Alpha's bedroom to access the elevator.

I prayed someone was down there. I needed answers and I didn't want to spend hours watching security footage. The doors slid open, and I stepped out. "Hello?" I called.

Kyson stuck his head out of a room several doors down from River's. "Who are you?" Kyson asked wearily. I pulled the mask off my face, and he immediately relaxed. "Cruz, I am so glad to see you."

"You may not be in a few minutes if I don't start getting answers." I growled out. "Where are Miles and Gin?"

"They are currently unconscious in the room." He pointed to the room he just exited.

"What?" I snapped.

"River was gone when I woke up. The purple light was flashing, so I figured she went up to the office. I found Miles with a bullet hole in his chest. There was a bandage over it and River's medicine box opened next to him. I followed her scent down the hall. I found where it looked like a fight had broken out."

"The broken table and picture?" I asked and he nodded. "Where was Gin?"

"I found him so badly beaten, that I was worried he was dead. He was outside." Kyson ran his hand down his face. "I had the pack doctor look at both of them. Miles will recover, thanks to whatever River had put on him, but we still aren't sure about Gin. Neither have woken up yet."

We walked into the room, and I looked at both men. I ran a hand through my hair. I should have left more men here. The problem was, I didn't trust any others. Now River was missing, and I have two men down, one might not make it.

"Any word or clues as to where River is?" I asked as I looked down at Gin.

"No, but I have watched the cameras. Two men came in and grabbed her. She fought hard and was winning until one of them hit her in the head with a bat. She continued to try to fight until the other man stabbed her with something."

"I know."

"You know?" Kyson said angrily.

"She called me. I listened to everything from the time she yelled in pain to the time they took her." I glanced at him. "I gave her an emergency phone that only called out to me."

"So, what now?" Kyson asked.

"I need to make several calls." I walked out of the room and pulled my phone out of my pocket.

I made calls to Fox and Martinez. I was calling in everyone. I was hoping that the Alpha King could protect his family while staying safely tucked away at the beach house. They all said they were on their way, and they would arrive within the next week.

Miles had regained consciousness not long after my calls were made. He had called River up to talk with her about a matter brought to him by a pack member. Before he sent the code, he and Gin did a sweep of the area. All was clear. Gin never reported any hostiles. Miles claimed the men had no scent. He heard the door creak and when he turned around, he was shot. The next thing he remembered was River putting pressure on his wound, and pain. He told River to run.

"From what I was told, you are lucky to be alive." I told him.

"No doubt thanks to River and her magic potions." Miles coughed. "Where's Gin?"

"Gin is on the floor at the base of the bed. He has been beaten pretty badly. Kyson said the pack doctor doesn't know if he is going to make it."

Miles cursed. "We never saw it coming. They didn't trip any of our alarms. They had no scent, Cruz. There was no warning."

"I know, Miles. Get some rest. Aunt Monica will never forgive me if you come home like this."

I patted his shoulder before checking on Gin. He wasn't doing very good. He might have stood a chance if he was a werewolf instead of being human. I left the bunker with instructions for Kyson to stay with Miles and Gin.

River's scent filled my nose when I entered the office. I crossed the room and picked up the blanket she used whenever she was in here. I closed my eyes as I breathed deeply. "Where are you, River?" I whispered.

*   *   *

I was watching the security video for the fifth time in the twenty-four hours I had been back. Seeing River fighting against two men two times her size fueled my anger. She had been doing a great job defending herself. Then Darius had hit her with a bat. I was going to make him suffer. The silent alarm triggered. I switched to the video feed of the driveway. Two SUVs were approaching the pack house.

I closed down the laptop and headed for the front door. I replaced my mask before pulling the door open and stepping out onto the porch. I pulled my guns from their holsters as the vehicles came to a stop. I wasn't going to waste my time if these people weren't friendlies.

A man slowly stepped out of the first vehicle's driver's seat. He held his hands up so I could see him as he slowly moved around the hood of the car. "Geez, Shadow. Are you trying to scare everyone?" Martinez asked.

I holstered my gun and walked down the stairs. "That depends on who is 'everyone'." I said. "I don't have time nor patience to play around."

"Care to bring me up to speed?" Martinez raised a brow.

"Not out here." I scanned over the vehicles. "Who did you bring?"

"Who do you think? Your family is as stubborn as you are. Not to mention the whole ruling families of this pack. I still can't believe you sent me alone to try to tell them what to do." Martinez gestured to the occupants of the vehicles. I watched in irritation as the Alpha, Beta, and Gamma families exited the SUVs, along with my family.

I didn't say anything as I spun around and stormed inside. I had almost reached the office when Molly pulled on my arm. "Not now, Molly." I yanked my arm away from her and continued into the room. I watched as everyone filed in. Gamma Easton closed the door. "I'm out of patience, so here is the gist of it. River has been taken and I have a man at deaths door, thanks to Dax and Darius Wood."

"Dax Wood?" Gamma Easton pushed to the front of the crowd of people.

"Yes, and his son, Darius. They are working with an unknown woman. As far as we know, they are eliminating all the royal family to put River and Darius on the throne while framing Kyson for the murders."

"But River has a mate." Gamma Carly said, coming to stand next to her husband.

"I'm sorry, who are you?" Alpha Max asked. "Forgive me for questioning you, but I don't put my trust in a man when I don't know who he is."

"That is wise of you." I leaned back on the desk.

"Dad, that's Shadow." Nash said as he pushed past everyone and ran to me. I crouched down to his level and gave him a hug. Before I could let him go, Belle was hugging me. "Did the bad guys really get River?"

"Afraid so."

"Why didn't you stop them?" Belle asked in alarm.

"I wasn't here when they took her. The two men protecting her nearly lost their lives. One is only alive because River managed to bandage him before they grabbed her, but the other man..." I shook my head as I stood. "He is human and isn't doing so well."

"Where is River's medical kit?" Gamma Carly asked, rolling up the sleeves of her shirt.

"I believe Kyson took it down with him." I answered in confusion.

"Good. East and Max, I will take Jackie, Nash, and Ana with me. Let me know if you hear anything." Gamma Carly gave her husband a kiss and left the room with the other three.

"Where are they going?" mom asked.

"Probably to see if they can heal my men." I ran my hand through my hair. "Alpha Max, do you have another safe room that the Storms can stay in until this whole mess gets sorted out?"

"East, can you show them to the safe room?" Alpa Max asked.

Gamma Easton studied me for a long moment before giving a nod. Molly gave me a concerned look before following the Gamma and our parents out of the office. When the door closed, I let out a frustrated sigh. I wanted to hit something.

"Who is the woman with Dax?" Max asked.

"Like I said, she is unknown. We have a video of the three of them, but her back is facing the camera. We couldn't even get a partial face to run through facial recognition." I turned my back to him as I moved back around the desk and opened the lid of the laptop.

"Why are you here? Shadow is known for being ruthless and lethal. I met a young man who works for you, but I don't like it. Working in the shadows. The human president has even expressed concern over you and your abilities. You are a threat to everyone." Max crossed his arms over his chest. "Although I am grateful that you saved Ana and Nash and that you are working on finding my niece."

"I have a personal interest in this case." I didn't look up as I typed in my password.

Max was quiet for a long moment. "Who do they have that is so important to you?"

I pulled up the video that Nash had taken on Alpha Max's phone. "Now, do you recognize any of these people?" I turned the computer around so that he could see the paused video.

"That is definitely Dax. I would recognize him anywhere. I have never seen the other man." He narrowed his eyes as he leaned closer to get a better look. "Is this the best image you have of the woman?"

"Yes."

"Is there audio where she is speaking?" I turned the computer back around and restarted the video. I let it play as I watched Max. He had his eyes closed as if he were concentrating. "I think I might know who that is. I think East and Carr should hear it too. I don't want to make any assumptions."

I told him that I knew about the bunker, and he finally opened the elevator. Everyone was there when we stepped off, including my parents. I motioned for Kyson to follow me into River's room. Once we were inside with the door closed, I felt safe enough to take my mask off.

"I am going to need you to help me with something." I said quickly, not knowing how much time we had.

"What's that?"

"No one knows who I am. I need to keep it that way." I lowered my voice. "So, when I have my mask on, I am Shadow."

"Got it. Miles is doing a little better. Mom is focusing on Gin though. She asked if she could take off his mask and I told her she would have to ask you."

I turned and left the room. When I entered the makeshift sick room, Gamma Carly had several jars open and was smearing something on Gin's chest. She barely glanced up at me. "Ky said to ask you if I can remove his mask. It will make it easier for him to breathe."

"The mask is specially designed for us. It works similarly to an oxygen mask, so he is probably better off keeping it on." I said.

"Can you tell me what happened to him?"

"He was beat by two werewolves."

"You are the fearsome Shadow?"

"I am."

"Why do you have humans on your team?"

My hackles rose. "My men are highly trained. We are good at what we do. The men that attacked him had no scent and knew the pack well enough to get passed our defenses."

"I didn't mean to offend you. Just trying to understand." Gamma Carly glanced over at me again. "You don't smell right either. I can tell you are a werewolf, but there is something messing with your scent."

I smiled at that. Maybe there was something to River saying I stink. She mentioned something about the oil. I gave myself a mental shake. I needed to concentrate.

"The mask stays on him." I said before turning and walking from the room.

"What is going on?" Dad asked as he walked up to me.

"I am going to show Gamma Easton and Gamma Carly a clip to see if they are able to identify someone, and then I am going back up top. The rest of my team is on their way. Hopefully, I have a lead by then, and as soon as they get here, we are shipping out. Everyone of you will stay down here until I return." I walked over to the kitchen counter and opened the laptop.

I played it for Easton. He reacted similarly to Max. He immediately recognized Dax, and the woman sounded vaguely familiar. At this point, everyone had gathered near the kitchen. Gamma Carly came out to take a quick look. She replayed the video twice more.

"That is obviously Dax." she said. "The woman, she sounds like...but she said she moved to the Southern Kingdom after graduation." Carly looked up at Easton.

"So, you think it is her then?" Easton asked.

"Who?" I said in irritation.

They looked at me with concern in their eyes. "That would be crazy. I mean, she wasn't the nicest person to be around, but she wouldn't stoop so low, would she?" Alpha Max stared at the Gammas in shock.

I was losing my patience, and I slammed my fist down on the counter, causing everyone to jump. "Someone better start talking fast because my patience has about run out." I growled. Pain slashed through the back of my head, and I grabbed the sides of my head with my hands. I leaned over the counter as I fought the urge to scream. Minutes passed in agony before it subsided. When I felt like I could breathe again, I straightened up. "Do you know the woman's identity or not?" I asked as everyone stared at me in confusion.

Chapter Seventeen

River

My head pounded and I fought the urge to groan. Something inside screamed at me to be cautious. I slowly became more and more aware of my surroundings. The ground I was laying on was damp, cold and hard. The air was chilled and musty. I kept my eyes closed as I listened for any sound. I was the only thing breathing in this place. I took a deep breath but smelled nothing other than stale water and rot.

    I opened my eyes slowly, taking in what was around me. The floor and walls were made of dark grey stone. There was a puddle of water near the wall several feet in front of me. I sat up and my head began to spin. I closed my eyes again and took slow deep breaths.

    When I opened my eyes next, a man was standing several yards from me. "How are you feeling?" he asked.

    I stared at him without speaking. Nothing made sense. Where was I? Who was this guy? I looked down at my wrists. Thick metal cuffs were connected to heavy chains that connected with a ring in the floor. My ankles were in similar shackles.

    "Where am I?" I croaked. My throat was so dry that I started to cough. The man brought me a glass of water. I gratefully accepted it.

    "How do you feel?" The man asked again.

    I looked up at him. He had blonde hair and blue eyes. He had broad shoulders and thick muscles. He looked like a fighter. I knew him. I know that I knew him. I just couldn't remember how. I looked back down at the chains, and caution bells rang in my head.

    "My head hurts." I whispered.

"You got quite a bump on your head." The man took the empty cup from my hand. "I will send in Greta. She will be able to help your head. We wouldn't want you feeling poorly at the wedding."

I watched the man disappear up a flight of stairs. Wedding? What wedding? I scooted myself back against the wall. I had to move slowly because every move sent a new wave of pain shooting through my skull.

It wasn't long before a wrinkly old woman shuffled down the stairs. She walked right up to me and set a basket down. "Other than your head, what injuries do you have?"

"I don't think I have any." I said quietly.

The woman grabbed out five vials. "Are you familiar with magic?" the old lady asked.

"I am not." I said in confusion. Did magic exist? Wasn't it just some made up thing in children's stories?

"Magic is powerful. Capable of doing many, many things. But one must be careful when using magic because magic has a price. Usually, the price for using healing magic is intense pain." The woman said as she dipped a sponge into a large jar. "Turn around."

Not knowing what else I should do, I turned around. Greta immediately started pressing on my head until I cried out in pain. Then there was a coldness being spread on that spot. Tears rolled down my cheeks. Just barely touching the area was excruciating. Greta helped me lay down on my side before offering me a drink. I took several sips. She took the cup away and I heard the sound of shuffling feet moving away from me.

When I woke again, I could sense someone with me. I slowly sat up and turned to face whoever was there. The blonde man and Greta stood there watching me. I was in a different room. This room was like a dungeon with stone walls. I was chained to the wall instead of the floor.

"How are you feeling today?" the man asked.

"I don't know." I said softly.

"River, I need you to be honest with me." The man took a step closer. "Where is Kyson?"

My brows knit in confusion. "Kyson?" I said slowly. The name sounded somewhat familiar, but I couldn't place it. "Who is Kyson?" I asked.

The man turned to the old woman. "What did you do to her?"

"I did nothing but heal the bump on her head." Greta scoffed.

"Why am I chained to a wall?" I asked as I ran my hand over the metal shackle on my wrist. The skin underneath hurt.

"River, what is the last thing you remember?" the man asked while coming to crouch down in front of me.

I closed my eyes and tried to think. All I could see was a tall man with black, no blonde hair and blue eyes. It wasn't the same man that was in front of me now, he was different. He was dangerous, yet soft and protective. I opened my eyes and met the curious gaze of the man questioning me.

"I don't know. I remember us talking and the pain in my head." I answered.

"Before that?"

I shook my head slowly. "I don't know." I rubbed my forehead. The man called me River, and I knew that was my name. It felt right. But there was nothing else. No memory of anything beyond waking up in this damp, cold room. "I can't remember." I whispered softly.

"Do you know who I am?" the man asked. I shook my head as I watched him. I could see him mulling over something in his mind. He finally smiled. I didn't trust this man. "I'm Dax Wood. I'm sorry we had to chain you down here, but you were trying to hurt yourself and we were left with no other option. Why don't we get you out of here?"

I nodded and Dax unlocked the shackles. My wrists and ankles were raw. How long had I been down here? It had to have been a while to create such sores. He put a hand on my lower back as we climbed the stairs. He guided me down a narrow hallway and into a living room. Nothing looked familiar. I felt so out of place. So unsure of where or who I was.

A man and woman were sitting in chairs. The room was cozy with a stone fireplace in the corner and a thick rug in the center. The furniture was made of logs. The whole place was bright with natural light.

When we entered, all attention turned to us. Before any of the two people could say anything, Dax spoke up. "River, I want you to meet my wife, Marissa, and my son, Darius." The man and woman looked confused as they slowly stood. I shrank back a little as I wrapped my arms around myself. "Do you not remember them as well?" Dax asked. I quickly shook my head. "Not even Darius? He is your fiancé."

My stomach clenched as fear filled me. I didn't know these people and I sure as heck didn't trust them. I was just chained in the basement for crying out loud. I may not remember who I was, but I knew I didn't belong with these people.

I tried to take a step back as Darius approached me with a smug grin on his face. He was blonde like the man from my memories, but his eyes were brown, not blue. Dax's hand on my back prevented me from moving. Darius pulled me into a hug, and I stiffened. He buried his face in my neck and took a deep breath.

I was shaking with fear, and he pulled back. His eyes settled on my neck for a long moment before looking at my face. "Darling, what's wrong?"

"She has no memory." Dax said. His voice was sympathetic, but there was also a hint of...excitement. "It seems that she hit her head in that fall she took when she tried to jump off the cliff. She can't remember anything."

"You poor dear." Marissa rushed to my side. "Why don't we get you upstairs so you can get a shower and into clean clothes. You will feel much better, I am sure."

I allowed her to lead me out of the living room and up a flight of stairs. She talked nonstop about wedding plans that were supposedly in the works. My anxiety rose higher and higher, though I kept a smile on my face. She showed me to a room and pointed out where clothes and towels were before leaving.

I slowly walked to the closet. All that was inside were dresses. I grabbed a white and dark green sundress before jumping in a quick shower. A small button was stuck to my skin just below my armpit. I touched it but pulled my hand away quickly. What if the Woods put it on me? What would happen if I pressed the button? I couldn't risk it right now. Not until I got more answers.

As I was brushing my hair, I noticed a mark on my neck. I leaned closer to the mirror to get a better look. The mark had four distinct dots. There were lines that looked like vines connecting the dots in an odd-shaped square.

I ran my fingers over it softly. Pain slashed through my mind as the blonde man approach me slowly. I was backed up against the wall as his head dipped toward me. He smelled like rain. Just as sudden as the vision appeared, it was gone. I sank to the floor and took several deep breaths. Who was the man?

After several minutes, I got back to my feet. I looked around the bedroom for any clue as to who I was. There wasn't anything personal in the room. The closet was filled with clothes and shoes that were my size. The bathroom had everything a girl would use, but everything felt wrong. I didn't belong here. I returned to the closet and went back through the clothes. All dresses. I remembered that I hated dresses.

Sighing, I put on a pair of sandals. I needed more information. Unfortunately, the only people with information were the ones downstairs. I slowly opened the door and listened. I could hear muffled voices coming up the stairs. I slowly made my way closer so I could hear what they were saying.

"She really doesn't remember?" Marissa asked.

"She seems completely lost. I don't think River is that good of an actress. She would have rather fought us than pretend to be dumb." Dax laughed. "Why do you think Darius took a bat to her head?"

"This could play in our favor." Darius commented.

"Her bond is still strong with her mate. Are you sure her husband is dead?" Greta asked.

"I watched the man walk into the building myself." Darius scoffed.

"Their bond must have been strong for it to be holding on for so long after his death." Greta mused. "You can't mark her until the previous bond breaks, or it will kill her."

"What about her wolf?" Dax asked.

"Oh, I took care of that." Greta chuckled. "I gave her a tea that suppresses a werewolf's wolf."

"Since she doesn't remember who she is, we have time. Darius can romance her, so she isn't so reluctant to take the throne with him." Marissa whispered. "When she is done getting cleaned up, take her for a walk around the meadow."

"Yes, mom." Darius sighed.

I moved silently back to the room. I opened the door and closed it. I walked hesitantly to the stairs but didn't try hiding my approach. I only descended a few steps before Darius appeared at the bottom with a huge grin on his face. I stopped moving and just stared at him. I wasn't safe here, but I didn't know where to go. I barely knew my first name. And what were they talking about when they said 'wolf'? Did they take my dog?

"Would you like to get some fresh air, my Darling?" Darius asked.

As much as I wanted to run as far and as fast as I could away from here, I needed to be patient. I gave Darius a small smile as I slowly made my way to his side. I flinched when he grabbed my hand but didn't pull away. His grip was so tight it was almost painful. He guided me outside, and I blinked at the brightness of the sun. When my eyes adjusted, I took in my surroundings.

We were in a large meadow. The grass reached nearly to my knees and wildflowers were everywhere. I ignored the itchy sensation as the blades of grass scratched my legs. I ran my free hand over the flowers as we passed. I recognized one of the plants. I couldn't remember its name, but knew that the leaves were capable of weakening the effects of certain potions. As we walked by, I grabbed a small handful of the leaves. This dress had pockets, and I slowly put the leaves inside the one on the side away from Darius.

"You seem scared of me." Darius commented.

I could feel his eyes on me, but I kept my eyes focused on the flowers around me. "I don't know you." I stated.

"We could start over. I wouldn't mind helping you fall in love with me all over again." Darius pulled me into his arms and pressed his lips to mine.

I shoved against him, and he pulled back with irritation in his eyes. "I'm not comfortable with this." I took another step away from him. My hands were shaking, and I felt like I had just betrayed someone. An image of the blonde hair, blue-eyed man popped into my mind again. He was staring at me with a teasing grin. I blinked several times to clear the image. "I want to go back inside." I whispered.

Darius grabbed my hand in a painful grip as he pulled me after him. He pushed open the door with such force, it slammed into the wall with a bang. Dax stepped into the hallway with a raised brow. "Is everything okay?" he asked, looking between us.

"I just want to go lay down." I whispered in a small voice.

"Go ahead upstairs. Do you remember which room is yours?" Dax gave Darius a hard look. I nodded my head and quickly ran to the room. Before I closed the door, I heard Darius saying that I refused to let him kiss me, and Dax yelling at him for pushing me. "This matter has to be delt with delicately."

I closed the door but there was no way to lock it. I ran to the bathroom and locked myself inside. I sank to the floor and began to cry. Darius hadn't given me much of a choice. He had ambushed me. I shouldn't be feeling so guilty. I hadn't wanted him to kiss me. I had given him no signal that would warrant him thinking I wanted him to.

A knock came on the bedroom door a while later. My tears had dried up and I was just sitting on the tile floor. I didn't get up. Instead, I pulled my knees to my chest and hugged them.

"River?" Marissa called from the other side of the bathroom door. "You didn't come down for dinner. Dax said you had a rough afternoon, so I brought you up something to eat. I am just going to leave it on the bed for you."

I heard the bedroom door close, but I still didn't get up. I remembered the leaves I had stuck in my pocket and pulled them out. I had only managed to grab five, but it should be enough. I put them in my mouth and chewed. They were bitter. I gagged several times, but pushed through until the leaves were a flavorless paste. I spit it into the toilet and flushed.

When I finally left the bathroom, the food on the tray was cold. A quiet voice in my head screamed at me to not eat or drink anything they gave me. I spent the next thirty minutes breaking apart the food enough to flush it all down the toilet. I took a drink out of the faucet before going to the closet to find something to sleep in. I scowled at the options I found.

Do these people think I would only wear dresses? The nightgowns barely reached mid-thigh. I crawled under the covers and let the tears fall. I finally started to doze when I felt the bed dip and an arm slide around my waist. I took a deep breath expecting to smell rain, but I didn't. I screamed as I jumped out of the bed.

I pressed myself against the wall as a dark figure stood. The light clicked on. Dax and Marissa were in the doorway and Darius stood near the bed. "You are my fiancé, River. Sharing a bed is inevitable."

"I don't know you." I snapped back.

"Darius, we told you to give her more time." Dax growled.

I didn't wait to hear anymore. I didn't feel safe in this room, not when there was no lock on the door. I ran to the bathroom and slammed the door. Once I was sure it was locked, I climbed into the bathtub. I needed to get away from here. Before I knew what I was doing I pressed the button under my arm and held it for five seconds.

Chapter Eighteen

Cruz

I just finished bringing my team up to speed on River's abduction, the Woods and Marissa's involvement, and the plan to terminate all the royals to force River to the throne. It had taken them a week to get here, and I was a time bomb ready to go off. "So, this River girl is what their whole plan hinges on?" Fox asked.

"It seems that way." I said stiffly.

"Do we know where they have taken her?" Tango stretched his legs out in front of him as he reclined back in the chair.

"Not yet." I paced the small space behind the desk. "Spur is keeping eyes on a cabin where we suspect the Woods and/or Marissa are holding up."

"I have never seen you so out of sorts, Shadow." Cheese observed.

"How pretty is this River?" Tango's smile widened.

"Has our fearless leader finally fallen victim to a pair of beautiful eyes?" Fox chuckled.

I spun around to face them with fire in my eyes. I was seeing red as Caspian surged forward. My men grew quiet as they stared at me with wide eyes. "She is my wife." I growled out.

For the next two and a half weeks, my men and I prepared ourselves to move out as soon as we found even a hint of where River could be. Cheese was exhausting every resource he had to try to locate her. I was at the end of my rope. She had been missing for nearly four weeks at this point. I was talking with Tango about sending him up to help Spur keep an eye on the cabin when my phone rang, and I picked it up. "Shadow." I snapped.

"I take it you have no leads on Finley?" Spur asked. I only growled in response. "Well, I think I might have found her."

"Where?" I clenched my fist.

"The cabin. Our two guys showed up and carried a body inside. The unconscious person had a bag over their head, but the figure was tiny. I would guess a female or a teenage boy. Whoever they carried had chains on their wrists and ankles." Spur explained.

"We are on our way." I ended the call. "Spur thinks he found her." I started moving to the door and they followed me. "I will not stand for anyone talking about her so disrespectfully." I ground out. "I will give you the coordinates for where Spur is, and I will meet you there."

I sent Cheese the location as we walked. As soon as we were outside, I shifted into my wolf. I looked back at my men to see stunned expressions before sprinting into the trees. I would get there much faster in wolf form than riding in a car. This also gave Caspian an outlet for our anger.

I arrived back at the camp within a day and a half. Caspian had pushed hard the whole time. Now that we had a lead on where River was, we had to get to her.

I shifted back to human and grabbed the water bottle Spur offered me. "You might want to oil your hair again. Your sweat has taken most of it out. Did you run all the way here?" Spur eyed me.

"Caspian wasn't about to sit in a car and twiddle our thumbs." I said as I grabbed the oil tin out of the bag I had left. "Any movement?"

"An old lady and a woman arrived yesterday." Spur returned to looking through his binoculars. "What the...?" Spur muttered. "Shadow, what do you make of this?"

I took out my set of binoculars and laid down on my stomach next to Spur. I looked at the house. My jaw clenched when I saw River holding hands with Darius. Caspian growled and tried to surge forward. River turned her head away from Darius as she looked out over the meadow. Her skin was pale and her whole body was tense.

She looked like she put something in a pocket of the dress she was wearing. "It has to be an act. Look at her wrists. They are raw." Spur muttered. "She snuck that handful of whatever in her pocket." I agreed.

"She isn't acting like her normal self. Even her walk is off." I commented. Just then Darius pulled River to him and kissed her. Pain stabbed my heart. I gritted my teeth to keep from making a sound. River shoved away from him with a panicked expression. Darius grabbed her hand and dragged her back inside.

"That man is going to die!" Caspian roared.

"We can't go in there guns blazing." I yelled at him. *"They might hurt River."*

"She was just lip-locking with someone else!" Caspian surged forward, but I forced him back.

"She wasn't happy about it, Caspian. I know you can feel her panic and guilt. Just calm down so we can figure out a way to get her out safely."

"You okay, Shadow?" Spur asked hesitantly.

"I will be once River is out of there." I huffed. "Get some sleep. The team should be here in the next couple of hours. We will do two-hour shifts."

I was just getting up from failing to sleep for the two hours I was supposed to be resting, when four figures materialized out of the shadows and joined Spur at the lookout spot. I was glad they were here. I wasn't sure I could wait much longer. Spur let everyone know what was going on.

"We are going in tonight." I said, and everyone looked at me.

I dished out assignments. Marco, Tango, and Spur were to circle around the back and come in from behind, ensuring no one escaped. Cheese was staying at camp to give us a bird's eye view with the sniper rifle. Fox was with me as we approached the front.

I was grateful for the moonless night as we approached the cabin just after midnight. I heard the soft pops of silencers and knew my men were doing their job. Fox picked the lock on the front door as I scanned the area. A tap on my elbow let me know we were in.

The house was dark, and we moved slowly, clearing each room. River's scent grew stronger as we reached a door in a side hallway. We silently made our way through the door and down some stone stairs. My anger grew when we reached the bottom. River's scent was really strong down here. There were chains connected to the wall, but the shackles were empty. I was both relieved and worried at the same time.

A frightened scream reached us, and I froze. Fox and I looked at each other before running up the stairs. In the hallway, we slowed our steps as we approached the stairs leading to the second floor.

"We have an S.O.S. signal coming from the house." Cheese said through the coms. I shook my head. Now she pushes the blasted thing. Why couldn't she have done so weeks ago?

"Non-lethal." I whispered.

Fox followed me up the stairs, but I paused just short of the landing. I peeked around the corner. Three people were in the doorway of a room at the far end of the hall.

"Darius, you can't push her too fast." A woman scolded.

"She will be mine eventually, she might as well get used to it." Darius snapped.

"Darius, go back to your own room!" Dax yelled.

Darius stormed from the room and stomped down the hall. I ducked back behind the corner and pressed myself into the shadows by the wall. Darius passed us without so much as a glance. A moment later, a door slammed.

"River? You can come out now, honey." The woman said in a soothing voice. There was no response.

"Let her have some time." The older woman said. "She will be feeling better by morning."

I moved into the hall and shot the old lady in the neck with a tranquilizer dart. I heard Fox move down the hall in the other direction. I caught the woman and eased her to the ground as I heard the pop of Fox's gun. I turned to see the two stunned faces of Dax and Marissa. Dax charged at me, and I slammed my fist into his face so hard that I felt his nose break. Shooting him this close with the darts would hurt. Good. I put two in him for good measure as I saw Marissa drop.

"All clear." Fox said quietly into the com.

A chorus of 'all clear' came from the others. I moved to the bathroom and tried the handle. Locked. I didn't bother picking the lock, I ripped the handle out of the door and pushed it open. River shot up from laying in the tub. Her eyes were wide with fear as she stared at me.

I took a step closer, and she whimpered. Her whole body was shaking. "River." I said softly.

"Please." She whimpered out. She was completely terrified. There was no recognition in her eyes.

I turned around and spoke to Fox. "Have everyone loaded up. I want to be gone in the next hour. The four on this floor need to be taken back to the North Wind Pack. Alpha Kion is expecting them." Fox nodded and I returned my attention to River. "Babe, are you all right?"

She squeezed her eyes shut as she pressed the back of her hand to her forehead. When she opened them again, she looked confused. "I-I don't think I know you." Her voice was soft and uncertain.

I pulled my mask off as I took a step closer to her. She pressed herself more into the wall. What had they done to her? "That's okay. We can figure that out later. Why don't we find you something else to wear and get you out of here?"

She looked down at herself before raising her eyes to me. "All they have are dresses." Her nose scrunched in disgust.

"Not a fan?" I asked as I smiled. "I don't think I have ever seen you in anything but shorts or jeans."

She studied me for a long moment. "Is your hair always black?" she closed her eyes and shook her head.

"That depends on who you ask. Would you like to change first, or do you want to stay in that?" I took a small step closer to her.

"I guess a dress would be better than this." she muttered. I offered her my hand. She tentatively put hers in it. Warmth spread from the contact, and she gasped.

"You are okay." I told her as I slowly moved back into the bedroom. "No one is going to hurt you. Where are your clothes?" I kept my voice soft.

"The closet." She was staring at our joined hands.

"I will be right here. Go ahead and change." River raised her eyes to meet mine. There were so many questions swirling around in her eyes. I gave her a gentle nudge, and it seemed to pull her out of her thoughts.

She was in there for only a few minutes when I heard a soft growl of frustration. "Um...Sir?" she asked hesitantly.

"I'm here." I smiled.

"I can't...I mean...Could you help me?"

I replaced my mask and walked into the closet. River stood with her arms wrapped around herself protectively. Her cheeks were red, and her gaze was focused on the floor. She had on a dark green dress. "What can I help you with, River?" I asked, giving her some distance.

"I-I can't zip up the dress." She whispered.

I took two small steps towards her. I gently turned her around. She was trembling. "Relax, River." I whispered in her ear. I zipped up the back of her dress and forced myself to take a step back. She turned around and then grabbed her head and cried out in pain. I pulled her to me and held her tight. Her whole body was tense for several minutes before she relaxed against me. "Are you okay, River?" I asked, stroking her hair. I was beyond worried about her. She seemed to have no memory and now she was experiencing random pain.

Chapter Nineteen

River

I was scared, terrified as I remembered something. The man that had come into the bathroom stood behind me as I lay in my bed. All I wanted was for him to stay. He finally got into the bed and pulled me close. He rolled me over to face him and I breathed in his comforting scent. Rain. How did someone smell like a rainstorm? I was safe with him. Protected from all my fears. The more I cuddled closer to him, the tighter he held me.

The memory faded along with the pain it brought. I blinked several times to clear my mind. The black-haired man held me as he stroked my head. I breathed deeply and was surprised to smell rain. I pulled away from him and looked up at his face. His beautiful blue eyes were filled with worry as he studied me. "River, are you okay?" he asked again.

"I think so." I said softly as I took another step away. I felt a stab of disappointment but pushed it back. I didn't know this man, even if he was showing up in my thoughts as a blonde.

He studied me for another moment before nodding. "Are you ready to go?"

"Go where?" I asked.

"First, to the North Wind Pack. Then we will take you to the Silver Moon Pack where your parents and brother are."

I furrowed my brow. "What is a pack? Aren't packs like an animal thing, not a human thing?"

The man's worry only intensified. I could feel it. "River, what do you remember about yourself?"

A tear slipped down my cheek. "My name is River." I closed my eyes. "And I think I know about plants."

"Oh, River." The man breathed out as his arms encircled me. I buried my face in his chest. I could feel his pain and sorrow. I don't know how, but I could. All I wanted to do was take it all away. To make him happy.

"Shadow!" A man called.

"In here, Spur." Shadow didn't release me.

"Oh good, you found her." Spur sounded relieved. "How is she?"

"She is…okay." Shadow answered.

"Great. You can hold your wife later. Right now, let's get her somewhere safe." Spur's voice sounded like it was moving away from us.

I stiffened at the mention of 'wife'. The memory of Greta asking if my husband was dead came back to me. I looked up quickly and studied the man in front of me. He met my gaze and seemed to sense my rising anxiety.

"River, it's okay if you can't remember anything right now. We can work on that. But Spur is right. We need to get you somewhere safe." Shadow released his hold on me, and I felt the immediate loss of his warmth. "Do you trust me enough to do that?"

I stared at the hand he was offering me. My gaze lifted and locked with his. I gave him a small nod and I could almost see him smile. The mask prevented it, but his eyes softened. I clung to his hand as we walked through the house and outside. The sky was still dark, and I couldn't see anything around us. I tripped and Shadow caught me.

"River, can I carry you? We have a bit of a walk before we reach the cars." Shadow asked. I nodded. "Sorry, Babe. Not good enough. I want verbal confirmation. I don't ever want you to feel like I am pushing you into something you don't want to do or aren't comfortable with."

I couldn't believe the difference between this man and Darius. From what Spur said, Shadow was my husband, yet he was practically forcing me to set my own boundaries so he wouldn't make me feel uncomfortable. Darius claimed to be my fiancé but tried forcing himself on me twice. I watched as Shadow waited patiently for me to answer.

"Okay. You can carry me." I whispered. Shadow moved slowly as he lifted me into his arms. He began walking again as I put my arms around his neck.

We walked for a little while before Shadow spoke again. "River, are you hurt?"

"They said I jumped off a cliff and hit my head. I heard them talking about hitting me with a bat, but I don't remember." I resisted the urge to bury my face in his neck. "Greta said magic has a price and said it would hurt. She put something on the bump, but it didn't hurt any worse than her pressing on it."

"That explains it." Shadow muttered.

"Explains what?"

"Don't worry about it, Babe." Shadow whispered. "Any other injuries?"

"I don't think so. I don't remember much passed waking up yesterday." I sighed.

"That bump on your head is what probably took your memory. I'm not a doctor, but I'm sure everything will come back to you as you recover." I wasn't sure if Shadow was trying to comfort me or himself. "Lay your head on my shoulder, Babe. You will be more comfortable."

I did as he suggested. He was right, it was more comfortable. I was so tired, and for some reason this man was comforting. I was safe with him. I closed my eyes and allowed myself to relax. Shadow held me tighter and pressed a kiss to the top of my head. I felt so bad for him. I couldn't imagine how hard it would be if our roles were reversed.

I was almost asleep when Shadow stopped walking. "Glad to see your wife is unharmed." A young man said quietly.

"She had a blow to the head that has taken her memory, Cheese." Shadow said in a clipped voice. "Are we good to ship out?"

"Yes, sir. Spur said that he, Tango, Marco, and Fox would transport the prisoners to the North Wind Pack in the next thirty minutes. He said you wouldn't want to caravan with your wife close to them."

"Let's go." Shadow said as he set me down. I bolted upright and glanced around. I was inside an SUV. I continued to look around until my eyes settled on Shadow. I hadn't realized I was searching for him until I found him. "You always wake up when I put you down." There was a smile in his voice.

"Maybe you should stop putting me down then." I blurted out before slapping a hand over my mouth. My eyes widened in surprise, but Shadow laughed.

"Are you asking me to join you back here instead of sitting in the front?" Shadow asked, there was a spark of mischief in his eyes.

"I uh...I..."

"River, it is okay if the answer is 'no'. I was teasing you." Shadow said softly. "Just tell me what you want me to do."

I looked between the front of the car and Shadow. I caught Cheese watching me in the rearview mirror. I had no idea who that guy was, and it made me nervous. I turned back to Shadow. "Could you sit back here with me?"

Shadow sat in the seat next to me and closed the door. He told Cheese to drive, and we were on our way. I curled against the side of the car as I stared out the window into the dark night. Shadow adjusted his large frame in the seat to get more comfortable, and he let out a long sigh. I glanced over at him. His eyes were closed, and he was breathing deeply.

I took the time to study the man that was supposedly my husband. His hair was as black as ink. Somehow that didn't seem right. His skin was tan, like he spent a lot of time outside. His shoulders were broad, and he was strong. Shadow was very handsome. But what I didn't understand was why his face was the same in my little snippets of memory, but now he had black hair instead of blonde.

I closed my eyes and leaned against the window.

I was on top of a hill looking down on a clearing. A small building was in the middle of it. I watched as Shadow moved to the building and slipped inside. Thirty seconds later, the building exploded. I screamed as I jerked awake.

"River!" Shadow yelled as I was pulled onto his lap. "Keep driving." He snapped.

He held me close as I shook. The fear of seeing him enter the building, only to have it explode, was too much. I clung to Shadow as I sobbed. He stroked my head as he whispered in my ear. "It's okay, River. You're safe." I shook my head. "I'm here, Babe. Everything is okay."

"I-It was you." I finally got out.

"Me?" he asked, pulling back to see my face. He studied me for a long moment. "That dream again?" He kissed my forehead. "I wasn't the one in the building, River. I was more than a football field's length away when it exploded."

I buried my face in his neck and breathed deeply. The smell of rain and something else filled my lungs. I loved the rain, but whatever that other smell was, was repulsive. "You stink."

Shadow chuckled. "You tell me that frequently."

I started to sit up but froze. I grabbed the collar of his shirt and pulled it down. He had a similar mark on his neck to the one I had. His only had two dots, but they were connected with the same looking vines. I ran my finger along it. "What is this?" I asked.

"River," Shadow tucked my hair behind my ear. He ran his finger along the mark on my neck. "Would you be okay if we had that conversation once you are feeling a little better?"

I looked into his eyes. I could tell he wanted to tell me but was holding back. "Okay." I whispered.

"Lay down. I will wake you when we get there." Shadow suggested.

"There isn't enough room." I said looking at the bench. It was the size of a small couch.

"There is more room than when we slept together last time." Shadow whispered close to my ear.

Pain shot through my head again. "Ah!" I grabbed my head. The image of a blonde-haired Shadow without his mask smiled down at me as I lay on a small couch. He leaned over me before kissing me. I wrapped my arms around his neck. His kisses moved from my lips to my throat. Another flash of pain. I sighed out his name. Cruz. I was cuddled up to his side as he combed his fingers through my hair. His phone rang and he had to go. He pulled me to my feet and held me as I was wrapped in nothing but a blanket.

I gasped as the pain went away. Shadow was watching me with concern. I searched his eyes as my cheeks heated. "What is it, River?" He asked in concern.

I stared at him with wide eyes. We had...I mean if we were married it would make sense that we would but...my cheeks felt like they would catch fire. I glanced at the front and met Cheese's gaze in the mirror. His eyes were bright with humor. I was so glad that no one could read my mind right now. I could almost feel Shadow's calloused hands on my skin and tangling in my hair. The sensation of us making out and...I shook my head to shake my desire to press my lips to his.

I quickly scooted off Shadow's lap, needing to put physical distance between us. Just having his arms holding me against him was triggering the memory to play on repeat. I curled up against the window again. I closed my eyes as I tried to banish that memory and go back to sleep. The problem with that was the fact that the only real memories I could remember were of him.

We had been driving for a while. I was beginning to doze but wasn't quite asleep. Cheese cleared his throat. "Does she really not recognize you?"

"It appears that way." Shadow said.

"She's cute." Cheese said.

"Watch it, Cheese." Shadow growled.

"I'm just surprised that she doesn't recognize you. Spur said you two were disgustingly cute together. He also mentioned that you two would be shooting barbs at one another in some sort of flirty fighting. Other times you two couldn't seem to let each other go." Cheese chuckled.

"I would watch what you say." Shadow told the young man. "She has this annoyingly cute habit of making everyone think she is asleep while she listens into conversations she shouldn't."

I couldn't stop the giggle that bubbled up. I glanced over at Shadow, and he winked at me. I closed my eyes again as the occupants of the car fell silent. Eventually the gentle rocking of the car lulled me to sleep.

Chapter Twenty

River

"River. Baby, it's time to wake up." Shadow's voice broke into my dream. I slowly opened my eyes. I became aware that the vehicle had stopped moving and the sun was shining. I looked over at Shadow. His eyes were even more blue than I had originally thought. He was a lot cuter too. He was standing in the open doorway watching me. "We made it to the North Wind Pack."

I sat up straighter and looked around. I slowly slid across the seat and Shadow stepped back, giving me room to get out. This place seemed familiar. Hope swelled within me. Snatches of memory of me walking along these streets flashed quickly through my mind.

"River!" A man called.

I turned quickly to see a man descending the steps of the huge house we were parked in front of. I had no idea who he was. I stepped closer to Shadow. He would protect me. Almost like he knew my anxiety, he moved his body partially in front of mine, blocking me from the man.

"What is going on?" The man asked in confusion. He stopped several feet away when Shadow's posture stiffened like he was preparing for a fight.

"Might we take this conversation inside?" Shadow stated calmly.

"Take this inside?" The man huffed. "My nephew called to tell me that his sister had been kidnapped four weeks ago after we had seen that their parents were killed in a plane crash. He said that she was being held somewhere near my pack and to expect her and a group of men in black masks within a few days." I could feel that man's anger rolling off of him. It felt like a weight was being set on my chest. "I want answers."

"Put your aura away, Alpha Kion." Shadow said in a bored tone. "Your aura doesn't work on me, and Cheese here is a human."

"What do you mean by aura and human?" I asked as I put my hand in Shadows.

He turned to me, and I felt his worry as if it were my own. "As soon as we are able to have a private word, I will answer any questions you have."

Alpha Kion looked between us before his eyes settled on me. He looked worried, too. "Come with me."

I clung to Shadows hand as we followed Alpha Kion inside. Cheese wordlessly took up the rear. We walked down a long hall until we reached a door. Pain slammed into me again and I felt strong arms surrounding me as a memory played in my mind.

I knocked on the door and pushed it open without waiting for a response. Alpha Kion sat behind his desk. He jumped to his feet when he saw me. We talked about our families as we caught up on lost time. He mentioned Prudence had been asking about me and wondering if I was coming back to learn more about healing.

I gasped for air as the memory and pain faded. I looked around. We were still standing in front of the door. Three men watched me in concern. I was leaning against Shadow, and he was gently rubbing my back. When my breathing slowed, he told Alpha Kion to continue walking.

When we stepped into the room, the familiar sights and smells hit me, and I closed my eyes. I knew this place. I slowly let go of Shadow so I could walk around the room. I ran my finger along the decoratively carved mantel as I made my way to the window. I knew what sight would meet me when I looked out. The gardens sat below the window. The dragon fountain was the centerpiece of this particular view.

"I know this place." I said softly.

"Of course, you do." Alpha Kion said. His tone wasn't mean but was filled with confusion. "You lived here for a year and a half before going home. You make monthly trips up here."

"I don't remember." I whispered as I continued to stare out the window.

"River received a blow to the back of her head." Shadow stated, and I could hear how hard talking about this was for him.

"I can't remember anything beyond waking up in chains in the basement of a cabin and the people there claiming I was their son's fiancé." I said as I turned around. "I am getting snatches here and there. Small moments. Nothing to really tell me much about who I am or who any of you are."

"I would like to know who you two are." Alpha Kion turned to Shadow.

"My name is Shadow, and this is one of my men, Cheese. I have four others who will be arriving soon with four prisoners. An old woman, Marissa, Darius, and Dax Wood."

"Dax?" Alpha Kion said in surprise.

"You know him?" Shadow asked. I noticed that his eyes were on me, even though he spoke to Alpha Kion.

"Know him? My father hired him to track down and kidnap River's mother. He was the second son of an Alpha. He wanted more power than a simple pack would give him. When he learned that Carly was a royal descendant, he became obsessed with her. After all the smoke cleared with my dad, and I became Alpha, Dax came to me asking questions about Carly. He became angry that she had found her mate. I haven't seen him since."

"Well, he is on his way here for you to judge his crimes." Shadow crossed his arms over his chest.

I had so many questions. Alphas and packs? Who were these people?

"River?" I jumped when Alpha Kion's voice sounded directly beside me. "I will show you to your room so you can rest."

"What about Shadow and Cheese?" I asked, looking back at them.

"I will have rooms made ready in the guest wing."

"If you are feeling up to it, River, we can have that talk." Shadow uncrossed his arms. I nodded quickly. I needed answers and I knew that he wouldn't lie to me.

We followed Alpha Kion up two flights of stairs. He stopped at a door, and I opened it. I smiled as a sense of familiarity washed over me. Shadow walked in behind me and took a seat on a chair in a small sitting area. Kion looked ready to protest but I closed and locked the door.

"You got me in a locked room. What's your plan now?" Shadow asked as he took his mask off.

A memory of him saying the same thing hit me. It was there and gone so quickly, I barely registered it. "I have so many questions." I rubbed my temples and closed my eyes.

Shadow's hands were soft and warm as he grabbed my wrists and pulled them from my face. "Do you mind if I shower first?" he asked.

"Oh. Sure?" I blinked and took a seat.

Shadow followed me and crouched down, so we were eye level. "I don't want you to freak out so I'm going to tell you this now." My heart began to race. "I have an oil in my hair to turn it black. My hair is normally..."

"Blonde." I said with wide eyes.

He gave me a smile. "That's right. I shouldn't be long." He stood and walked into the ensuite.

True to his word, he was in there for only ten minutes. He looked completely different when he walked out. The smell of rain hit me, and I felt like I was home.

"All right, Babe. What is your first question?"

Shadow answered everything I asked without trying to hide anything from me. I was a little freaked out when he explained that the world was filled with many different kinds of people: humans, witches, werewolves. He told me I was a werewolf and that he was a hybrid, three-fourths wolf, one-fourth human.

He didn't know why my wolf wasn't with me right now. He said he could sense her, but I couldn't reach her. I asked again about the marks on our necks, and he sighed.

"River, werewolves are blessed with mates. One person that is born to be their equal. They have a distinct smell that only the other can smell. When they touch, warmth and sometimes a tingling sensation will originate from that spot. When they find each other, they mark one another. The marking process involves biting into one another's necks, leaving a mark that seals their mate bond."

"And we marked each other?" I asked lifting my hand to my neck.

"*We* didn't. Our wolves did." Shadow chuckled.

"I'm confused. Aren't we mates? It would explain why you smell like rain."

"Do I?" He sniffed his shirt, and I swatted his shoulder. "You usually just tell me I stink."

"It might be the oil you had in your hair. It put off a weird smell. The scent of rain is so much stronger now than before your shower." I shrugged. "Now, explain what you meant about our wolves."

"Being a hybrid, no one knew when or if I would be able to shift. Caspian, my wolf, was trying to shift the night we met. He had tried before several times but was never able to. You said that Maya, your wolf, was panicking because you could feel some of the pain I was going through. My mother was the first hybrid, she only shifted after my dad marked her. I guess you had heard the story, and Maya took control of you and marked me."

I could see it happening as Shadow explained. I could even hear my conversation with Maya. I remembered the pain we had experienced while watching him fight with Caspian.

"I wasn't planning on marking you. We didn't know each other. I wanted us to spend time together before I marked you, but I was scheduled to leave on a mission. You agreed that everyone telling me to mark you was insane. You said all you knew of me was that I was a soldier with a bad attitude. Caspian took over and marked you. The stupid creature marked you so deep, you almost passed out."

"I think I remember hearing something about the different depths of mating marks." I ran a hand through my hair.

"Yeah, a normal mark, like the one you gave me, allows us to feel each other's emotions. Caspian's level of mark is incredibly painful for the giver and receiver." Shadow said.

"Why would he do that then? If it was painful for you as well, it seems silly to do it."

"Caspian and I don't go into something halfhearted. Our mark on you signifies our complete devotion to you. It sealed our bond to one another immediately and is stronger than a normal mark." I rubbed my temples as I tried to process all the information I was given. "I think that is enough for right now. You look completely exhausted, River. You should head off to bed."

My head snapped in his direction. "Where are you going?" I asked without thinking.

Shadow smirked at me. "I am being a gentleman. I am heading to my guest room." I chewed my bottom lip as my anxiety rose. If Shadow left, would I be safe? "Everything will be fine, River."

"I don't want to be alone." I admitted.

"What are you saying?" Shadow lifted a brow in challenge.

I scowled at him, which caused his smile to widen. "Please stay in the room with me, Shadow." I rolled my eyes.

Shadow grabbed my hand and pulled me to the bed. He grabbed a pillow and tossed it on the floor by the chairs. I sat on the bed and watched him toss an extra blanket over there too. He finally looked at me. "My name is Cruz. At least when I don't have the mask on."

"Is there a last name that goes with that?" I smirked at him.

"Good-night, River Storm." He raised my hand to his lips before walking to the pile of bedding he had tossed on the floor.

I watched him make a bed and lay down on it. "Why are you on the floor?" I asked.

"I am not going to share a bed with you until you are ready for it." He looked over at me. "You have been through a lot over the last four weeks, Babe. You don't even recognize me, not that I am angry about that. The mate bond is making you feel somewhat comfortable with me, but I won't cross that line. I love you too much to push you into something you aren't fully comfortable with."

I blinked in surprise. He just said he loved me. Were we even at that level of our relationship, yet? From what I had been able to gather, we were barely getting along. "Cruz?" He glanced at me. "Did we fight a lot?"

Cruz chuckled and he closed his eyes with a smile. "I wouldn't call it fighting, but we verbally sparred a lot. Nothing hurtful. Everything we said was typically sarcastic and somewhat playful."

"Were we friends?"

"I don't know, River. Our relationship was complicated. We had just barely met, and then we were bonded to one another. I'm sure you found me irritating at first, and I didn't want a mate, but our bond kept pulling us together. It was hard to say goodbye every time I had to leave on assignment. We have only known each other for a month. Friends? I think we were headed that way."

Did he not realize that he had just told me he loved me? I crawled into bed, and I heard Cruz get up before the lights went out. He let out a long breath. I whispered a good-night, and he did the same.

*   *   *

Morning came and I felt more confused than I had before I had gone to bed. Memories flooded my brain in fragments all night. Growing up with a brother, Kyson. Visiting a giant mansion. Studying for my nursing degree. Spending time with an old woman named Prudence. Cruz getting dressed in all black. Cruz laying on a small couch battered and bruised from a plane crash.

I sat up and hugged my knees to my chest. Cruz was standing on the other side of the room with his back towards me. It looked like he was on the phone.

"They can't just swarm her. You need to tell them to let her have some space. I won't have them overwhelming her." He ran his hand through his hair. "Sir, with all due respect, I understand you are her father. But I will not see her come to harm. That includes mentally or emotionally. So, if they can't respect River's space, I need them to stay at the Silver Moon Pack."

I got off the bed and walked over to Cruz. From my recovered memories, I knew we were married and that he was protective of me. I touched my hand to his back. He tensed slightly as he turned to me. I wrapped my arms around his waist. His arm came around me and he rested his chin on my head. Cruz took a deep breath, and then he relaxed.

"I understand, sir. Believe me, I get how difficult it is but imagine how hard it is for her. When you get here, just have patience." Cruz hung up the phone before wrapping his other arm around me. We stood like that for several minutes before Cruz pulled back. "Your parents and brother, and I can imagine Alpha Max, are on their way. Alpha Kion has set the trials for tomorrow."

I chewed my lip as I looked down at the floor. "What if I don't remember them? What if I don't regain any of it back?"

Cruz tilted my chin up, so I was looking in his eyes. "River, if you don't remember them now, it doesn't matter. Things will come back over time. Trust me. I know how frustrating it is not knowing who you are or anyone around you. Once Maya is back, she can help you remember." Cruz looked so earnest, desperate for me to believe him.

"But what if it doesn't?" I blinked back tears. "I'm broken, Cruz. You deserve something better."

He released me and took several steps back. "If anyone deserves better, it's you. If you want to know what kind of man I am, I will tell you." He paced farther away from me before turning to face me. "I am a killer, River."

"Cruz, that's not what I meant. I can't even remember you. I don't know how long we have been together. Were we happy? Was I a burden? All I know is that we are married, but that's it. It's not fair to you." I said desperately.

"Nine weeks."

"Nine weeks?"

"That is how long we have known each other and how long we have been married. Five weeks together with me leaving a few times on missions for days at a time. And four weeks with you missing. We were finding our way, still finding our footing with each other. You have never been a burden. Not once."

"I wish I could remember, but I can't." I felt a tear slip down my cheek. "I feel drawn to you. Like I have to be with you, but I don't know why. I can't be the person you need." I shook my head. "I think I need space." I whispered.

"I understand." Cruz said. It was like his whole body deflated, yet he still stood tall.

"No, you don't." Tears were coursing down my cheeks. I could not believe I was pushing away my only source of comfort. The only person I knew was my ally.

"That's the thing, River. I really do." Cruz gave a sad smile before heading for the door.

"Cruz!" I called. My heart felt like it was breaking watching him go. He paused with his hand on the doorknob. "I just need to figure out who I am without you distracting me."

Cruz crossed to me and pressed his lips to mine. I melted against him as I returned the kiss without hesitation. His hand cupped the back of my head as he deepened the kiss. I was falling hard for him, and I knew I had been before my amnesia. He slowly broke our kiss, and I could almost feel how hard it was for him. He rested his forehead on mine with his eyes closed. "I thought we agreed you were the distracting one." He whispered.

Us on the couch with nothing on but the blanket, flashed in my mind again. I didn't want Cruz to go. I needed him. And that is what scared me. I had no idea who I was, but I couldn't seem to function without Cruz nearby. He was like a drug. The fact that I craved his presence, his touch, was a frightening concept. He was so kind and sweet with the patience of a god. He didn't seem irritated with me for wanting some time to work through my memories.

I wanted to remember who I was. It wasn't fair to him that he was giving me everything, while I could give him nothing. "Just give me two months." I whispered. I raised my hand to his cheek and took a deep breath.

"I can give you two months, Babe, if that is what you need." His thumb gently stroked my cheek, and I leaned into it. "River, I made you a promise the night you got the last call from Darius. I always keep my promises." He pressed a long kiss to my forehead and left.

What promise? I didn't remember any promise. I climbed back into bed and cried myself to sleep. When I woke up, I felt completely drained. I sat for a while staring out the window, not seeing anything. Suddenly, the image of an old lady popped into my mind. Prudence. I slipped my shoes on and ran from the room.

Chapter Twenty-One

River

I knocked on the cracked wood door. Minutes passed with no answer. I was ready to return to the packhouse when it finally creaked open. An old woman stood there. A smile spread across her face when she saw me. "My dear girl, come in, come in." She shuffled further into the small cabin, and I followed her. "You have been exposed to some powerful magic, River. I can sense it coming from you. Why don't you come tell me all about it?"

"Are you Prudence?" I asked.

"Of course it's me. Are you seeing okay?" Prudence squinted her eyes as she studied me.

"I um...I hit my head pretty hard. I don't remember anything." I rubbed my arm.

"There is a story there. We have never stood on ceremony, so spill it." Prudence pointed to a chair, and I sat.

I told her everything I could remember. Mostly it involved Cruz. When I got to waking up in chains, the old woman sat forward. She listened intently as I told her about Greta's treatment of my head and what I had overheard. When I was finished, she sat back and looked to be deep in thought.

"You said that when she treated your head, it hurt when she pressed on it." Prudence asked. I nodded. "No additional pain or the pain intensifying?"

"No."

"Hmm." Prudence tapped her fingers on the arm of her chair. "And you said that she gave you something to suppress your wolf?"

"That is what I overheard her saying to the Woods." I said nervously.

Prudence slowly got up from her rocking chair and shuffled to a large cabinet near the fireplace. She started pulling all sorts of jars and pouches out of it. I walked over to the table she was setting them on.

"What are all these?" I asked.

"Your knowledge will return. Why don't we get Maya back? This Greta woman gave you a powerful concoction to suppress your wolf, and I'm guessing your memory as well. You can sit while I fix up an antidote. In the meantime, you can tell me more about this Cruz of yours."

I sat down with a sigh. "He seems like a really nice guy. This morning, he was warning my family about my lack of memory and telling them to give me space. I can't seem to get him out of my mind." I huffed. "That's the problem, all I can think about is him. Most of the snippets of my returning memory are of him. I think I know more about Cruz than I do myself."

"He is your mate. You are bonded to him. He is a piece of you." Prudence commented. "Where is he now?"

I laid my head down on the table and groaned. "I told him I needed space, and to give me two months to sort some things out. He said he understood, and he left."

Prudence clucked her tongue and gave me a glare. "He must really care about you to be able to walk away right now."

"What do you mean?" I asked as I sat up and watched her combining several liquids into a pot over the fire in the fireplace.

"As your mate, his instinct is to protect you. That mark of yours is deep, making the bond stronger. You are vulnerable right now, River. You are no better than a human without your wolf and he knows it. That is why he told your family to give you space. He was protecting you from being overwhelmed." She looked up from stirring the mixture and gave a smile. "You were attacked, kidnapped, and held hostage. He just got you back, yet he is giving you what you want, even if it goes against his instincts."

"Like I said, he is a great guy." I sighed.

"Do you remember anything about magic, dear?" Prudence asked as she ladled out a cup of the brew she had been working on.

"Greta said magic has a price. The cost of healing is pain."

"That is correct. What we are doing is healing your mind and freeing your wolf. You will be in extreme pain for several minutes as your mind heals, so I need you to lay down on the cot."

I moved to the cot and sat on the edge of it. "What is the price of freeing my wolf?"

"The price of breaking sealing magic is paid by the one you love." Prudence said seriously. "For a werewolf, their wolf becomes weak for a while."

"I would be weakening Cruz?" I shook my head. "I can't do that."

"There is no other choice, River. If Maya is suppressed much longer, she will die."

Why had I told Cruz to leave? He should be here with me. He should be able to have a say in this. I covered my face and took several deep breaths to try to calm my anxiety. Cruz would tell me to do it. I knew he would do anything for me.

I laid down and tears blurred my vision. *Forgive me, Cruz.* I whispered in my mind as Prudence lifted my head enough for me to drink. I waited for the pain to come, but it didn't. The only thing I felt was a little dizzy. I looked over at Prudence who was watching me with a puzzled expression.

"Did it work?" I asked after several minutes of nothing happening.

"There should have been pain." Prudence's brows knit together.

"It was the transference potion, River. Cruz drank the other half." A soft weak voice said in my head, and I sat up.

"Transference potion?" I asked.

"You took a transference potion?" Prudence asked in surprise. "Who drank the other half?"

"Cruz." I breathed out. I ran from the cabin. I needed to find him. I needed to know if he was okay.

As I rounded the corner of the packhouse, I slammed into a huge figure and was knocked to the ground. I looked up to find a giant man in all black wearing a mask. One of Cruz's men.

"Where is Shadow?" I asked, getting to my feet.

"Shadow? He left a few hours ago. He told Spur he was in charge and left."

"Where is Spur?"

"Follow me." The man said as he turned around and began to walk. I had to jog to keep up.

We entered the packhouse and took the second hall on the left. I followed him through a thick wood door and down stone stairs. I had never been down this way before. I grew nervous when we reached the bottom. The air down here was musty and cold. There were prison cells lining the walls. It wasn't long until we heard voices coming from one of the cells. The giant gestured for me to stay put before he entered the room.

A minute later another man came out. "Is everything okay, River?" he asked quietly as he grabbed my elbow, guiding me away from the cell and back the way I had come.

"Where is Shadow?" I asked.

"He left." Spur said in confusion. "He said you were aware of it." I ran my hand through my hair anxiously. "What is going on?"

"Did you know about the transference potion?" I whispered, coming to a stop and turning to face him.

"Gin mentioned you giving Shadow something that made all his pain from your healing stuff transfer to you."

"Yes, it is a two-way potion. Any magic that affects me, he pays the price."

"Okay." Spur said slowly.

"I just took a potion to help with my memory. It was supposed to be incredibly painful." I grew anxious. Was Cruz driving? Oh gosh. What have I done?

Spur cursed and pulled out his phone. He pressed several buttons before holding it to his ear. His expression became worried as he looked at me. He lowered the phone and opened his mouth as if to say something, but then he closed it.

Cruz didn't answer. I shook my head and ran back up several flights of stairs until I got to my room. I slammed the door behind me and began to pace. Where was he? I was close to panicking. He had to be okay. I needed him to be okay. My memories were starting to filter in. With magic no longer blocking them, they were coming back as if watching a movie. I didn't want two months anymore. I wanted Cruz to be with me so that I would know he was okay.

*   *   *

Cruz

Caspian was beyond furious with me. He didn't want to give River even a month to sort things out. He wanted to help her recover her memory. I fought with him every step of the way to my guest room. I couldn't do this. I couldn't give her the time she wanted and needed, and at the same time, stay close to her. Caspian would never let up trying to get back to her.

I knew how frustrating it was to lose one's memory. After my first plane crash, I had woken up with no clue as to who I was. I was in so much pain and barely alive. However, the people that had found me thought I was playing dumb and tried to extract information from me. I had been scared and thought I was going to die in that hole. Caspian attempted to shift and heal us between sessions. I was in a constant state of torture for twelve days.

Caspian had helped me remember enough to call Miles. He had tried to help me remember my family and who I was. It had been frustrating. I ended up purchasing two houses, both on the beach. One I rented out for some extra income. The other was my personal home. No one knew about it, not even Miles. It had taken me several months before I felt whole again. I still didn't have all my memories but I had come to terms with that.

River asking for a few months was understandable. No matter how much Caspian fought me on this, we were giving her that time. I went through my bag, pulling out the emergency phone, S.O.S. transmitter, and an arrow. I quickly found an Omega who helped me locate a box, pen, and paper.

I boxed up the items, tossing in a few final items at the last minute and wrote a note. I slowly opened River's door. Peeking in, I saw she was asleep on the bed. Silently, I put the box and letter on her bedside table. I couldn't help watching her for several minutes.

I needed to go. I bent down and placed a kiss on her temple before whispering close to her ear. "I love you, River. I can give you your two months, but after that time is up, I will be back for you. You are perfect for me, no matter what you think." I kissed her forehead and left.

I stopped by my room, grabbed my bag and walked downstairs. I found Spur in the lobby. "Cruz, all prisoners are locked up to await their trial."

"Good." I transferred my bag to my left hand.

"Going somewhere?" Spur eyed my bag.

"I'm heading out. You are in charge of the team for the rest of this mission."

"I don't understand. Why are you leaving right after finding River, especially in the state she is in?" Spur crossed his arms over his chest.

"She is upset and frustrated over the loss of her memory. She said she needs space and asked for two months to sort through things." I told him quietly.

"And you, knowing exactly what she is going through, are giving her time with no hesitation." Spur nodded. "But you can give her space without having to leave, can't you?"

I shook my head. "Caspian doesn't agree with me. He is fighting to get back to her. I can't stay here and give her space; Caspian won't allow it." I looked at the empty stairs that led up to the bedrooms. "Keep an eye on her for me."

"That's it, then? You are just walking away?" Spur asked angrily.

"For now." I clenched my jaw. "I promised her two months. But when that time is up, I will be back. Even if her memory hasn't returned, she will just have to deal with the fact that I'm not going anywhere."

"What is your plan while you are gone?" Spur asked.

"Our government is snooping around, trying to figure out who we are. I plan on paying them a little visit. Once that is done, I have my own things I need to sort out." I turned and walked out the door.

Every step I took down the road was torture. My feet felt like they were filled with lead. I needed a distraction. I pulled out my phone and hit my first contact.

"O'Brien."

"Miles, I am checking in and letting you know I am going to be shipping out with the tide for the next two months." I said without preamble.

"That might be a little hard after you talk with your sister." Miles sounded confused.

"I wasn't planning on calling her." I made it to the fork in the road, just outside of the North Wind Pack borders and took the one heading south.

"I would if I were you. You will die a slow painful death if you don't." Miles warned.

I sighed. "Is she with you?"

"Yes."

"Put her on."

Miles called for Molly, and I waited. "Cruz!" She yelled and I pulled the phone from my ear.

"What is going on, Molls?" I asked, trying to hold back my frustration.

"Everyone is getting ready to leave for the trial tomorrow. Kyson and I will be there. I can't wait to see your face when I tell you something." Molly said excitedly.

"Sorry, Molly. I won't be there. I will be unreachable for the next two months, but Miles thought it a good idea for you to tell me something before

I go." I felt a little guilty. Molly loved surprises and she lived for dramatics. I hated to disappoint her.

"Oh, where are you going? Is River going with you?" Molly asked in surprise.

"River, is needing to stay behind this time." Caspian howled mournfully at my words. "What is your news, sis?"

"Oh, I...um...I found my mate." She said. She still sounded confused, but her excitement was coming back.

"That's great, Molly." I smiled. "Do I know the guy?"

"As a matter of fact, you do." she giggled.

I stopped walking. "Who is it?"

"We didn't want to say anything with Nash and Ana missing, and then you and River. Then there was the plane crash. Everything has been so crazy for the past four months. But we decided that if we wait for the perfect time, then it's never going to come. I just want to be with him. I'm sure you can understand that." Molly started to ramble.

"Who is it?" I interrupted her.

"Paxton Williams." She sighed dreamily. "We are going to get married next month."

"Paxton? The jerk I knocked out before I married River?" I asked in surprise.

"He is no bigger jerk than you are. He sees River as a sister, and some stranger that broke into the house, marked her. His emotions were already high with Nash and Ana coming home." She defended.

I took a deep breath and let it out slowly to calm myself. Speaking of emotions being high. "If he makes you happy, then I am happy for you, Molly. I really am. But I am going to need a specific date. Like I said, I will be unreachable as soon as I am done talking with you. And can I assume it will be at the Silver Moon Pack?"

"Yes, Paxton is the future Alpha. We want it to be here so the whole pack can be a part of it." Molly said. "Hey, sweetheart, what day should we get married? We won't be able to reach Cruz after this phone call, so he needs to know."

"Whenever you want, my love." Paxton said with a smile in his voice.

These two were making it hard to control Caspian. "Molly, my time is running short. I really hate to rush you, but I need to get going." I said, as I began walking again.

"What about the tenth of August?" Molly asked.

"That is eight weeks away." Paxton commented. "Sounds good to me. That will give us enough time to get everything put together."

"August tenth at the Silver Moon Pack, got it." I said.

"When should we expect you?" Molly asked.

"I will be there late on the ninth." I heard Molly's disappointment as she responded, but it couldn't be helped. River would be there, and the two months wouldn't be up yet. "I love you, Molly. And congratulations." I ended the call and turned off the phone before shoving it into my bag.

I had been walking for a few hours now, and Caspian was still complaining about allowing River to have some space. At the next pack, I was going to purchase a ticket south or rent a vehicle. I didn't trust Caspian enough to shift. Giving him even an ounce of control would end with us back in the North Wind Pack.

Suddenly my head felt like it was going to explode. I dropped to my knees as I grabbed the sides of my head. "Caspian." I growled out. What was the beast doing?

The pain only grew, causing me to yell in agony. I was vaguely aware of Caspian writhing on the ground as he yelped and whined in pain. I didn't know how long I lay on the ground squeezing my head, when my vision began to fade. The pain hadn't subsided. My last thoughts were of River. Who would care for her if I died?

Chapter Twenty-Two

River

Alpha Kion and Spur came to see me a little after dinner. I had taken my meals in my room, away from everyone. My memories were slowly starting to come back, thankfully without the pain. But I wasn't ready to face the world. They let me know that my family was going to be arriving within a few minutes, and it was up to me if I felt up to greeting them outside.

Only Spur knew that I had visited Prudence to get my memory back. I wanted to keep it that way for now. I didn't want to get anyone's hopes up if it didn't fully work. So far, I remembered a good amount of my childhood. Which made me feel a little better.

Spur and Alpha Kion were still waiting for my response to see if I was going to meet my family at the front porch. "I will go outside with you, Kion." I said, slipping my shoes on.

"Shall we?" Kion gave me a kind smile as he motioned for me to join him in the hall.

I glanced back into the room. My eyes, once again, strayed to the box on the nightstand. It had Cruz's scent on it, but I hadn't been able to bring myself to open it. What if it was a final good-bye? I would be shattered. I hadn't even read the letter on top. I never should have told him to go. I swallowed hard before exiting my room.

Spur walked behind me as I followed Kion. I glanced back at him. He was scanning the hallway, looking alert. He almost seemed like a guard. When we stepped outside, I noticed several more men in all black stationed around the front of the house. A security team? I glanced at Spur. He looked relaxed, but also ready for a fight. I moved to his side, and he looked at me quickly before turning his eyes back to scanning the area.

"What are you doing?" I asked.

"My job." Spur said.

"Did we know each other before I was kidnapped?"

"A little. You were usually engaged in either verbally sparring with Cruz or kissing him." Spur shrugged.

I felt my cheeks heat and I looked down the long driveway. "I know enough that babysitting me isn't part of your job description." I whispered.

Spur turned his full attention to me. "Cruz asked me to look out for you, and I will not let him down. That man has saved my life at great risk to his own many times. If making sure you are safe while he is away is how I can repay even a fraction of what I owe him, I will do it. Tango, Marco, Cheese, and Fox won't leave either. They didn't see you and Cruz together before, but by his actions over the last few weeks, they know how much you mean to him."

I turned and watched each man for a while. "Thank you, Spur." I whispered. "Why did he leave? I asked for a little space, not for him to completely disappear."

Spur sighed. "He was having a hard time controlling Caspian. When we talked, his eyes were flickering between dark blue and his normal blue. Caspian adores you and didn't want to be away from you."

"That doesn't tell me why he left." I glared at the ground in front of my feet. I know I was the one that said to give me time, but I felt abandoned.

"Cruz knows how frustrating it is to not remember anything. He hasn't told me much about what happened, but he still has a gap in his memory. He can't remember the years between age fourteen and eighteen. Gin said Cruz remembers training to be an FBWHA agent, but it took a while to get even that back. Miles said that he tried to help Cruz regain his memory, but Cruz only grew more and more frustrated when he couldn't. Miles helped him purchase a beach house so that Cruz could take some leave and figure some things out."

"If he knew how frustrating it was, why didn't he stay to try to help me through it?" I huffed. "I know I told him I needed space, but still."

Spur chuckled. "Cruz disappeared for several months. Miles didn't even know where he went. The beach house where he assumed Cruz was staying, was being rented out to a family for the summer."

"Where was he?" I looked at Spur.

"He never said. When he came back, he had a barely sober Gin in tow, and told Miles to start training him." Spur glanced at me. "What I am trying to say, is that Cruz knows the frustrations of amnesia. Even though it was killing him, he wanted to give you space. He had needed that, too, during his experience. Caspian wasn't having it though. In order to keep his word to you, he had to go. He asked me to watch out for you until he comes back. Cruz is a man of his word, River. He will come back after your asked for two months."

I hoped Spur was right. We lapsed into silence as we waited. Ten minutes later, several vehicles pulled up in front of the wide porch steps. I closed my eyes and took a deep breath to calm my rising anxiety as the doors started to open. Uncle Max and Aunt Jackie were the first to exit the cars, followed by Nash and Ana. Max held tightly to the twins who tried to run to me. Paxton held hands with a pretty blonde girl with blue eyes. She reminded me of Cruz. Behind them was a tall man with brown hair and a blonde woman who looked like an older version of the one holding onto Paxton.

I blinked back tears when I saw mom, dad, and Kyson. Everyone stood back as they watched me with various expressions. Most looked like they wanted to run to me. Spur nudged me toward them, and I looked back at him. He gave me a small nod. I turned back to my family as they continued to stand by the vehicles.

I slowly walked down the steps and went straight to my mom. "Mom." I whispered, and she pulled me into a tight hug as she began to cry. I held her tightly as my own tears began to fall. After several minutes, Mom pulled back and I looked at my dad. "Daddy." Dad pulled me to him. My parents' familiar smell filled my nose. I hugged dad tighter.

"We weren't sure if you would remember us. From what we were told, you barely remembered your name." Dad whispered.

"I remember snatches, mostly from when I was young." I told him.

"Hey, River." Kyson smiled at me.

"Ky." I breathed out and hugged him.

I was greeted with tears from each member of my family. The two blonde women and brown-haired man stood off to the side and watched patiently. Paxton was the last person I hugged. When he released me, he had a huge grin on his face.

"River, I found my mate." Paxton motioned for the young woman to come over. She practically bounced to his side. "This is Molly Storm. You met her before but…"

"Storm?" I said quietly as my brows knit together. That was the name Cruz had called me when I asked about his last name. "You are Cruz's family." I stated.

"I'm his sister." Molly smiled. "Do you remember, or are you connecting dots?" She wasn't being unkind, just curious. I immediately liked her. She treated me like a person and not some fragile piece of glass.

"Connecting dots." I smiled at her. "That, and you look a lot like him."

"Where is my elusive brother?" Molly asked, looking around.

"He isn't here." I tried not to show how upset I was, after all, it was my fault that he had left.

"Oh, I know. He called this morning to let us, well Miles, know that he was going to be unreachable for the next two months." Molly rolled her eyes. "I just thought you might know where he ran off to."

I didn't know what to say. "Agent Storm was called away." Spur said from behind me.

"Wouldn't I know about it, Spur?" A man I hadn't seen yet was standing several feet away.

"Agent O'Brien." Spur said stiffly. I glanced at him, and he looked a little flustered.

"I think it is time for us to have a debriefing, Spur. Cruz didn't sound himself and all his missions go through me. I haven't reassigned him."

"With all due respect, sir. Cruz doesn't work for you. You may be the go between, but he can pick and choose his missions." Spur crossed his arms over his chest.

"What are you saying?" O'Brien snapped.

"Storm is unavailable for the next two months. That is all you need to know." The giant man walked up.

"Marco, what has gotten into you guys? I am not the enemy." O'Brien looked ready to pop a blood vessel. "Where is Cruz?"

"The man is a ghost." Another masked man walked up. "Some of Shadow must have started rubbing off on him because the man is slippery and hard to keep track of. Maybe you should see if Shadow wants to recruit him."

"Tango." O'Brien growled. "I want to know where Cruz is. His mission was to find and bring down the people targeting the royal family. If he isn't completing that, he is AWOL."

"I mean, that is a pretty broad mission assignment. Just because he isn't currently present, doesn't mean he isn't working. For all we know he and

Shadow took off to follow another lead since Martinez wasn't here to go with him."

"Don't, Fox. I am not in the mood for your mind games." O'Brien pinched the bridge of his nose. "He said he was unavailable for two months. I know you all know more than you are saying. What is he up to?"

"I told him to go." I whispered. "He left because of me." Everyone went quiet. I wasn't going to explain more than that.

"River, I have some questions about Paxton." Molly finally broke the silence. "I know you might not remember everything, but I was hoping to get some juicy stories from you."

"Hey!" Paxton said.

I gave Molly a grateful smile. "Sure, why don't we go where he won't try to correct me to make himself look less like the idiot he is."

Molly laughed and hooked her arm through mine. We ignored Paxton's complaints and went inside. When we were out of earshot of everyone, I glanced at her. "Thank you."

"No problem. I know you don't remember me, but we were becoming friends until Cruz showed up and stole you from me." Molly gave me a big smile.

After we were in my room with the door closed, I felt a little better. I didn't want anyone to ask me why I had asked him to go. Molly released my arm as she looked around the room. She crossed to the sitting area and took the chair I had sat in the night before. I took a seat on the one Cruz had occupied.

"Why is Cruz's scent so strong in here?" Molly asked as she continued to look around.

"He spent the night in here last night." I felt my cheeks burn.

"Oh, then I am a little confused." She said slowly.

I sighed. "I don't remember him."

"Liar. You remember him enough." A female voice said in my head. It was louder this time, but still weak.

"We talked last night. He answered my endless questions. Besides what he told me, I remembered that we are married. I get snatches of memory here and there. I don't even know what events happened first." I tried to explain.

"So, you were feeling comfortable enough with him to let him sleep in here with you?" Molly watched me.

I covered my face with my hands. "He was going to go to his guest room, but I asked him to stay. I didn't want to be alone, and I felt safe with him. He slept on the floor."

"Hmm."

"By morning, I felt like I knew him more than I knew myself. Most of my returning memories were of him. I couldn't be who he needed me to be. I'm broken, Molly. I don't know who I am. He deserves someone who can give him all of them, like he can give all of himself to them." Tears burned my eyes, and I blinked, trying to keep them from falling.

"Did he say he needed more from you?" Molly asked softly.

I shook my head. "He kept telling me, it was okay. That everything would be okay. We would work through it."

"Where is Maya?"

"My wolf? She was locked away with magic. I think she is coming back, but Prudence said she is weak." It wasn't exactly the truth, but Maya and I were paying the price for breaking the magic keeping her suppressed. "I asked him to give me space for two months. I didn't mean for him to leave completely. Spur said Caspian wasn't liking that Cruz agreed, and in order to give me time, he left." Tears ran down my cheeks. "I made a mistake. Such a huge mistake. I should never have told him to go." My eyes caught sight of the box on the nightstand just over Molly's shoulder.

"It will be okay, River. You seem to be getting some of your memories back, and Cruz will return. He is a man of his word." Molly touched my hand and gasped. "Did he leave you something?" She asked quickly.

"Yes." I said in confusion. "I haven't looked at it yet."

"You should. Right now, or at least before the trial." Her eyes were wide. "Please."

I stood and retrieved the box. "Do you know what is inside?"

"Not everything." Molly still looked shaken. "Did Cruz tell you much about our family?" I shook my head. "Our mother is a hybrid. She is half wolf, half human. She has a gift because of it. She can control her pack aura. Cruz and I are also hybrids and have different abilities. He hasn't told us what his is, but I can see the different outcomes of a single choice."

I blinked at her in surprise. "And you saw something when you touched me?"

"You were debating opening the box, weren't you?"

"I am afraid of what he said. What if he says he won't be coming back?" I stared at the box in my hands. It wasn't very big. It was about nine inches long, five inches wide, and stood four inches tall.

"You need to open it, River. Before the trial. If you want to do it alone, I can go find Paxton." Molly stared at the box.

"I think I want to open it alone." I whispered.

Molly stood and gave me a hug. "You won't regret it. I promise." She gave me one last smile and left.

I sat for several minutes just staring at the box. I chewed my lip as I debated just setting it aside and ignoring it again. Something about Molly's insistence had me slowly reaching for the letter on top. With shaking hands, I unfolded the paper.

River,

I need you to know that I would never leave you if I could help it. You are not broken, no matter how much you feel like you are. When I had to leave you before, I gave you three items, and I am giving them to you again. I put a shirt in there as well. A mate's scent helps calm and comfort the other. I added one more thing. I pray they bring you some measure of peace.

Always yours,
Cruz

I dropped the letter on the floor and quickly pulled open the box. Sure enough, there was a shirt. I pulled it out and pressed it to my nose as my tears began to fall again. Rain. I laid the shirt across my lap and reached back inside. A phone, a quarter sized button, a coin, and a bullet.

I set the phone and button aside. I examined the bullet in confusion. It wasn't a bullet. I didn't know what it was, but somehow I knew it wasn't a bullet. I put it carefully next to the phone and turned my attention to the coin. It was just a normal coin.

A memory of sitting in Cruz's lap with his arms protectively around me resurfaced. I was scared that they were going to kill Cruz and take me. "You are mine, River, and I am yours. You can't separate two sides of a single coin. You are my wife, and as such, I will protect you with my last breath. I will always be here for you." Cruz said firmly. I closed my eyes and nodded before laying my head on his shoulder. "Always remember that."

I blinked several times. The promise. I stood and moved to the door and opened it. Not surprisingly, Spur stood in the hall. "I need you to put a hole in this, close to the edge." I held up the coin. Spur took it with a confused expression. I didn't explain or wait for him to ask. I closed my bedroom door and went back to the items.

I put the phone, button, and bullet in my pocket before slipping the shirt on over mine. It reached mid-thigh. Another memory of me holding hands with Cruz as I wore nothing but his shirt as we walked up to my room after showering in the locker room, surfaced.

I shook my head to clear my thoughts. I really did make a mistake telling him to go. All I wanted was for Cruz to be with me.

"*Cruz is our other half. We won't feel whole without him.*" The female voice said.

"*Maya?*" I asked in surprise.

"*Hi, River.*" Maya said with a tired smile. "*I am so happy to be able to talk with you again.*"

"Oh, my gosh! I am a werewolf!" I laughed.

"*Of course you are. I know we can't remember much, but I can tell you, we aren't ones to mope. So, Cruz had to leave in order to give us the time you wanted to figure things out. Let's make the most of it and do what we planned on doing before finding our Alpha mate.*"

"Which is?" I asked with a smile.

"*Help others. Heal those who need healing.*" Maya said firmly. "*Being a Luna will restrict what we can do in that regard. After the trial, let's go home and work at the hospital.*"

Chapter Twenty-Three

Cruz

"Wake up, Cruz!" Caspian yelled in my head. *"Use caution."*

I was immediately awake, but I didn't move a muscle. Using our ability, I saw all around us. We were in a small, one room shack. An elderly man and teen boy sat at a small table in the corner. Their heads were close together as they discussed what to do with me. The contents of my bag were laid out on the floor. I didn't have time for this. I sat up and started gathering my things while keeping an eye on the two in the corner.

"Excuse me, sir?" The boy asked.

"Which way did you two take me?" I ignored his question. When neither one answered, I tried again. "From where you found me, which way did you go to bring me here?"

"South." The old man said.

"Thank you for your hospitality." I gave them a nod and headed for the door.

"Just a minute. You were screaming in agony for nigh onto an hour, even after you seemed to lose consciousness." The old man got to his feet. "I know magic when I see it."

"Your point is?" I asked. Magic? Is that what it was?

"Magic that powerful could kill a man or beast. We took a great risk in bringing you here. You owe us compensation." The boy stood next to the man.

"You did take a great risk bringing me here. Not by whoever had attacked me, but by me. It isn't wise to bring someone to your home when you know nothing about them. You are lucky I am not in the mood to clean up the mess I usually leave behind." I continued to the door.

"Who are you?" The old man's voice shook.

"I am a shadow. A ghost. A monster." I stepped outside and shifted into my wolf. Caspian let out a loud howl before grabbing my bag and running in the direction of home.

He finally accepted that what we were doing for River was what was best for her. It would take about a week to get home like this, but it would allow us to blow off some steam. Now that Caspian was on board, I let him have full control and shut the world out.

* * *

The salty ocean air grew stronger. I smiled and pushed myself faster. The moment my paws hit the sand; I shifted back to human. I took a deep breath. The scent that once helped center me, now made me only think of River. I shook my head, picked up my bag, and walked to the front door. I pushed it open and looked around.

The place was exactly how I had left it, other than the dust on everything. It had been several months since I had been here. I owned the mile strip of beach extending in each direction with the house at the center.

I didn't bother turning on lights as I made my way upstairs to my bedroom. I pulled off the dusty sheets, grabbed a blanket from the closet, opened the doors leading to the deck, and plopped back on the bed. I listened to the sound of the surf as I stared up at the ceiling.

I closed my eyes in an attempt to force myself to sleep. First thing in the morning I was going to start planning my visit to The Board.

Chapter Twenty-Four

River

I got dressed in a pair of dress pants and blouse. Mom had brought them for me. The pants felt a little tighter, but I was stress-eating all night. I put the phone and small button into my back pocket and the bullet in the front right. Something told me to always have them with me. I gave myself one last look in the mirror. My fingers touched the coin I now wore around my neck.

A knock sounded at my bedroom door, and I crossed the room. I pulled it open and smiled when I saw Spur and Cheese. "Good morning, gentlemen." I began walking down the hall. I slept better than I thought I would. I had worn Cruz's shirt as pajamas and his scent had been calming.

"*Remember to be quiet and unsure of yourself. We don't want them to know we have our memory back.*" Maya warned.

I slowed my steps a little and took a deep breath. I remembered a lot more during the night. It had been like watching a movie about my life. I remembered school and working with Prudence. Getting my degrees. Marking Cruz and our rocky start. He had been a pain in the butt. But whenever I needed him, he was there. I still don't remember meeting the Storms, though.

A large crowd was gathered in the entrance hall by the time I made it downstairs. Mom grabbed my hand and gave it a squeeze. "They will be opening the door for seating in a moment or two. Kion is one of five on a panel to judge the proceedings." I nodded my understanding.

I had been sitting between my mom and Molly for hours now. Greta had been found guilty of illegal use of witchcraft. One cannot use magic in order to take away another's wolf or magic. She also broke the law by assisting in kidnapping me. Mom and dad were called before the panel to answer questions about their history with Marissa and Dax. Darius was called forward and my stomach clenched.

"State your name." Kion said.

"Darius Wood."

"You are an Agent of the FBWHA. Is that correct?" Kion asked, and Darius answered in the affirmative. "How do you know River Storm?"

"Storm?" Darius sounded confused, but his hands clenched at his sides. "To my knowledge, River's last name is Shepherd."

"She is married to Cruz Storm." Councilwoman Bethany said.

"If that is the case, I don't know why she would agree to marry me." Darius winked at me, and I felt like I was going to throw up.

"I have their marriage certificate here. Signed and dated nine weeks ago. For a man of your resources, I find it odd that you were unaware of Mrs. Storm's marital status. Especially, since she also has her mate's mark on her neck."

"She said she watched him go into a building before it exploded." Darius shrugged.

"And you believed her? Her mark is still very much intact." Councilman Berry asked incredulously.

"I had no reason not to doubt her claim. River's mark is deep. Deeper than I have ever seen. I just figured that the bond was taking longer to fade because of that." Darius's eyes never left mine. "And Cruz Storm is dead." I looked down at the ground so he wouldn't see me glaring at him.

"Have you ever heard of Terror Root?" Prudence asked from her spot next to Kion.

"I have. It is a rare poisonous plant." Darius said slowly.

"The plant can be quite dangerous; however, the roots can be prepared to create a sweet treat that makes the consumer speak nothing but truth for five minutes." Prudence explained. I covered my mouth to keep from giggling. I remembered Cruz's experience with Terror Root. "I ask the council to allow me to give Mr. Wood one in order to get the truth from him, since he has spoken mainly lies thus far."

The council agreed, and Darius was forced to eat a piece of root. He glared at Prudence as she slowly returned to her seat. "Now, Mr. Wood, how did you learn of Mr. Storm's supposed death?"

"I watched it with my own eyes. I was the one to push the button to trigger the explosives when I saw him enter the building. River confirmed it after we brought her to our cabin. She kept having nightmares about his death." Darius's jaw clenched and his face turned red.

"Why was his death necessary?" Kion asked.

"He stood in the way of me marrying River."

"Why did you need to marry River? Surely, you could have found your mate or taken another chosen mate." Bethany asked.

"River is my ticket to the throne. The royal family was easy to take care of. Cruz Storm is proving to be a thorn in my side. Him and Shadow both." Darius sneered.

"You are responsible for the deaths of the royal family?" Kion asked in surprise.

"Dad built the bomb, Mom planned the event and got the flight scheduled, and I planted the bomb."

The room fell silent, and Darius looked ticked. He turned eyes of hatred to me, and I sat frozen. A wave of nausea hit me, and I stood up. Molly looked concerned as I pushed past her. I needed air. I made halfhearted apologies to those I rudely shoved past.

I took deep breaths once I burst out of the door. A hand touched my back gently, and I turned to see Molly. She rubbed my back in slow circles, and I took several more deep breaths. She guided me off to the side when the doors opened, and people started filing out. I closed my eyes and leaned against a pillar.

I saw Mom and Dad talking with Kion and a few others in the center of the entrance hall, once everyone had cleared out of the room. I closed my eyes again. Suddenly, there were men yelling right before Molly went sliding across the floor and I was grabbed. A sharp metal blade was pressed to my neck. My eyes scanned the room, looking for anyone to help me, but they were all powerless right now.

"Darius, lower the knife." Spur said slowly as he stepped closer. He was calm, but I could see in his eyes that he was worried. He was too far away to be of any real help.

I grabbed Darius's forearm and tried to pull it away. "Not this time, Darling. You are mine. We need you."

I swallowed and the tip of the knife stabbed my neck, and I winced. A second later it felt like something was slowly running down my neck. Tears filled my eyes. Why on earth had I told Cruz to go away?

"Darius, River is bleeding, just take the knife from her throat." Mom said desperately.

"You think you have the right to talk to me, Gamma Carly?" Darius laughed. "After what you did to my mother, taking your daughter will be quite rewarding."

"Explain to me what I did that would warrant you doing this." Mom said, throwing her arms out to the side.

"You stole her mate from her, for starters. But that all worked out for the best in the long run. Dad and Mom were able to get you out of the Silver Moon Pack and to Alpha Kane without too much trouble. Easton refused to give her a chance after you disappeared. He was too concerned about finding you. Then you took over the pack when you returned. Everyone knew you were the one in charge, even after Luna Jackie came along. She couldn't stand your brainwashing anymore and left. I came along a few months later. When mom found dad again, he took her as his chosen mate. You made it so he couldn't return to his pack. Dax Wood had to disappear."

"So that is what this is about?" Mom asked in disbelief. "Revenge on me because your parents made poor choices?"

Darius dipped his head toward my neck and took a deep breath. "How painful do you think it would be to place my mark on yours." He whispered.

A memory of Cruz giving me the bullet and showing me that it was actually an arrow flashed through my mind. I pulled the bullet from my pocket while Spur tried again to get Darius to let me go. Darius only laughed at everyone.

"Darius, you know very well that marking her would kill her. You said you needed her alive." Fox stepped out of the shadows to my right.

Darius jumped, pulling me closer to him. I whimpered as the knife scratched my throat. I adjusted my hold on the bullet-arrow. *"Okay, now I'm getting angry."* I told Maya.

"I can't heal you if you do this, River. You have to get it in the perfect spot." Maya warned.

I made eye contact with Spur. I was several inches shorter than Darius. If I did this right, I could stop Darius and not totally damage my own shoulder. I felt Darius drop his head again. I put the bullet to my shoulder and pressed the sides of it. Darius's teeth grazed my skin just as I felt pain explode through my shoulder. I screamed and squeezed it again, collapsing the arrow. I fell forward while Darius sank to his knees.

Spur scooped me up before I knew what was happening. I whimpered in pain when someone began pressing on the front and back of my shoulder. "Geez, River. Cruz is going to kill me when he finds out that you intentionally stabbed yourself with this." Spur said as I felt my hand get pried open and the arrow taken away.

"He was trying to mark me." I said through clenched teeth.

"Tango was right behind him." Spur pressed hard and I cried out.

"If he wasn't going to kill Darius in the next millisecond, he would have marked me. All he had to do was break the skin." I opened my eyes and looked up at him. "And Cruz doesn't need to know. He will kill me if he finds out I did that."

Spur chuckled. "Looks like we both will be digging our graves. Cruz has the uncanny ability to know everything you don't want him to."

"Where is she?" Prudence called. "That was quite the dramatic display, River." She said from beside me. "Why don't we get some healing salves on you, since Maya is probably too weak to heal you."

*   *   *

Molly accompanied me today for my check-up. My shoulder was healing nicely. I would have a scar, but internally, everything was good. Maya had been able to help with healing this last week. She wasn't able to do much, but she was gaining her strength back.

We weren't able to shift yet. I couldn't wait until we were able to. I missed it. My memory came back a month ago. I had tried to find Cruz, but he was gone. No one knew his location. Molly even tried calling him on the phone he had given her, but he didn't answer. I didn't even try to use mine after she told me she got no response. I was tempted to push the S.O.S. transmitter, but I didn't want to give him a heart attack. He was going to be getting enough of a shock when he got back.

Other than impaling myself with the arrow and getting my memory fully restored, several more developments popped up. I needed to talk to Cruz. Miles received a call about two weeks after the trial saying the Shadow Project was terminated. All active agents were to disband and report to Miles for their next assignments under their real identities. Miles tried reaching out to Cruz, with no luck.

Molly and I were walking back to the packhouse from my appointment. It was a hot day, and I was tempted to take a trip to the waterfall. "Cruz should arrive late tonight." Molly said conversationally.

My heart sped up and I glanced over at her. "Did he call?"

"No, he said he would be here late on the ninth." Molly shrugged. "I imagine he is going to try to keep his distance, since the two months isn't up yet."

"We are a week shy of it." I laughed.

"Cruz is nothing but a man of his word. If he said two months, he will give you two months."

"Do you think he will be mad when I tell him?" I asked nervously. I didn't want any surprises or secrets between us.

"Hard to tell." Molly laughed. "Cruz has been completely unpredictable when it comes to you."

Great. Just what I wanted to hear. I spotted the turn off for the falls. "I am going to the waterfall for a little bit. I should be back by dinner."

"Your shoulder hurting that much?"

"Physical Therapy is always brutal." I gave her a hug and jogged down the path. I had to do human physical therapy with Marco several times a week for my shoulder. I swear he was attempting to kill me. I was always hurting and sore afterwards. A soak in the waterfall helped relieve some of the pain.

I kicked off my shoes, took out my cell phone, and slowly walked into the icy water. It was somewhat refreshing with the heat of august but still freezing. I swam to the waterfall and dove under to sit on the small shelf just behind the water curtain. There was no way I would be able to climb to the cave. Sitting here though, I felt like I could be alone. Spur, Fox, Marco, Tango, or Cheese were always nearby.

That was one reason I couldn't wait for Cruz to return. I wanted my independence back. I tried to go for a run the other day, but I couldn't relax because I had my shadows tailing me. The more time passed, the more irritated I grew with them. It wasn't their fault that Cruz was gone, but they reminded me of him. Even without their black gear and masks.

Gin, who I learned was Jameson Edwards, went back home. He recovered enough that Martinez took him home to spend time with his wife and baby. All the guys went by their real names now. Spur was actually Spencer. Fox was Judd. Marco was Mark. Tango's name was Nick and Cheese was Micah. To keep themselves busy, they were upgrading the security around the pack and would take turns traveling to the Royal Pack to do the same.

I had been there for ten minutes and was about to get out when I saw a large figure pulling its clothes off at the side of the pool. The water distorted everything, so I couldn't make out who was there.

Chapter Twenty-Five

Cruz

I didn't realize how bad I had been speeding until I pulled in front of the Packhouse. I still had a good hour or two before the sun set. I should have left later in the day, but I was too keyed up to sit around any longer. I couldn't face her yet. Not until I had better control over myself.

I parked my motorcycle in the trees and walked through the forest until I heard the waterfall. I scanned the area but didn't see anyone. I pulled my shirt off as I slipped out of my shoes. I didn't have any extra clothes, other than my suit for the wedding tomorrow. I didn't even bring it with me. I sent Miles a message to have it ready for me.

I moved closer to the water's edge. Nothing like freezing oneself in order to focus your thoughts. I dove in and stayed under for as long as I could. I tried to tamp down my excitement to see River again, but it was difficult. Caspian even suggested using a powder we had learned about a few weeks ago to deaden my sense of smell, so I wouldn't be able to smell River.

I took it before starting my drive. It was like how it was before I met River. Well, not exactly. I literally couldn't smell anything right now, which messed with my ability to taste. It had been five days, and I was ready to taste food again. I ducked down under the water. I didn't stay under as long this time. After resurfacing, I wiped the water from my face.

I needed to figure out where I was going to take a warm shower. The only rooms I knew the locations of were River's and Alpha Max's. I could always go to the gym.

"Cruz?" I froze at the sound of River's soft whisper.

I turned around and there she was, a mere two feet from me. Her green eyes were wide with surprise and her teeth were chattering. "How long have you been here?" I asked in concern.

"Long enough to want a hot shower." She gave me a small smile. "I was about to get out when I saw someone jump in. I didn't know who, since I was behind the waterfall and couldn't see details.

"Come on, let's get you out. I think your lips are turning blue." I grabbed her arm and pulled her towards the shore.

"P-prob-bly." River was shivering like crazy. "With M-Maya s-still weak, I forget how m-much she warmed m-me."

I grabbed my clothes quickly and grabbed her hand, pulling her behind me. "Where is Spur?"

"He probably saw you and figured he could be off babysitting duty." River said. "Thanks for that, by the way."

I smiled. "Anytime, Babe. Which door will get us up to your room with the least likelihood of being seen?"

River pulled me to the left of the packhouse. We came to the door, and she typed in a code before opening it. We slipped inside. We walked down the hall with the gym before hurrying across the entryway and down the hall with the offices. She pulled me into her father's office. I could feel her hand shaking in mine. I needed to get her warmed up fast. She activated the elevator. We stepped in and she pressed the button for the basement.

"Molly and I are sharing a room. There are so many guests here, we had to double up." River said when she saw my questioning look.

I walked her to her room but stopped at the threshold. "Take a shower and warm up. I will see you at the ceremony." I took a step back and she spun to look at me.

"I need to talk to you before the wedding." River wrapped her arms around herself as she stood there shivering. She was in a large sweatshirt and sweatpants. Her hair almost looked black with it so wet.

"Please get in the shower." I said, taking another step back.

"How has Caspian been?" River asked, and I stopped retreating.

"He's been completely fine, other than the constant complaining." I answered in confusion.

"Good. A little help, Caspian. I need to talk to the two of you, but I need to warm up and I can't have Cruz disappearing again." River smirked at me.

"You little..." I started to say, but Caspian surged forward. I tried to keep him back, but he was determined. River took a step back and gestured us forward. I growled as Caspian stepped into her room. She closed and locked the door behind us before moving to the bathroom. Oh, she was going to get it.

"Stay here. I shouldn't be too long." She closed the door, and I heard the water turn on.

It took me several minutes to take control from Caspian. He was laughing and wagging his blasted tail. I stormed into the bathroom. A startled squeak came from the shower when the door hit the wall. "River." I growled.

"I'm almost done." she said quickly.

"Whatever you need to say can wait until next week. I promised you two months and I won't break that promise." I stormed from the room but stopped when I heard River a few steps behind me.

"This can't wait until then, Cruz!" She yelled.

I turned to face her. She was wrapped in a towel and her eyes were ablaze, even with the tears pooling in them. My gaze dropped from her eyes to the necklace she was wearing. It was a coin on a leather cord. A spot larger than a silver dollar was on her left shoulder. As I looked closer, I realized it was a fresh scar.

"Do you like it?" River asked angrily. "I have a matching one on the back." She turned, and sure enough, there was an identical scar.

I moved to her quickly. She sucked in a sharp breath when I ran my finger over the scar on her back. "What happened, River?" I asked as a pit formed in my stomach. She should have healed from whatever caused this. Maya should have been able to heal her.

"The arrow you gave me came in handy after the trial." She whispered. I swallowed hard but remained quiet as I continued to look at the injury. "They trapped Maya, Cruz. They used magic and locked her away. That same magic was making it so that my head injury wasn't healing and that is why I lost my memory. There was too much swelling."

River turned to look at me. I ran my fingers over the mark on her shoulder. "After you left, I went to see Prudence. She gave me a potion that would break the magic holding Maya and heal my head. I realized a few things at that moment."

"Which were?" I asked softly, looking into her eyes. "That you would have accepted any cost it would take to free Maya so she wouldn't die." I nodded my head in confirmation. "The cost was that my mate's wolf would become weak for a while. The second was going to be excruciating pain to heal my head."

"I think I know when you took that potion." I said, remembering walking and dropping to the ground in agony.

"I'm sorry about that. I didn't remember that we had taken the transference potion. So instead, you got the pain and Maya became weak. She was already bad off from whatever they did to her. It is taking her longer to recover. I can't even shift right now."

"That explains why this isn't healed, but how did it happen?" I asked, trailing my fingers down her arm until I could lace them through hers. It felt so good to be touching her. I had missed her more than I ever thought I could miss anyone. Not even staying busy kept my mind from her.

"Darius's trial didn't exactly end like anyone thought it would. They were all convicted. Darius broke free somehow as they were moving him back to a cell. He grabbed me. He laid out their whole revenge reasonings. Spur and the guys were trying to get into a position to get him, but he had a knife to my neck. I remembered the moment you gave me the three items and showed me how to activate the arrow. So, when he tried to mark me..."

"You put it to your shoulder because you couldn't reach him otherwise." I said and closed my eyes. I rested my forehead against hers and took a deep breath. I groaned and stepped back.

"What's wrong? I'm healing fine and Marco has been helping me with physical therapy." River looked worried.

"I can't smell you." I said and walked a few steps away. My anger towards Darius was building and I couldn't use River's scent to help calm me down.

"What do you mean you can't smell me?"

"I used a powder to deaden my sense of smell so it would be easier." I began pacing.

"You are impossible, Cruz. You know that?" River snapped at me. She stormed from the room. She came back in and tossed a white powder in my face. I had been taking a breath when she did, and I started coughing. "Good, now go rinse it off before it starts burning."

I stumbled to the bathroom and into the shower. *"Do you think she has her memory back?"* Caspian asked as he laughed.

"My guess is she has gotten back enough of it." I said as I scrubbed my face.

Chapter Twenty-Six

River

I paced the bedroom as I waited for Cruz. I was so blasted nervous. I had put on a long cardigan, since I didn't have any large sweatshirts down here. I felt Cruz's eyes on me, and I stopped my pacing.

"River, I am beyond happy that you are okay, but we have a week left. I should go." Cruz started moving to the door with quick steps and I was close to a panic attack.

"Cruz, that wasn't what I needed to tell you. This can't wait until next week, or after the wedding, or even the morning. I need you to stop trying to leave and just listen." I followed him out into the common area. His steps slowed, but he was still moving toward the elevator. "You can't be serious right now?" I growled out when he pushed the button.

"You asked me for two months, River. I understand. Amnesia sucks. I needed time too. I will see you at the ceremony." The doors slid open, and Cruz stepped onto the elevator.

"Wait until the doors are closing." Maya growled.

He turned to look at me as the doors began to close. "I'm pregnant, Cruz." The doors fully closed.

I went to the kitchen and began cooking spaghetti. There was no way I was going to be eating with the family tonight. I was so angry with Cruz right now. The butthead wouldn't even let me tell him face-to-face.

"What do you mean you're pregnant?" Cruz asked, hesitantly.

"I thought you didn't want to see me until the wedding and that you didn't want to talk for another week?" I didn't turn around as I snapped my handful of spaghetti noodles in half before dropping them into the pot. I walked over to the pantry and reached for the sauce. A shot of pain went through my shoulder, and I cursed as I dropped the jar. It shattered and sauce was everywhere.

I was lifted off the ground and Cruz set me on the counter. He reached behind him and turned the burner off. He turned back around, placing his hands on either side of me. "I never once said I didn't want to see or talk to you, River. It has been complete torture not seeing you or hearing your voice. It's just easier to give you the space you needed when I wasn't having to fight myself and Caspian."

"I haven't needed space for almost seven weeks." I whispered.

"Are you hurt? Did you get cut by the glass?" Cruz asked as he searched my eyes. Our faces were mere inches apart.

"No, I'm fine." I sighed as I rested my forehead against his shoulder.

"River, are you really…?" his voice trailed off.

I straightened up and grabbed his hand. He let me move it to my stomach. I was pretty big for being only thirteen weeks along. Cruz's gaze dropped, and I heard him let out a puff of air. When his eyes returned to mine, I felt a tear slip onto my cheek. "Yeah, I'm really pregnant." The tears began to fall faster. Cruz put his arms around me, and I started to cry harder.

Cruz buried his face in my neck as he cradled my head. "I'm so sorry I left." He whispered.

I sniffled as I put my arms around his neck and wrapped my legs around his waist. "I'm sorry for telling you to go." I pressed my lips against his. "I did enjoy the shirt though."

Cruz rubbed his nose against mine. "I thought you might." He kissed me. "I missed you." He kissed me again. "How have you been? I mean, with the baby?"

"It was a bit of a shock to be sure." Cruz gave a short laugh. "I went through phases."

"Phases?" Cruz asked as he tucked my hair behind my ear.

"I was scared, resigned, completely ticked off that you would leave when I only asked for space, angry that I couldn't get a hold of you. Seriously Cruz, who leaves for two months without a way to contact them?"

"I gave you a phone, River. I would have answered for you."

"You said it was an emergency number."

"I think you being pregnant classifies as an emergency, Babe. I would have immediately come back if I had known about the baby."

I pulled back so I could see him better. "There is one more thing."

"More than you impaling yourself." He asked and I nodded. "More than us having a baby?" I nodded again with a smile. "I'm listening."

"Well, I guess there are four more things." I corrected and he raised a brow in question. "First, you are going to have to clean up the sauce and make dinner because PT was brutal today. Second, you have to be the one to tell Molly that I am not going to be sleeping upstairs tonight."

"Is that so?" Cruz smiled. "Where are you sleeping?"

"That is the third thing. *We* are sleeping down here, in my room, in the bed." I smiled at him.

Cruz chuckled. "I can do that. What is the fourth thing?"

"So, you said that we are having a baby." I licked my lips nervously. "That isn't exactly true."

Cruz pulled back with his brows pinched together. "What do you mean?" He suddenly grew tense, and his eyes began to flicker. "I'm going to kill him." He growled as he tried to pull away from me.

I tightened my legs and arms around him. That wasn't what I was trying to say at all, and now he was going into crazy beast mode. "Cruz, look at me." I said desperately. I cupped his face, forcing him to look at me. "The babies are yours."

He froze as he stared at me. "Babies?" He breathed out.

I nodded slowly before pressing my lips to his. "I love you, but you need to calm down and not jump to horrible conclusions."

"You love me?" Cruz smiled.

"Mmhmm. Just like you love me." I smirked at him.

"Do I now?"

"You said so the night you rescued me." Cruz's brows drew down as he thought. "You said you loved me too much to push me into something I wasn't fully comfortable with. It was cute that you didn't even realize you said it."

"I do love you, River." He kissed me. "But I am still waiting for you to tell me what you meant when you said babies."

"I guess that would be something important for you to know." I kissed him again. When he tried to pull back, I held his face to mine. He began to tickle me, and I let him go as I laughed. "Okay, okay. You win." I laughed. "Five." I said with a straight face. Cruz looked like he was going to pass out. "Are you okay?" I asked as he stared at me with a deer in the headlights look. I slowly got off the counter. "Maybe you should sit down." I laughed.

"Five? Are you serious?" Cruz asked breathlessly.

"No, I'm not." I smiled at him.

It took him a minute before he registered what I said. The look in his eyes said I was going to pay for the 'five' comment. I took off running for the elevator as I laughed. I managed to make it around the first couch before I was grabbed from behind. I squealed as he picked me up and carried me to the bedroom. He kicked the door closed before he dumped me on the bed.

"I obviously believe the fact that you are pregnant," Cruz stared down at me with his hands on his hips.

"Are you calling me fat?" I asked in mock horror.

"For the love." Cruz muttered.

"I thought you said it was hot when I was mischievous?" I asked as I stood and walked over to him with a large grin on my face. I had missed this. I had missed him.

"I see you have regained more of your memories." Cruz put one arm around me while putting his other hand on my stomach.

"Twins." I kissed his cheek. "We are having twins."

"Do I need to get out the Terror Root to make sure?" Cruz asked.

"I promise, Cruz. There were only two babies in there at the last ultrasound." I laughed.

Cruz kissed my temple. I laid my head against his shoulder, just enjoying the feeling of being held by the man I loved. Then my phone rang. I tensed slightly before reminding myself that Darius was no longer a threat.

Before I could reach for my phone, Cruz pulled it from my pocket. "Storm."

"Cruz?" Molly asked confused, and I smiled.

"Is there something you need?" Cruz asked.

"Okay, so you are with River, then? Spencer came back from the waterfall saying that River was with you, but no one can find either of you."

"Is there something you needed or are you just checking up on River?"

"Just making sure she is safe." Molly started to say more, but Cruz cut her off.

"River is safe for now. And don't worry, she will be there when the ceremony starts." Cruz hung up the phone and tossed it on the bed.

"I have to be there before the ceremony starts to get ready." I smiled up at him. "And you aren't wearing this, are you?" I asked, tugging on his dirty shirt.

Cruz gave me a wicked grin before tugging his shirt off. "Is this better?"

I rose on my toes to whisper in his ear. "Nice try, Sweetheart but I'm starving."

Cruz laughed as he grabbed my hand. "If I'm making dinner, I need you to sit at the bar to keep me company."

I smiled as I watched Cruz finish the spaghetti. We talked about what we had been up to since he left. He was reluctant to give too many details when he mentioned having a meeting with his superiors. I knew there was more to the story than just a simple meeting. We sat at the kitchen bar and ate. Cruz did the dishes when we were done.

"What time is the wedding?" Cruz asked as we cuddled on the couch watching a movie.

"The wedding starts at ten, but I am supposed to be up with Molly by six." I yawned.

"Uh, yeah...that's not happening." Cruz pressed a kiss to my head.

"Cruz, I am the maid-of-honor. I'm supposed to help your sister get ready."

"She will understand. Molly knows how demanding I am. Plus, I have been without you for roughly three months, if we aren't counting the couple of hours after the rescue." Cruz pressed a kiss to my neck.

"Tomorrow is your sister's wedding day. She will be presented as the future Luna of the pack. It's a big deal." I turned to look at him.

"I don't envy her position. Thank the stars we never have to be where she is."

"What do you mean? You are an Alpha." I sat up and scooted away from Cruz so I could see him better. He let out a groan of protest.

"My dad and his twin, Dallas, are co-Alphas. Thankfully, Dallas has a son that is far more suited to the role than I am."

"You aren't going to be Alpha of some pack?" I was getting excited, but I tapped it down just in case I had misunderstood.

"Is that a problem? Did you marry me thinking you were going to me Luna?" Cruz pulled me closer. "Sorry, Love. Our future is going to be far less chaotic."

"I married you because Maya and Caspian practically forced us to." I poked him in the chest. "And one of my biggest issues with you, was the fact that you were an Alpha."

"You have an issue with me being an Alpha?" Cruz chuckled. "That was one of my better qualities for the ladies."

"I don't want to be a Luna. I want to help heal people. That's why I went to college and got my nursing degree."

"How do you see the rest of your life going?" Cruz asked seriously. He angled his body so that he was facing me more after turning the TV off.

"I want you to not go on crazy dangerous missions anymore. I need you and don't want to sit around wondering if you will ever come home again. I want to live in a small town where my time is mostly demanded by our kids and not hundreds of people." I laced my fingers with his. I knew I was asking a lot of him. To give up the career he loved. It was unfair of me.

"Does a house on our own private strip of beach fit your vision? It's about an hour from the Maple Grove Pack, twenty minutes to the nearest town, and two hours from the city. Our nearest neighbor is over a mile away."

"I have never been to the beach." I said with wide eyes. "But it sounds amazing. What about work?"

"Shadow has been retired instead of hunted. My meeting,"

"Not a meeting." I corrected, and he scowled at me. The corner of his mouth twitched as he fought a smile.

"My *meeting* persuaded The Board to back off of everyone involved with the Shadow Project." Cruz ran his hand up my arm until he was cupping my face. "Now, I am in charge of training the new recruits for Miles. My team is almost complete, I'm just missing one person."

"Who?"

"I need to find an on-site nurse."

"Are you asking me to work for you?" I raised a brow.

"Not for me, River. Beside me." He placed a light kiss on the tip of my nose. I kissed him and he smiled, pulling me closer.

It was late. The lights were out, and we were lying in bed. My head was on Cruz's chest and his arms were around me. One of his hands rested on my belly, his thumb was slowly going back and forth.

"Cruz?" I asked softly.

"Hmm?" He sounded close to sleep.

"Be honest with me, what are your thoughts about the fact that I'm pregnant?" I was nervous for his reply, but I needed to know.

"I think I am still processing. Shocked is one word to describe it. We weren't exactly in a place in our relationship where I would say we were ready for this. I'm still not ready for this, River. I never thought I would have a family. I always pictured myself having a short life. Going out on a mission and not coming back. A wife was a foreign concept I was just beginning to accept. Kids? I'm not really father material." Cruz's heart began to beat faster, and I could feel his anxiety rising the more he talked.

"Cruz." I said firmly as I turned my face up to look at him, resting my chin on his chest. When he looked at me, I continued. "You are great with kids. Nash and Ana adore you."

"I know nothing about babies. My training didn't cover this."

"Neither did mine." I laughed. "I always pictured myself living in a tiny house in the middle of nowhere healing people, like Prudence. A husband was an inconvenient thought. Kids were never even a possibility."

Cruz took a deep breath and let it out slowly. "I guess we will have to help each other through this." He pressed a kiss to my forehead. We settled back into silence. I was almost asleep when Cruz spoke again. "Your scent is different. It used to be just the salty ocean air. Now…it has a hint of something sweet and citrusy to it."

"The doctor said you might be able to smell the difference once you got back. I guess he went to school in the south and learned that the deeper mate's mark allows you to smell the slight difference between me and the baby, when I am far enough along." I laughed. "The added scents are the babies."

"Hmm."

"Go to sleep, Cruz. Six o'clock comes early."

"Not happening." He muttered, pulling me closer.

Chapter Twenty-Seven

Cruz

Something soft and warm pressed to my lips, pulling me from a deep sleep. I breathed in. River. I kissed her back. "Morning." I mumbled as she sat back. I blinked my eyes a few times to clear the sleep from them.

"Cruz, we need to get up." River smiled at me.

"I told you six was too early today." I tucked her hair behind her ear.

"It's eight." She laughed. "Now come on. I need you to get up so we can get dressed."

I groaned as I sat up. "We are sleeping in tomorrow until I say it's time to get up." I looked over at her. She was pulling my shirt on as she laughed.

"I hate to break it to you, but if I don't get food in me before seven, your little surprises," she rubbed her belly. "Have me throwing up for hours."

"My surprise?"

"I sure as heck didn't do this to myself." River smirked at me.

"I didn't do it myself either." I shot back. "You were an equal participant. I would go as far as saying you started it."

River gasped as her eyes widened. "Are you blaming these two on me?"

I got off the bed and put my arms around her. "That depends. If they are little demons, then yes, you are responsible. But if they are complete angels, I will take full credit."

River laughed as she put her arms around my neck. "Feeling a little calmer about impending fatherhood?"

"At the moment." I kissed her.

In truth, I was still freaking out about it. From the moment she said she was pregnant as the doors closed between us; I have been terrified at the very idea. Caspian was unsure about the whole thing too. I was a killer. A man that knew nothing about caring for the well-being of another. I wasn't the type of person parents wished for as a role model for their kids. Nash and Belle were the youngest kids I have interacted with since I was a teen.

"You are still freaking out, aren't you?" River pulled back and studied me.

I let out a tense breath as I buried my face in her neck and held her close. River didn't say anything. Her arms around my neck tightened. We stayed like that for a long time. "I'm not father material, River." I whispered. "I am a trained killer. I have ended more lives than I could count." She ran her fingers through my hair. It had grown several inches, and my natural curl was apparent.

"And I just killed a man my stabbing him in the heart with an arrow through my own shoulder." River whispered. She leaned back and looked me in the eye. "Cruz, I think you will be just fine."

I closed my eyes. "You seem so certain."

"I am." She ran her hand along my scruffy jaw. "You are loyal, a protector, and despite your intimidating exterior, you are a softy at heart."

"You just described a guard dog." I smiled. Mom had us kids helping her with all the rescue dogs that came through her animal shelter from the time we could walk."

"Well, you are a werewolf, is there a difference?" River smirked.

"Ha. Having helped my mom train a few guard dogs over the years, I can tell you that there is a big difference between me and a Pitbull." I kissed her neck, and she giggled. A phone rang and I sighed. The world awaited. I walked over to the nightstand and picked it up. "Storm." I said as I turned around to watch River.

"Where are you?" Miles asked. "I have your uniform. I went to your guest room, River's room, and the Gamma's office."

"Just take it and everything River will need to get ready to the locker room by the gym." I told him. I smiled when River's mouth fell open as she stared at me with wide eyes.

"Cruz, I can't. I have to help Molly." River protested.

"How am I supposed to know what River is going to need?" Miles asked in disbelief.

"We will be there in thirty minutes. Ask Molly or Gamma Carly what she will need. But we need it there." I hung up the phone.

River let out a huff of frustration. She was smiling, even though I could tell she was a little irritated. I remember her saying she got sick if she didn't eat something when she woke up. I grabbed her hand and led her out to the kitchen. I passed her a piece of fruit before pouring both of us a bowl of cereal.

She was still in just my shirt. It was way too big and reached mid-thigh. If I didn't already know she was pregnant, I wouldn't be able to tell. That little belly of hers was hidden by the baggy fabric.

We were in the elevator when River turned to me. "There is one more thing I should mention."

"Babe, I don't think I can handle any more of your surprises." I said cautiously.

"No one knows I'm pregnant." River said quickly.

"How have you hidden this," I rubbed her stomach. "From everyone?"

"Baggy shirts and sweatshirts. With Maya weak, I have been cold, so no one has questioned it."

"Why didn't you tell anyone? You shouldn't have had to deal with this alone." I said in concern.

"Okay, Molly knows. She knew before the trial, but didn't say anything." I gave her a look and she talked fast. "She touched my hand and saw the outcome of me deciding whether or not to open that box you left me. After I was stable and healing, she came to see me. She said that she saw only one outcome where both me and the baby survived. She said a lot of them ended with me losing the baby."

Before I could say anything, the doors slid open. The room was blessedly empty. We were crossing to the door when River pulled me to a stop. "I wanted you to know before anyone else. That is why I had to talk to you before the wedding. The dress Molly wants me to wear is more form fitting than we thought it would be, considering my new size. There will be no hiding the fact that I'm pregnant." She whispered.

"Are you wanting to tell everyone before, or are you just wanting to walk down the aisle?" I asked.

"Even though I have had several weeks to process this, I am still freaking out about it." River let go of my hand and paced away from me.

I followed her, wrapping my arms around her. I pressed a kiss to my mark, and I felt her shiver. "River, everything is going to be okay. We will tackle this mission like all the others I have been on."

"We are not going to kill the wedding guests." River said flatly, and I chuckled.

"I was talking about being parents." I turned her to face me. "With each one of my missions, I prepared to the best of my ability, and then let the chips fall where they may. I also expected to be flexible because not everything goes as planned."

"Wise words for a man who doesn't think he will be a good dad." River muttered.

"I really don't think I will be, but I will do my best to not be a complete failure." I gave River a quick kiss. "We need to get going if we want to be on time."

Holding hands, we stepped out into the hallway and began walking toward the gym. We passed several startled people who gave us disapproving looks. River moved closer to me, and I smiled. The woman was bashful. I pushed the door to the gym open and stopped when I saw all my men, plus Miles, standing around.

Cheese saw us first. He stood suddenly, straightening his dress uniform. "Agent Storm." He visibly swallowed. "I want to thank you for extending the offer in your unit. It will be an honor serving with you." I had to work hard and not smile at that. Cheese, Fox, Marco, and Tango still didn't know I was Shadow.

"How are you doing, River?" Spur coughed before asking.

"Much better." River said as she leaned against me. I put my arm around her.

"Looks that way. Is there a reason you are in Cruz's shirt while he is only in pants?" Tango asked with a confused expression. "I thought...but isn't Shadow..."

"Still have doubts that Cruz was able to keep his identity guarded?" Spur laughed.

River put her arms around my waist. "It still boggles my mind that men of your station couldn't tell."

"Wait...No..." Marco squinted his eyes as he stared at me.

River laughed as she put her hands over my mouth and nose. "See?" she said. I spun us around so that I was between her and the guys. She let out a startled squeak at the abrupt movement.

"My shirt doesn't cover enough for you to be raising your arms up like that." I whispered in her ear.

She gasped and shoved away from me. "I have been lifting my arms up all morning putting breakfast and dishes away." She glared at me. I grinned at her, causing her to scoff and march into the bathroom. "You are impossible!" She yelled as she slammed the door.

"Come on, Babe. No one else was around this morning." I called after her.

"I see you two are getting back to your earlier routine." Miles commented.

"Flirty fighting." Cheese laughed.

"We are finding our way." I turned to look at him. "Is my uniform in the other bathroom?"

Miles laughed as he headed for the door. "Nope."

"I'm happy you all accepted my invitation to work with me on training the new recruits. Work starts September first, so enjoy your downtime." I gave a nod to the guys and went into the locker room. Time was starting to run short, and Molly would definitely kill me if we were late.

* * *

It was going to be close. We got a little sidetracked on top of it taking River longer to get ready than I had thought it would, but it was worth it. She was a vision. She had curled her hair and pulled the sides into a braid that ended in a decorative clip at the back of her head. Most of the curls cascaded down her back with a few loose ones falling around her face. She was wearing a thin strapped sage green dress that hugged her belly before flowing to the floor. If I had to guess, the dress wasn't supposed to be so form fitting, but it still looked great on her.

We rushed outside, but everyone had already gone. "We can take my bike." I said as we jogged down the lane.

"I'm not getting on that." River pulled free of my hand. "I am in a dress, Cruz."

"Sweetheart, there is no other way for us to get to the wedding on time. We are pushing it as it is."

"I can't in this dress. Maybe if it had a slit in it, but it doesn't."

"Hold still, Babe." I said, pulling the knife from my belt and sliding it down the fabric.

"Cruz!" River gasped.

"A slit. Now get on." I smiled at her, and she glared at me. I took my uniform jacket off and put it around her before getting on in front of her. "Hold on tight, Love."

I started the bike and as soon as I felt River's arms come around me, I shot down the road. Her grip on me tightened. I was going to need to get another helmet before we headed home. I hated that she wasn't wearing one now. Even though we weren't going crazy fast, anything could happen. Caspian stepped forward and used our ability to see any potential obstacles that could cause us to crash.

Caspian was in the same boat as me. We loved River and would do anything for her. But we were both unsure about the whole fatherhood thing. There was no way we were backing out of it, but we were more afraid at the prospect of being a dad than going onto a hostile base to retrieve hostages.

The church came into view. There was a ramp to the side of the stairs and the doors were open. I rode up the ramp and stopped right outside the doors. We got off the bike and ran inside. Rounding the corner, I spotted dad, Molly, two other women in similar gowns to River's, and Belle.

"Cruz!" Belle yelled when she saw us.

"Hey, Belle." I smiled at her. "But keep your voice down, remember we are in a church." I tapped her nose and winked.

"Where have you been?" Molly hissed.

"I told you I would get River here before the wedding started." I gave her a kiss on the cheek. River handed me back my dress uniform coat, and I slipped it on. "I will see you ladies after the ceremony." I gave River a quick kiss before turning to find mom and a seat.

"Where are you going?" Molly snapped.

"To go sit down before this thing starts."

"You are escorting River. You would have known that if you had bothered to show up for breakfast." Molly scolded.

I glanced at dad who was staring at River with wide eyes. River moved closer to me, and I could sense her anxiousness. I put my arm around her and moved us to stand in front of Molly and dad.

"I will follow your lead, River." I whispered in her ear.

She looked up at me as she took the arm I offered her. "I told you we should have gotten up earlier."

"I wanted to sleep. I haven't been sleeping well since Spur and I left to check out the cabin." I retorted.

"You could have slept in and been here on time if you hadn't insisted on breakfast."

"Someone said they needed to eat in the mornings." I kissed her forehead. "Plus, you were the one who..."

"Stop being so distracting." River's eyes danced with mischief.

"Will you two start walking?" Molly laughed.

I glanced at her before looking in front of us. The doors that were previously closed were now open. The two bridesmaids were already standing at the front. All the guests had turned and were watching us. River's face turned red as we began to walk. We were halfway down the aisle when I glanced at River. "Do you regret it?" I whispered.

"What?" River glanced at me.

"The way we got married." I wouldn't blame her if she did. It was not the most romantic of ceremonies. We had both been angry with our wolves and weren't certain about each other. It all felt like some weird crazy dream.

We reached the front, and I kissed her cheek. "No." She whispered.

I stepped back and winked at her. Mom gestured me over and I took the seat next to her. My smile widened when she gasped. I knew what she had noticed. "Cruz, is River...?" She asked softly, but was cut off when the music changed, and we all stood to watch Dad and Molly.

The ceremony began and mom remained quiet as she watched Molly. My eyes were glued to River. She glanced at me, and her smile grew when our eyes met. This wedding could not end soon enough. I finally pulled my eyes away from River to watch Molly and Paxton mark one another. Caspian laughed that they didn't give each other a deep mark, like he had given River.

In the chaos of everyone getting up to leave, I slipped past several people. I managed to grab both River's and Molly's wrists. I congratulated Molly and told her I was taking River back to the packhouse. Molly nodded and kissed my cheek.

I pulled River out a side door and down the hall at a jog. "Where are we going?" River laughed.

"I told Molly the packhouse, but I am willing to go anywhere." I smiled at her.

I stopped once we got to my motorcycle. "What's the rush and why are you hiding?" River kissed me after I got on the bike.

"Mom and dad noticed." I said as I held her hand and she got on the bike behind me. I quickly unbuttoned my coat and took it off before passing it to River. "I need a few more minutes before the questions start and I would rather be together when they do."

"You are kind of cute when you are freaking out." River wrapped her arms around me, and I drove back down the ramp.

I stopped once we reached the waterfall. I helped River off the motorcycle, and we walked over to a grassy spot near the water's edge. We sat down and River let out a long sigh. She reclined back against my chest after I leaned back against a tree. I put my arms around her and kissed her temple. We sat in comfortable silence, just listening to the sound of the waterfall. My hand rested on her belly. I still couldn't believe we were going to be parents.

We had been out here for hours, and River had fallen asleep only a few minutes ago. I was in no rush to get back but knew we probably should. I kissed River's temple.

"You know, big brother, stealing my maid-of-honor all day is a jerk move." Molly called. My head snapped in her direction. Everyone was standing there. River's parents, my parents, Molly and Paxton, and Kyson.

"When did you get in?" Dad asked.

I sighed. "Last night."

"Why didn't you come say hi?" Mom asked with her hands on her hips.

"I was a little busy." I said. I felt River move slightly and knew she had woken up, but the little stinker was pretending to be asleep.

"We hardly see you anymore and you have become so distant." Mom stated, and I felt a little bad. I had become distant over the last few years. It was hard dealing with my nightmares and knowing that I could hurt them on accident if I had one while visiting. Not to mention all the secrets. I couldn't tell them anything about what I did. "So, what had you so busy that you couldn't even let us know you arrived?"

"I was finding out that my wife was pregnant." I shrugged. "I wasn't quite expecting that kind of news upon my return and was taken by surprise."

River laughed. "A little surprised?" She sat up and looked at me. "I thought you were going to pass out."

Everyone started talking at once, asking about the baby and how River was feeling. Molly finally called order to the chaos. She told everyone that there would be plenty of time to talk about the baby, but right now there was a wedding celebration taking place with no bride and groom.

That night, River and I went to bed early in her normal guest room. We planned on leaving at first light to head down south. No one knew about our plan to leave immediately after we had breakfast with the family. Neither of us could wait to get away from everything. To finally start our life together.

Epilogue

River

The ocean had become one of my favorite things. The sound of the surf was like a lullaby. It even helped get the kids to sleep. They were complete terrors to put to bed whenever we traveled anywhere.

I smiled over at the twins. I couldn't believe they were three already. They both had my brown hair and Cruz's blue eyes. Emerson was quieter than her sister, but she was a cunning little thing. She could get out of her crib and through most baby locks. And a daddy's girl through and through. Finley was my mini-me. She was bossy and was a non-stop chatter box, even though she barely talked in full sentences. Cruz mentioned frequently that I cursed his angel to be more like me because I gave her my nickname.

"Daddy!" Emerson yelled as she slapped her hand on the sliding patio door.

"Is daddy coming?" I asked her with a smile.

Cruz always ran his recruits by the house at this time of day, so he could say good morning to the girls. They were usually asleep when he headed out. Sure enough, thirty men were jogging along the beach in the thick sand. I opened the side door and both girls bolted down the short path that led to the beach. Finley reached it first and managed to open the gate before I could get there. Great. Cruz was going to have to replace it with another kind of lock, again.

"Stay with mommy." I reminded them.

That reminder only lasted until they recognized Cruz at the front of the group of men. They sprinted across the sand as they squealed. Cruz scooped Emerson up while Jameson grabbed Finley. Neither man broke their stride. It still amazed me that they could do that.

"Good morning, Babe." Cruz pulled me against him with his free arm and kissed me.

"Good morning to you, too." I smiled at him. "Good run so far?" I asked.

"What are you feeding these kids, River? They are growing like weeds." Jameson set Finley down.

Before work every morning, Cruz filled up several large cooler jugs so the men could get a drink while he talked with us. Jameson passed Cruz a water cup and he let go of me to take it, downing it quickly.

"They are trying to be as big and strong as the boys, so they can go run with their father in the morning." I laughed and gave Jameson a quick hug. "How's the family?"

"My in-laws are good in small doses." Jameson grinned.

"What do you mean mommy has a secret?" Cruz looked from Emerson and Finley to me.

"It's not a secret." I laughed. "You and you." I pointed out two of the recruits. "Babysitting duty. You get Finley, she is an escape artist, and you take Emerson. She will try to follow her dad."

I grabbed Cruz's hand and pulled him down the beach. Once we were out of earshot of the others, I stopped. "They called with the results." I said quickly.

"And?" Cruz asked anxiously as he grabbed my elbows.

I took a deep breath and let it out. "It came back positive."

"How does this keep happening?" Cruz asked, running his hand through his hair. "We are going to start having to live in different houses if you can't stop this."

"Like I'm the one at fault. You are the one with no self-control." I retorted. "And we are not living in different houses."

"Sweetheart, what are we going to do with three kids?" Cruz threw his arms out to the side.

"Oh, stop it. You adore your girls, and you are excited about this one. I can feel it through our bond." I scoffed at him.

His lips twitched before he straightened his features. "I think you got it all wrong." He took a step towards me. I took one back. I knew that look. He was scheming.

His lips twitched again, and I turned and ran. I only made it three steps before I was picked up. I screamed and tried to break his hold on me. I looked around and saw every one of his recruits watching us. Cruz dragged me backwards into the ocean and dunked us both. When we surfaced, I coughed several times. I finally stopped and glared at Cruz.

"I love you." He said before kissing me. I sighed as I wrapped my arms around his neck. I quickly got lost in the sensation of his lips on mine.

"Are you two done?" Jameson called, and I pulled away from Cruz quickly.

We made it back to the group and Cruz wrapped his arms around me from behind. The recruit I had assigned to watch Emerson cleared his throat. "No offense, ma'am, but I didn't sign up for the FBWHA to babysit while my commander kisses his wife." I felt Cruz stiffen behind me.

"Let me handle this, Love." I said softly. "You think I am taking advantage of you gentlemen?" I asked. "Distracting you from training?"

"Here we go again." Jameson muttered. This happened with every new batch of men. They were always shocked and put off by the way Cruz combined work and family. They usually ended up challenging me because I was less intimidating than Cruz was.

"I mean no disrespect, ma'am." He said again.

I scanned the faces. All of them were new. "I'll tell you what, recruit, if you can win a sparring match…"

"You are not sparring. Not for a while." Cruz said firmly.

"Okay, fine. If you can do more push-ups than I can, I will keep these little pitstops to five minutes." I pulled my hair into a ponytail. "Emerson, honey. Go stand by your father." I took off my shirt, so I was only in a tank top and shorts.

The man eagerly agreed. I offered him my hand to shake, and he took it. He was human. Maya laughed as we dropped into a push-up position. He began strong, but after thirty, his arms began to shake. At forty he was grunting and struggling. The guy dropped at forty-three. I continued until I failed. One hundred and twenty-two.

I stood and looked over at the men. "I can outrun you, heck, I can outrun those two." I gestured to Cruz and Jameson. "I can out pushup, pullup, spar, and pretty much anything you challenge me to. You will learn I am not someone who likes to be challenged. You all will be subject to watching the girls throughout your little vacation here. Nothing will help you be more observant than having to watch Cruz's girls. They get into everything, can escape most things, and conspire together to get away from you."

"Recruits, meet the nurse on staff, and also one of your fitness instructors, River Storm." Jameson laughed. "Just a fair warning, she is a werewolf with royal blood and has been trained by the warriors of the North Wind Pack in the Northern Kingdom. If you don't know the significance of that, you will once you get to that class in a few weeks. Not to mention that scar on her shoulder was from her intentionally activating a spring powered arrow into her own shoulder to stab the man behind her. She isn't one you want to tick off."

"Take them on the last leg of the run, Jay. I need to speak to River for a few more minutes. I will let you know what is going on back at the base." Cruz told Jameson. He nodded, and they all cleared out. "Girls, time to go inside." Emerson and Finley ran into the house. Cruz grabbed my hand as we followed the girls. "What all did the doctor say?"

"He said that I am pregnant." I smiled at him, and he shot me a look. "And we have an ultrasound appointment in two weeks." I said as I wrapped my arms around his neck.

"How many are you wanting? Cause at this rate, we are going to have a football team's worth." Cruz kissed the tip of my nose.

I laughed. "There is no way we are having that many kids."

"Mmm."

"We planned this one, so stop acting like it is a complete shock." I smiled at him.

"I need to get back to work, but when I get back home tonight, we are going to spend some time together. Just you and me." Cruz stroked my cheek as he smiled at me. "And stop scaring the new recruits. You completely destroy their self-esteem."

"I only break them down so I can build them up stronger. Your uncle has even commented on how the graduates seem to be more well rounded than before you let me take some of the classes."

Cruz gave me another kiss. "I will see you tonight, my love." Emerson and Finley came running into the room as he was walking toward the door. He gave them each a kiss before leaving.

I watched from the window with a smile on my face. He did this every time he left. He would make it almost to the gate, stop, hesitate, turn around, and come back inside. I laughed when he did just that. Cruz kissed me until the girls tried to wedge their way in between our legs.

"Stop being so dang distracting, woman." Cruz growled before kissing me again.

I laughed. "I love you, Cruz. Get to work."

He looked into my eyes and gave me a crooked grin. My stomach did a somersault. It was crazy that after four years of marriage, he could still put butterflies in my stomach with a single look. "I love you too, River." He gave me one final kiss and stepped back.

The girls and I stood on the porch and watched Cruz jog down the beach. He had been so scared of being a dad, but the moment Emerson was placed in his arms, he seemed to forget all his worries. He put his whole heart into fatherhood. The girls loved their daddy, and he adored them. He read to them every night and most nights the girls fell asleep listening to him. Cruz had been the one to bring up another baby.

I never would have pictured my life turning out like this. I loved everything about it. My favorite part was working with Cruz. We were a team in everything. Work, home, and the occasional mission. Two sides of the same coin, we were inseparable.

THE END

www.ingramcontent.com/pod-product-compliance
Lightning Source LLC
LaVergne TN
LVHW012017060526
838201LV00061B/4352